Out of Bounds

USA TODAY BESTSELLING AUTHOR

KARA KENDRICK

OUT OF BOUNDS PLAYLIST

So High School - Taylor Swift
Sweet Melody - Little Mix
Gorgeous - Taylor Swift
Linger - The Cranberries
Waves - Luke Bryan
Are You Gonna Kiss Me or Not - Thompson Square
Risk - Gracie Abrams
Worst Way - Riley Green
Bed Chem - Sabrina Carpenter
Birds of a Feather - Billie Eilish
Down Bad - Taylor Swift
Burn It Down - Parker McCollum
Lies, Lies, Lies - Morgan Wallen
End Game - Taylor Swift
You Make It Easy - Jason Aldean

For all the risk takers

PROLOGUE: SLOANE

Thirteen years ago...

"Trouble—"

I tear my gaze away from Mrs. Evans and the Pythagorean formula she's scrawling on the whiteboard and glance toward the whispering voice.

Cam Crawford.

One of the stars on my dad's high school football team —and my best guy friend. I raise a brow and mouth 'What?,' not wanting to risk detention for talking in class. Mrs. Evans is one of the strictest teachers in the school and she'll take no mercy on me, even if my dad is Coach Carter, the best football coach this school's ever had.

"Lunch?" he whispers and I nod, a smile tugging at my lips. I secretly love that Cam wants to have lunch with me in our special spot. He may also want help with the Lit homework due today, but that's fine.

Anything to spend time with him.

I shouldn't be crushing on him, I know. He's the most

popular, handsome guy at Thunder Creek High. A football phenom destined for the pros, according to my dad. But it hasn't stopped my stupid heart from falling for him.

Hard.

Not that I'll ever tell him.

God, no.

Instead, I'll be his friend. Be there to listen to all his football stories, sit around and help him memorize the running routes for the next game.

Then inevitably watch as he gives some other girl his Varsity jacket.

Because I'm Sloane Carter. Strictly relegated to the friend zone.

Add to that I'm the coach's daughter and my dating life has been doomed from the beginning. No one on the football team dares ask me out, fearing my father. The best I can hope for is getting asked out by a baseball boy and some of them are even scared.

So I take what I can with Cam and that's a solid friendship.

The bell rings and we all jump from our seats, shoving notebooks and calculators into our backpacks before tearing out into the hallway. Lockers slam and the linoleum squeaks beneath sneakered feet.

"Hey, Trouble—" Cam throws his long arm around me and matches my stride. "You gonna grab your lunch from your locker?"

I nod, heat licking through my body walking this close to him. He smells like the woods, and I have to resist leaning in and nuzzling his neck to get a better whiff.

That would be weird.

Instead, I pull up to my locker and twist my lock, whipping the brown paper bag out of the dark cavern.

"You have yours?" I ask, banging the metal door shut.

"Yep. Let's go."

Together, we head across campus and I'm acutely aware of all the stares following Cam's every move. He's the golden boy of Thunder Creek High, already signed and committed to the University of Alabama on a full football scholarship. I'm the coach's daughter, but no one's really all that interested in me.

Not here, deep in football territory.

We glance around before ducking behind the gym building, using the back door to access the weight room. Girls aren't supposed to be in the boys' weight room or vice-versa, but Cam's been sneaking me in with him since freshman year when we bonded over the cafeteria smelling like rotting milk and canned peas. The weight room's always empty at lunchtime, giving us a private place to dine. Sure, it smells only slightly better than the cafeteria, but I'll take sweaty socks over sour milk any day of the week.

Cam pulls up a weight bench and the two of us plop on the black plastic seat, leaning against the dark blue wall. He pulls a sandwich out of his matching brown paper bag and we eat in companionable silence for a few minutes. He's on his second sandwich when he asks about the Lit homework.

"Yes, Cam, you can use my notes. But you really should read *The Great Gatsby*. I think you'll like it—the writing's excellent." I reach into my bag and slide my notes out of my Lit folder. "You're missing out."

He shoots me a sheepish grin. "I know, Trouble. You're right. But Coach has me learning a bunch of new plays for the next game. Ran out of time to do homework." He shrugs his broad shoulders and I can't be mad about it.

I know my dad's running the team hard. He wants to win the state championship this year, has talked of nothing else all season long in fact.

"Thanks." Cam takes the notes and looks them over, his brow furrowed. "Wait, the main guy—Gatsby—gets killed in the end? And he never gets the girl?"

I nod, take another bite of sandwich. "Correct."

"Seems like a bummer."

"It's tragic. But that's what makes it great. The novel's a harsh critique of the American Dream."

"Hmm. That's a real downer, Sloane. I like happy endings." His marine eyes slide to mine and I'm suddenly lightheaded.

"Yeah, me too." I swallow hard, acutely aware of the thudding of my heart. I hope Cam can't hear it through the quiet.

He leans forward, the rough pad of his thumb brushing my bottom lip.

"You have a crumb."

"Oh." Heat floods my system, the skin at the side of my mouth burning where he made contact. "Thanks."

The word's a whisper, barely audible over the thrum of the air conditioning.

"Listen—after the game on Friday, you want to go out to the bonfire at the lake? A bunch of the guys from the team are going. You and Gracelyn should come."

He inches away from me, crumpling his brown paper bag into a tight ball and firing it into the trash can across the room. The ball disappears into the can and he pumps his fists in the air, victorious.

"Yes! A perfect shot." Cam grins at me, his perfect white teeth flashing in the fluorescent light of the weight room.

"Yeah, we can probably make it."

"Probably?" He cocks his eyebrow, the scar above his right eye rising. "C'mon, Trouble—it's one of the last bonfires of the season. We don't have many left together."

He reaches out, covering my small hand with his huge one and squeezing. "Please, Trouble."

His marine eyes lock on mine, wide and pleading, and my heart contracts.

How can I say no to him?

Because he's right—we don't have much time left together before we head our separate ways. It's our senior year; after this, everything changes, for both of us.

Just thinking about it makes my chest ache.

"Yes, Cam. I'll go."

"Good. You know I'll breathe easier with you there."

That makes one of us.

Because when Cam's around, I'm a mess. Four years together and he still has the same effect on me as the day we met.

Breathless.

The bell rings, the shrill clang bouncing off the metal weight equipment and the spell between us is broken. Cam hops up, grabbing both of our backpacks, looping his arm around my shoulders.

Light. Easy. Casual.

The absolute walking definition of *friend zoned.*

Cam Crawford's the love of my life, but there's no way I'd ever tell him.

CHAPTER 1
SLOANE

The feels-like temp's already hotter than hellfire and it's only the beginning of May.

May 12th, to be exact.

The day I'm supposed to be getting married under the stars at a swanky, tulle-draped courtyard in the French Quarter.

Instead, sweat's rolling down my back as I swat at flies the size of gumballs from a plastic lawn chair in my dad's back yard.

All because my fiancé decided to 'explore other options,' as he so delicately put it.

And by 'explore other options,' he meant bang a busty paralegal doggy-style over the shiny mahogany desk at his law office downtown six months before our wedding. A gruesome sight permanently burned into my retinas.

After we planned—and paid for—the whole damn wedding, complete with two hundred already-invited guests, a five-tiered vanilla buttercream cake from the fanciest bakery in New Orleans, and a sparkling champagne tower.

I really could have used that champagne to drown my sorrows, too.

Cool, cool. Instead, I have the option of embossed invitations as wallpaper in my childhood bedroom here in Thunder Creek, Georgia. I flove rose gold and blush on 120-lb cotton cardstock—it's a vibe, am I right?

Splashing lukewarm water from a Yeti cup at my face, I tip my head toward the blinding sun and squeeze my eyes shut. This really isn't how I envisioned spending my summer —living back home with my dad at almost thirty years old— but here we are. Both of us single as the day is long, watching *Wheel of Fortune* together on the lumpy sofa every night.

I guess I should be grateful I had somewhere to go after moving out of the apartment I shared with the cheating rat for five years.

Even if the current living space is cramped and stuck in a time-warp. I swear my father's changed nothing since I left for the University of Georgia, not even the worn paper coasters collected from Mustang's, the local bar.

A hot breeze rustles the leaves of the sprawling oak at the far corner of the yard and I grab my cell to scroll through my email again. On the off-chance that Ratface remembers the date of our wedding-that-isn't and penned me a Shakespearean sonnet of an apology.

Ha freaking ha.

I tap the glass and my phone blinks to life, a photo of me and my bestie flashing on the screen.

Gracelyn, another bright spot in this whole moving-back-home scenario. She's been my ride-or-die since grade school and last night was no exception. In honor of my not-happening-wedding eve, we hit up Mustang's, drained tequila shots, and danced until midnight. Just like the old days, before I moved away.

My stomach roils as I blink down at the black-and-white messages; maybe I took one shot too many last night.

Oh god.

Make that *definitely* took one shot too many last night. I stare at the Sent messages, my chest tightening.

To: c.c.crawford@chicago.profootball.com
From: sloanecarter@gmail.com

Subject: Hey, you!

Cringe. *Hey, you! Seriously?* For fuck's sake, Sloane…

A wave of nausea rolls through me, but I force myself to keep reading the email I vaguely recall writing in a drunken tequila haze last night.

Hi Cam,

I was just thinking about you and wondering how you've been and what you've been up to these past few years. I don't know if you heard, but I'm back home in Thunder Creek. In fact, I'm living with my dad. At least for the summer, anyway. Right now I'm lying in bed remembering how you used to throw pebbles at my bedroom window when it was past curfew and you wanted to talk out plays before a big game. Ha! How funny is that, a time before we had cell phones. So weird, right?

I always loved talking to you. You were so funny and cool. Also, hot, but I'm sure you know that. Every girl fawned all over you, so I'm positive you're more than aware of how gorgeous you were. Are. I've seen pictures...

Did you know I was supposed to be getting married tomorrow? Probably not because why would you? It's not like I'm famous and end up in the tabloids like you. Anyway, long story short, my ex is a cheating ratface and I called the wedding off. Hence, why I'm back home.

It's weird being here without you. I never told you this before, but I've always liked you. Like really liked you. As in not just friends. You probably don't think of me like that, but I always wonder what might have been if I told you how I felt back in high school. Would anything have happened between us? I dreamed of kissing you so many times, but never got up the courage to tell you or do anything about it. I know my dad being your coach was an issue and things could have gotten weird, but I still wish I did something back then.

I don't want to live with regrets now, though, you know? So I'm putting this out into the universe. Just in case.

Anyway, I wanted to let you know you were one of my closest friends and I miss you.

Love,

Sloane

Ohmygod. I can't have sent that message to Cam.

Maybe he didn't read it yet and I can get it back.

Hot panic floods through me as I click around, frantically trying to unsend the message.

Why? Why would I have confessed my true feelings to Cam Crawford now, via email no less?

After all these years, why?

The man is a pro football star, living his wild and best life in Chi-town, playing the sport he adores in front of a national audience. He's famous, in the tabloids every other day, with beautiful blonde models hanging off his bulging biceps. I'm an unemployed, walking, talking sob story with well-earned trust issues, living with my dad. Why the hell would he be interested in me?

I tap around, desperate for an Unsend feature, my stomach knotting tighter with tension as the seconds tick by. Giving Cam more time to read The World's Most Embarrassing Email.

"Dammit!" I finally give up, flinging my cell down on the grass. The metal vibrates and I snatch it up so fast I create wind.

No response to my email, but the front door camera's alerting me to motion on the porch.

My mouth goes desert-dry as I stare at the grainy black-and-white image of the visitor. Squinting at the phone, I shake my head. This cannot be happening right now.

No fucking way.

I scramble out of the lawn chair, kicking the flimsy plastic over in my haste to answer the door. Slinging my T-shirt over my head, I race across the grass, panting from the heat and exertion. Running into the kitchen, the artificially cooled air sends a chill through me, goosebumps rising on my arms.

Slowing to a brisk walk, I move through the house. With a deep breath, I smooth my hair away from my face, readjust my messy bun before flinging the door open.

"Cam?"

CHAPTER 2
SLOANE

can't believe Cam Crawford's standing on the front porch right now, all six-foot-five of him. And he's gorgeous as ever, an artfully broken-in gray T-shirt stretched taut across his broad chest, barely containing his biceps. Several days' worth of scruff frames a chiseled jawline, and his dark hair's floppy and ruffled, as if he's just run his hands through the slight waves. His eyes are still the deepest, most vibrant blue I've ever seen. Rimmed with dark circles, he's giving off a broody air. Less high school hotshot, more sexy pro baller.

"Cam?" I repeat his name again, trying to figure out if this is a dream or my new Karmic reality.

I typed the words and sent them out into the universe late last night, but I never actually believed Cam Crawford would materialize on my front porch after all these years.

"Hey, Trouble."

His voice is deeper than I remember, the gravelly tone sending hot pulses straight to my core as my old nickname rolls off his full lips.

The sweetest sound in the world, falling from that mouth.

I can't freaking believe it.

He got my email and instead of just hitting Reply like the average Joe, he flew back home to surprise me. He's here to sweep me off my feet like a modern-day small-town Cinderella and I'm wearing a ratty *Thunder Creek Mustangs* football T-shirt and a cheap string bikini from the Walmart.

Still, May 12th is a fucking magical day.

My stomach goes all fluttery and adrenaline surges through me as he locks his serious gaze on mine.

Yes! After a craptastic start to the year, things are finally looking up.

I lick my bottom lip, holding my breath in anticipation of what's about to happen. His *in-person* response to my love note. Possibly our very first kiss.

"Um—sorry to bother you like this—" He runs a hand through his dark hair, shuffling from foot to foot. "But is your dad home?"

I blink, my mind whirring, trying to process the words. "My dad?"

"Yeah. Coach Carter. Is he here?"

Cam shoves a hand in his jeans pocket as crushing disappointment settles like a 200-pound barbell on my chest.

Of course he's here for my dad. He always came looking for my dad.

The winningest football coach in town history. The man, the myth, the legend. Everybody's hero.

Dammit. Good to see nothing's changed.

Feigning neutrality, I hold back a sigh.

"He's still at school." I glance at my watch. "But he

should be home soon, usually around three-thirty. You're welcome to come in and wait."

I tip my head back toward the dim living room, stepping aside so he can enter. He brushes past me, our arms touching for the briefest of moments, and I catch the faint scent of him. The same masculine-smelling cologne, like he's come straight out of the forest, mixed with the slightest hint of salty sweat from the south Georgia heat.

The screen door slams shut, the bang echoing loudly through the quiet space. Kicking the main door closed behind me to preserve the precious AC, I turn on my heels and head to the kitchen. Cam trails behind and I wonder if he's checking out my ass, peeking from beneath the hem of my T-shirt. Just in case, I add in a little extra shimmy.

"Want something to drink while you wait? Water? Lemonade?" I offer, already reaching for a glass from the cabinet.

He shrugs. "Sure. Lemonade's good."

I set about fixing drinks, plunking ice cubes into glasses, then pouring a healthy serving of lemonade for both of us from the plastic jug.

"Thanks."

Taking the drink from me, the tips of our fingers brush, and I work hard to ignore the electric zing shooting up my arm.

"Coach still gets his lemonade from Ingles, huh? They always had the best lemonade."

"Yep. My dad sticks to the tried-and-true. 'If it ain't broke, don't fix it' is his motto."

I gesture at the table and he takes the hint, sliding out a chair and maneuvering his massive body into it. He leans back and the old chair creaks under his weight. Cam looks to be solid muscle now and I silently pray this isn't the moment that chair finally cracks under pressure.

Lifting the glass to his lips, he takes a long gulp, and I fervently try not to stare. I haven't seen Cam Crawford in years—not since he left for college—and now he's sitting at my kitchen table.

Did he read the message I sent?

He's not acting like someone who read the World's Most Embarrassing Email. But I can't be sure—maybe he's playing it cool?

The wall clock ticks loudly behind me, the only other sound the light clink of ice in Cam's glass. He sets the lemonade down and drums his fingers on the table in an agitated rhythm. I silently shuffle through various conversation starters, my chest tightening as the seconds crawl by.

Damn, this is more awkward than rereading that tequila-drenched missive I typed last night.

I sink into the seat next to him, carefully angling my legs beneath the table to avoid playing footsy. He seems preoccupied—and not with how best to declare his undying love for me.

"So—what brings you back to Thunder Creek?"

There's a clever line. Good one, Sloane.

Keeping his eyes downcast, he pauses.

Tick, tick, tick.

Several seconds go by before he breaks the silence.

"I got cut."

I inhale sharply, sputtering on the overly sweet beverage. A few drops of liquid splatter onto my shirt and I swipe them quickly away. Cam says nothing, his jaw tense.

"Shoot. I'm real sorry, Cam. That sucks."

"Yeah. It does."

He sighs, his huge shoulders lifting then sinking, exhaling his despair. A decade ago, I would have reached for his hand, but the gesture feels clunky and awkward now, after all this time.

"Um—so what happens next?" I tuck my leg up under me, biting at my lip. "Do you get picked up by another team or something?"

He resumes the finger drumming. "Maybe. I had a tough season, didn't make as many plays as I wanted."

"Oh."

"The coach said I have an attitude problem coupled with a bad reputation, whatever that's supposed to mean. I may have told him to fuck off."

"Wow, okay."

Rule number one in football—never tell the coach to fuck off. That would get you ten laps, fifty pushups, and at least a one-game suspension from Coach Carter.

Cam lifts his head, staring straight at me. "That coach is kind of a dick. I do not have an attitude problem."

I nod, noticing he didn't mention the reputation part. But no need to poke the bear. What do I know, anyway? I wasn't there and you can't always trust everything you read in the tabloids.

"So what's your plan? Do you go to some type of camp or something to get scouted?"

"Nah. My agent's working on it. But he suggested I take some time off to 'get back to basics.'"

"And that's why you're here, to see my dad."

"Yep."

Not to see me.

"So are you staying in town for the summer then?" I run my thumb up and down the smooth surface of my glass, wiping away the condensation and holding my breath for his response.

He shakes his head. "I don't know. Maybe? My folks moved to Denver to be closer to my oldest sister and her kids. Everything's kind of up in the air right now."

"Right." I bob my head in sympathy. "I know that feeling."

"Are you visiting? Didn't think you'd move back to Thunder Creek after college. I always figured you'd have some fancy corporate job, since you're so smart." He locks his eyes on mine and heat creeps up my neck.

Guess it's my turn in the hot seat.

"Not visiting, exactly. I'm kind of between things at the moment myself—" My voice trails off as I kick around the most positive way to say I'm jobless, homeless, and newly unengaged.

"Guess that makes two of us, huh?" He shoots me a half-hearted smile and I go all gooey inside.

Get it together, Sloane. The guy just lost his career, his passion. Stop mooning over him like a lovesick highschooler.

"Yeah, guess so." I swallow hard, my throat tight and dry in spite of the lemonade.

The screech of the screen door creaking open shocks me back to reality. Quiet time with Cam is up—Coach is home.

"Sloane! Whose Rover's in the driveway?" My dad's big voice booms through the small house and then he's standing in the doorway of the kitchen in his Thunder Creek High uniform of dark blue polo and khakis, the ever-present orange whistle dangling from his neck.

"Well, I'll be damned. Is that Cam Crawford, wide receiver for Chicago, sitting at my kitchen table?" My dad squints at us before rushing over and slapping Cam hard on the back, embracing him in a side hug. "You in town for a visit, son?"

Cam shifts awkwardly in the chair. "Not exactly, sir. It's kind of a long story."

My dad's eyes narrow. "Well, lucky for you, I've got time. It's Friday afternoon and I'm staring down the weekend. That means it's officially happy hour. Let's grab a beer and catch up out back. Hey, baby."

My dad drops a kiss to the top of my head on his way to the fridge, pulling out two bottles of beer. Popping the lids from both, he hands one over to Cam and then heads out back. Cam follows, leaving me alone in the kitchen, wondering if he ever read the email.

CHAPTER 3
CAM

hit.

What am I doing back here in Thunder Creek? After all these years, this isn't the triumphant homecoming I dreamed of.

But after the dustup in Chicago with the team, the only logical move I could come up with was coming home. Sure, I could have flown to Denver and stayed with my parents, but what can they do? They can't help me get my mojo back. And the last thing I need right now is a lecture from my sister Ansley on positivity. Hard fucking pass. I'd rather go get my tarot cards read or visit a psychic before I build a 'manifestation board.' That's some new age bullshit right there.

No, this is where I need to be, I feel it in my bones.

And in my dick, but now's not the time to focus on Sloane and how breathtakingly fuckable she is. I shouldn't fixate on those wide, hazel eyes, brighter and more sultry than I remembered. How her T-shirt slipped off her shoulder to reveal her smooth, tanned skin. The way the

Georgia humidity curled up the chocolate brown wisps of hair around her heart-shaped face. That tiny strip of ass peeking out at me as she sashayed barefoot through the kitchen.

Kinda wrong to be lusting after Coach's daughter, sitting out here on his deck, drinking his beer and acting all innocent. Like I hadn't been fantasizing about peeling off his daughter's clothes back there in the kitchen ten short minutes ago.

Like, all kinds of messed up.

What the fuck is wrong with me?

"So, son—what's really going on? And don't sugarcoat it, either. You've gotta tell me the God's honest truth, or I won't be able to help you."

Coach levels serious hazel eyes on me—the same mossy shade as Sloane's—and it's a little disconcerting. The question, coupled with the stare, has me stiffening and shifting uncomfortably in the hot sun. I pick at the label on the beer bottle, my toe tapping as I carefully select my words.

"I screwed up."

Wow. Real enlightening.

"I gathered as much. How bad we talking? You in trouble with the law?"

"What? No, nothing like that."

"Okay, then, so it's nothing permanent that can't be fixed. Get someone pregnant?"

I blanch at his bluntness, squirming. "Uh, no. I mean, not that I know of."

"I would hope you're smart enough to always use protection. In this day and age—and in your position—you have to keep things locked up. You understand what I'm saying?"

"Yessir, absolutely. Every time. Not that there have been many times…" I stammer, my face heating. Coach chuckles, shaking his head.

"Sure, son. This isn't a confessional, no need to go into all the details."

My gut churns and I silently pray he'll move on to a new topic.

"So it's not the law, not a woman. Trouble with the ball then?"

"Sort of—"

Coach takes a long swig of his drink before tipping his head to the side and studying me. The furrow between his brows is deeper than before, the skin around his eyes crinkled from the sun, but other than that, the man's barely aged since I last saw him back in high school.

He waits, comfortable letting the silence between us stretch, long and loud. I kick my toe at a patch of dirt, a puff of dust rising into the air. My throat's dry and tight. I take a swig of beer, but it doesn't help much.

"Coach said I had an attitude problem. That it wasn't worth dealing with my shit because I wasn't scoring. So he cut me."

My voice is low, my face burning with shame. This is worse than calling my mother and telling her the bad news.

Because Coach knows football. He understands exactly what those words mean. And just how badly fucked I am right now.

"All I know is ball, Coach." The familiar feeling of panic claws its way through my chest, gripping my throat, strangling my voice. I can't breathe, every muscle in my body tight, ready for action.

Except there is no action. Nowhere to run.

This is my new reality and I have no idea how to dig out of the pit I dug this past season.

Coach doesn't say anything, doesn't offer up weak platitudes about how everything will work out or things always get better. Instead, he reaches over and rests his large hand on my shoulder, squeezing lightly.

A sense of calm radiates from my deltoid all the way down my arm. Through my biceps, my forearm, until my fingers tingle, the pressure built up in my muscles releasing. Heat pricks behind my eyes and I blink hard, pretending to be sensitive to the bright sun. My chest opens up and oxygen surges into my lungs—it's the first deep breath I've taken in days.

"You sure there's nothing else? Besides a shitty attitude and a few fumbles? Now's not the time to bullshit me, Crawford."

I nod. "Yeah. That's the gist of it. I let my emotions get the best of me this season. Took my eye off the ball."

Coach sets his empty bottle down, scrubs his jaw. "That doesn't sound irreparable then. I think with a month or two of hard work, we can get you back into shape. You can train with me—we'll do two-a-days. Privates in the morning, then workouts with the high school team in the afternoon. Weight room most days of the week on your own."

A fire, hot and bright, lights in my gut as I digest his words, process the plan.

Yes. I can do this.

I'm going to make it back.

I can fix this.

"I'll expect you to help with the afternoon workouts. Show those kids how it's done in the pros." Coach narrows his eyes at me and I shoot him a wan half-smile.

"Sure, no problem," I say. Even if I'm none too sure I'm

the best man for the job at the moment. But it's not like I can say no.

"Where you staying, son? Your parents moved out West, right? You still got friends in town?"

I shake my head. "Not really, sir. I planned to rent a room, maybe stay at the inn."

"Nah. Don't need you wasting your hard-earned money on accommodations. You can stay here, with me and Sloane. There's an extra bedroom, no sense having it sit empty. Go grab your stuff. We can start training tomorrow. Have you back on the field by pre-season."

Coach slaps my back, his face set with determination. I'm torn between the rush of cool relief that Coach still believes in me and a fluttery panic at sharing close quarters with Sloane.

Sloane Carter.

The perpetually off-limits good girl of my teenage dreams and dirtiest fantasies.

And now we'll be spending an entire summer together under one not-all-that-big roof.

I'm not sure if I should be ecstatic or scared shitless.

CHAPTER 4
SLOANE

t takes every ounce of willpower I possess not to hover in the kitchen, ear pressed tight against the screen door, hoping to catch snippets of the man-to-man my dad's having with Cam.

I shuffle around for a while, but can't really hear anything over the low hum of the refrigerator. Then the AC kicks on and I give up entirely, heading out to the living room.

Plopping onto the sofa, I pick up my cell and text Gracelyn.

Sloane: GRACE! You'll never guess who's in my backyard right now…

Bestie: Tom Holland?

Sloane: Really? Why would Tom Holland be in my yard?

Bestie: IDK. You said I'd never guess

Sloane: LOL. Think more local

Bestie: That guy from last night at Mustang's? Rick something or other?

Sloane: Mercifully, no

Bestie: What? I thought he was kinda cute

Sloane: No. He had that odd smirk thing going. And wouldn't stop talking about how great Dallas is gonna be this year. And we all know that means he's delulu

Bestie: Truth. Okay, I give up. Who's there???

Sloane: Cam

Bestie: OMFG

Sloane: I KNOW

Bestie: Are you totally freaking out rn? Did you have sex with him?

Sloane: What? No

Bestie: Oh. I thought he came to profess his love for you and whisk you away to Chicago

Sloane: Not exactly…

Bestie: Ohhhh—spill

Sloane: He's kind of in a bad spot
right now

"Sloane?"

My dad's deep voice startles me and I almost fall off the sofa as he and Cam saunter into the living room. I slam my cell face down on the cushion, the vibration of an incoming message rattling against my palm.

Gracelyn's going to have to wait.

I flick my eyes from my dad to Cam, trying to read their expressions. My dad seems happy, his broad chest puffed up. Cam seems…I don't know. Confused, maybe? Not sad or anything, but not happy either, his brow wrinkled.

"What's up?" My foot bounces in the air, crossed over my knee.

"Can you throw sheets on the guest bed?" Dad asks, folding his arms across his chest.

I bite at my lower lip, my mouth going dry. "Uh, yeah. Sure, no problem."

I don't move, my bottom glued to the sofa. The metal of my cell continues to vibrate against my palm—Gracelyn cannot take a freaking hint.

"Cam's going to be staying with us for a while." My dad grins over at Cam like he's the prodigal freaking son and my insides twist.

Cam Crawford's staying at my house. In the only other room in the house, the bedroom next to mine.

Oh. My. God.

It's my high school dream come true.

Except now it's a freaking nightmare because I'm living with my dad at almost thirty years old.

FML.

"Go on, scoot." My dad pushes Cam toward the front door and I stand on wobbly legs, trying not to sway on unsteady feet.

I follow Cam's every move, staring at his broad back and very fine ass as he bangs out the front door.

"Sloane? You okay?" Dad interrupts my ogling, and I tear my gaze away from Cam's retreating backside.

"Uh, yeah. Of course. How long's he staying?" I hook a thumb in the direction of the driveway. "Like, a week or two?"

"I don't know. Might take longer to get him back on track. You okay with that?" He narrows his eyes at me and I swallow hard.

"Sure. Totally fine," I say, forcing a tight smile. I mean, I should be fine with it. A gorgeous pro football player staying in the room next to mine, with only a thin wall separating us.

And I probably would be fine if I hadn't sent that drunken email.

Maybe he never read it. He's not acting like he read it, at least. And now he probably doesn't have access to his team email anymore. I should just forget about the email, pretend it never happened.

The door swings open and Cam reappears, duffel in hand. Good gravy, the man is gorgeous. His wide, muscled frame fills up the entire space, golden rays of sunlight streaming around him. I can practically hear a romantic swell of music announcing his arrival as we lock eyes across the living room.

"Sloane will get you settled in. We usually order pizza on Friday night. Does that work for you, son?"

"Sounds great, thanks." Cam nods his approval and I force myself to move, ignoring the frantic flutter of possessed butterflies lurching around my stomach.

Cam looms behind me as we walk down the dim, narrow hallway. My bedroom's at the end, the guest bedroom adjacent, with a shared bath on the opposite side of the hall. The house was built in the mid-sixties, before the concept of the en suite became a thing.

"Guess we're going to have to pull straws to see who gets first shower," I joke, tipping my head at the small aqua bathroom.

"Nah. You can always have it. It's your house and all."

Heat rushes into my cheeks and I open my mouth to correct him—I mean, technically it's my dad's house and I'm a visitor here too—but then slam my lips shut before I say something pathetic. I've already spilled my tale of woe —no need to keep reminding him of my current solo status.

"Here's the extra bedroom." I sweep my arm at the door, ushering him into the room that's an exact replica of mine, just flipped with no window. "It's nothing fancy, probably not like your digs in Chicago—"

"It's great, thanks." Cam drops his duffel on the ground, his hulking frame taking up most of the space. My eyes flit to the bed and my heart flip-flops.

Stop it, Sloane. The man's at an all-time low and all you keep thinking about is jumping his bones.

"Uh—I'll go get the sheets and make the bed up for you."

I scurry out of the room, my entire body flaming.

This is going to be the longest summer of my life.

Grabbing the first set of sheets I lay hands on, I hustle back to the bedroom. Only when I unfold the sheets and start stretching the cotton over the mattress do I realize I'm staring at the smiling faces of the Jonas brothers in all their boy band glory.

OMG.

And why the fuck does my dad still have these sheets?

"Is that the Jonas brothers?" Cam asks, his voice tipping up.

I'd love nothing more than to crawl under the bed in mortification right now, but I'm not sure I'd be able to inch my way back out with any shred of dignity remaining.

"Um—yeah. You nailed it. Nick, Joe, and Kevin, keeping you cozy all night long." I straighten up, moving to the end of the bed to pull the fitted sheet tight.

"Cool." Cam's lips tip into a smirk and I'd love to melt into the beige carpet, becoming one with the semi-plush fibers.

I wave the top sheet up in the air with a flourish and decide to fully embrace the Jo Bro sheets. Too late to do anything about it now, so might as well go with it.

"Didn't my dad tell you about the available accommodations? This is the Jonas Brothers suite. If I dig around, I may even be able to find the matching pj's—although I'm not sure they'll fit you." I take the opportunity to eye him up and down, pretending like he may have a shot at squeezing into my Jonas brothers jammies.

"It's okay, don't go to any trouble on my behalf," Cam says, not missing a beat. "You've already done way too much."

"You sure?" I glance over my shoulder as I fluff the pillow, smacking Joe's grinning face. "Maybe I could find my signed T-shirt?"

Cam chuckles, waving his hand in the air. "Positive. This is more than enough." He tips his head at the sheets.

"Lucky for you, the comforter is long gone. Gracelyn and I spilled glitter nail polish on it and then tried to use nail polish remover to get it off. Spoiler alert—acetone eats comforters. We ruined it and I'm pretty sure I cried."

"Shame," he says with a straight face, his marine eyes glittering. It's the first time I've seen him genuinely happy since he walked into the house.

"I know. It was a vintage set. Probably could have sold it for a lot of money on eBay."

"For sure."

"You'll have to make do with this quilt instead. Real sorry about that." I pull the navy-and-white quilt up on the bed, smoothing out the wrinkles.

Satisfied, I straighten up and spin around to face Cam. "Feel free to use the dresser and the closet to unpack. They should be pretty empty." I gesture at the tall wooden dresser in the corner and Cam nods.

"Thanks." He shoves a hand into his pocket and I rack my brain trying to come up with some roundabout way to find out if he read the World's Most Embarrassing Email.

"Well, I guess I'll leave you to it—" I hold my hands up and shoot two finger guns at him, my voice trailing off. Somehow managing to be both cringey and awkward, all at the same time.

So much time's passed since we've seen each other that I'm not sure how to act around him anymore.

I wish things between us were the same as they were back in high school, before he was Cam Crawford, pro football player. When he'd stop by my locker every morning to say hi and catch up on the latest episode of *The Walking Dead.* Or when we'd sneak into the weight room during lunch—sometimes Cam would lift weights and I'd eat my sandwich in peace, avoiding the smelly cafeteria scene. Back when he'd pop over to the house to see my dad after practice and we'd end up talking for hours, about school and football and all our big grown-up plans.

Plans that didn't happen, at least not for me.

I force my legs to move, heading for the door. As I brush past Cam, he reaches out, taking gentle hold of my wrist.

"Hey—" The low rumble of his voice sends a hot bolt of electricity shooting straight through me and my breath hitches. My gaze drops to his huge hand encircling my arm, the rough pads of his fingers creating a flame burning beneath my skin. His touch familiar, but somehow different, more charged.

"Yeah? You rethinking the Jonas brothers' shirt?" I tease, but Cam doesn't smile at my joke this time, his face serious.

"Thank you." He swallows hard, his throat bobbing with the effort, and it's a monumental struggle for me to even breathe as the rough pad of his thumb tingles against my skin.

"It's no biggie." I shrug, my heart pounding against my rib cage.

"It is to me. It's good to see you, Trouble."

Blood roars in my ears as Cam gazes at me with an intense stare, sending shock waves rippling through me.

"You too, Cam." I force the words out, my voice hoarse, like I've been at Coachella screaming for the last few days.

He lets go of my arm then, breaking the connection, and I somehow make myself move forward, out of the room. I head down the hall, sinking down onto the edge of the bed. Every inch of my body's sparking and I'm acutely aware of the dampness between my legs.

It's going to be a long, hot summer, sharing such close quarters with Cam Crawford.

CHAPTER 5
CAM

It's downright painful being in such close proximity to Sloane, even after all these years. I knew coming back to town would be risky, but I hadn't counted on this, on her. The two of us being back in Thunder Creek at the same time. And certainly not on us living together.

Sitting at the kitchen table together, pretending to be all nonchalant, is almost impossible when all I want to do is stare into those wide hazel eyes sprinkled with gold flecks. Memorize every angle of this grown-up version of her, the curves and the dips. Touch her smooth skin, run my thumb across her cheek, trace along her bottom lip. Lean in so close I feel the heat radiating from her body just before I press my mouth to hers.

I swallow hard and instead train my eyes on the melted triangle of cheese on the plate to keep me from staring at those full, pink lips and chasing the wild fantasy.

Coach talks about the team and his summer training plan, but I barely catch a word he's saying—all my attention funnels to his daughter.

Time's only made her more beautiful, more perfect—but she's still as off-limits as ever.

Maybe more so, seeing as how I need her dad's help something fierce.

Besides, I need one-hundred percent of my attention focused on football. No distractions. Not even one as gorgeous as Sloane.

Especially not one as gorgeous as Sloane.

Keep your eye on the ball, Crawford.

"What do you think about that, Cam?" Coach pauses, pizza slice frozen in mid-air as he waits for my response.

Shit. What was he saying?

"You remember the Wild Mustang, right? Three receivers on one side, tight end stuck to the O-line?"

I nod, vaguely recalling the formation.

"Don't worry, I'll grab you a playbook after dinner so you can refresh your memory. I'm sure there's a lot swimming around up there right now." He taps a finger to his own temple.

There definitely is, and unfortunately, most of it's not about football.

"Thanks, Coach. Going through the playbook should jog my memory. Last thing I want to do is go out there and mess up your team, get them all confused on plays."

"Understood. You know, let me get that for you right now. Be right back." He shoves away from the table, heading out of the kitchen toward his room on the pressing mission.

Leaving me alone with Sloane.

I'm not sure if it's relief, apprehension, or indigestion flooding my gut—maybe a combo of all three.

"My dad's really amped that you're here." Sloane purses her lips and I can't quite figure her expression. I'm dying to shoot back, *"What about you?,"* but the question feels too bold, too big for the small room.

Instead, I take a long swig of water, trying to calm my nerves. The cool beverage does nothing besides add to the jostling pizza-and-anxiety mix swirling around my stomach. Sloane shifts in her chair, absentmindedly winding a stray lock of hair around her finger, waiting for me to say something, anything.

"Wish I was here under better circumstances." I cast my eyes down, my chest tight. A familiar feeling now, and I don't like it one bit.

She leans toward me, into my space, and my heart pumps harder. She smells like summer—coconutty and sweet—and blood rushes south as the scent of her fills my nostrils.

For fuck's sake, Crawford. Get it together or you're gonna be blue balling all summer long.

Her small hand wraps around my forearm and squeezes reassuringly. Not helping the dick situation at all, but my chest loosens a touch.

"I'm sure my dad will help get things all straightened out." Her voice is soft and comforting and I grasp at the words like they're a life raft and I'm on the damn Titanic post-iceberg collision.

"Here we go." Coach bustles back into the room and Sloane slides her hand away from my arm so fast there's a slight breeze. A thick paper booklet hits the table beside my plate and a flood of memories rush back as my eyes trace over the familiar dark blue lettering: *Thunder Creek Football.*

"You've got some homework, son." Coach thumps the playbook. "Good thing you've got all weekend. Tomorrow morning's conditioning and then we take

Sunday off. Come Monday, I'll expect you to be up to speed."

"Yessir." I thumb at the paper, nerves firing.

Coach sinks back into his seat and silence fills the room. I stare at the playbook, not daring to lift my eyes to Sloane's.

"Everybody finished? I've got clean up." Sloane starts stacking empty dishes, not waiting for an answer. Coach touches her on the arm.

"You okay, baby? I'm sure today was hard for you." Sloane winces, staring down at the floor.

"Yeah, I'm fine. Right as rain, actually." Her voice tips up into the forced-cheery range and she shrugs, narrow shoulders drooping.

"Better off now than later," Coach says, patting her arm. "All for the best."

She nods and huffs out a breath, then pivots toward the sink, turning her back on us.

"Yep." She turns on the faucet full blast, aggressively rinsing the plates, and I wonder what exactly they're talking about.

But I don't dare ask. Whatever it is feels personal.

"All right. I'm gonna go catch the ESPN highlights. You two are welcome to join." He hooks his thumb in the direction of the living room.

"Maybe later," Sloane says, still scrubbing.

"Okay." Coach squeezes her shoulder, then grabs his beer and ambles into the living room not giving me so much as a backward glance.

Because he trusts you with his daughter.

The thought weighs heavy on my mind as Sloane sashays past me, gliding from the sink to the table, then back again. She's wearing the same T-shirt from earlier, but threw on a pair of tiny denim shorts before supper. The type that's so short the pockets hang lower than the frayed hem, leaving miles of upper thigh exposed.

Good god, this is going to be a long, hot summer.

Sweat beads on my lower back as my eyes travel up her legs, landing on her juicy ass. An ass I'd definitely like to caress, squeeze, maybe even smack.

But no matter how badly I'd like to hit that, Sloane's still the coach's daughter.

Firmly off-limits, an unspoken rule for every member of the Thunder Creek football team.

Date anyone you want, as long as it's not Sloane Carter.

And I'm betting that rule still stands, especially with me accepting shelter and coaching from her father.

Besides, I can't afford to fuck this up.

There is no back-up plan.

Football is—and always has been—the whole plan. Now's not exactly the time to take my eye off the ball.

"Cam?" Sloane's voice interrupts my worrying. "Can you bring me the rest of the silverware, please?"

She tips her head at the knife sitting next to the pizza box and I snatch it up, standing.

"Sorry, I should have offered to help with the dishes." I meet her at the sink, handing over the knife, and she gives it a good scrub before rinsing the bubbles away.

"It's fine. You're the guest." She swipes at the hair flopping over her eye with the crook of her arm, pushing the dark fringe out of her way.

"Technically, I suppose. But I need to pull my weight around here, if I'm going to be staying for a while."

"Agreed. How about I let you take out the trash?" She shoots me a cheeky grin, and I can't help but laugh.

There's the Sloane I know, always quick with a comeback. It's one of the many things I loved about her. That and her smile, a smile that stretches from her mouth all the way to her eyes, instantly making you feel better, special.

Like you were the only person in the room, quite possibly the world.

Something always floated in the air between us, but I never had the balls to act on it. There was a hard line drawn when it came to Sloane Carter, and not one member of any Thunder Creek High football team ever crossed that line. At least, not to my knowledge.

Does that line still exist?

Because she's not a teenage girl anymore.

Now she's so much more, all curves and woman. And the chemistry that flowed between us back then still feels as strong as ever.

You cannot go there, Crawford. No matter how good she looks in a T-shirt. Or how great she'd look out of it. You're here to get your shit together, land a new contract, and play pro ball.

I clear my throat.

"Deal."

"The trash goes out around back. Pick-up's Monday, so we have to take it to the street Sunday night. And by we, I mean you." She flashes her white teeth at me and I pretend to grimace.

"Fine. I'll try to remember."

"Don't forget. Because we have big ole' bugs here during the summer and they'll start partying in the garbage. Maybe you blocked that fun little nugget from your memory."

"Oh, trust me, I didn't." I heft the trash bag from the can, cinching the plastic tie.

She shuts off the water, wiping her hands on a dishtowel. "I'm going to grab a quick shower. Holler at my dad if you need anything."

"Will do."

Spinning on her heel, she glides out of the kitchen and I'm glad Coach is glued to the television screen, fully engrossed in the latest sports news. Because I have a raging hard-on that's impossible to conceal, courtesy of his darling daughter.

I'm not sure how long this cozy little arrangement's going to last—and it's only night one of quite possibly the longest summer of my life.

CHAPTER 6
CAM

I toss and turn all night, the Jonas brothers doing nothing to calm my nerves. All the negative thoughts run through my head, on freaking repeat. During the day, I manage to silence that voice, that doubt. But at night, in the stillness and quiet, it won't shut the hell up.

I fucked up.

What if I don't get picked up by another team?

Is this the end of my career?

All I know is football.

Without football, I have nothing. I am nothing.

I'm so fucked.

Round and round I go, until I'm so tightly wound I'll never get to sleep. Then my thoughts drift to Sloane in bed down the hall, and that's not much help, either.

I should stay away from her, leave the situation exactly how it stands.

Friends.

She's the coach's daughter and I have nothing to offer, anyway.

I need to focus forward, on the future. Not get sucked back into the past, the what-ifs, the could-have-beens.

I'm so fucked.

Finally, the first weak rays of sunlight slant through the blinds and I give up on the idea of sleep altogether. I rise and throw on a T-shirt, gym shorts, and sneakers, then hit the bathroom to brush my teeth. Tiptoeing down the hall, I'm careful to be quiet and not wake Sloane.

I spot Coach already sitting at the kitchen table, sipping coffee and scrolling through his cell.

"Morning, son." He glances up from the screen. "You want to eat breakfast before practice? Toast, a banana? Cereal?"

"A banana works, thanks." I snag the fruit from the bowl sitting on the counter, muscles already humming and ready to go.

"Glad to see you're up. We should get going, hit the field before it gets too hot. You ready?"

"Sure."

"There's a jug of water in the freezer. Grab it and let's go. We'll take my truck."

Coach shoves away from the table, setting his mug in the sink. I take the frozen water jug out of the freezer and together the two of us head out.

The air's warm and thick with humidity, the low hum of mosquitos buzzing off in the distance. My skin's getting sticky already and we haven't even left the driveway. Coach unlocks the truck, the beep echoing along the quiet street. I climb in and try to relax, taking a deep breath and counting to three as I exhale. Coach backs down the drive and heads toward the high school, a country tune playing on the radio. He hums under his breath, fingers thumping the steering wheel in beat with the music, totally at ease. A sharp contrast to me, every inch antsy and fired up. I'm grateful he doesn't try to strike up conversation and is content listening to the music.

We whiz through the neighborhood, the only vehicle on the road at this early hour. The sky's streaked pink with the dawn as Thunder Creek High comes into view. I suck in a breath, a flood of emotions rolling through me—nervous excitement, nostalgia, apprehension, dread, defeat. Everything's spinning together and I'm as confused now as I've ever been.

I haven't been back home since I turned pro, right after college. Thunder Creek still looks the same—same old houses, same old buildings. The high school's no exception, the chain-link fenced parking lot, the white two-story building with the blue metal roof, the iron statue of our mascot, a mustang bucking on hindlegs in the courtyard.

Everything about this place is the same, as if time stood still here.

The only thing different is me.

Throat tight, I swallow down my regrets. Now's not the time to focus on my screw-ups; I've done plenty of reflection on those over the last few days. Right now, I need to focus on making things right, getting back to basics and finding a new team. That's why I'm here.

We park behind the school and I trail behind Coach toward the football field. Even though I'm older, taller, and stronger since the last time I set foot on these grounds, deep down I still feel like the same high school kid as I trudge over the dew-soaked grass. Coach unlocks the gate, shoving it open for me, and we step onto the track.

"Welcome home, son." He slaps me on the back and the tightness in my chest loosens up a touch. "Run a mile for warm-up and then we'll do some drills."

"Yes, sir."

I stretch my hamstrings and quads for a minute and then get going, running along the track at a moderate speed. The air's stagnant and sweat beads at my temple, on my brow, my low back. After the first lap, I start to relax and lean into the work. Get lost in the rhythm of my breath, finding my pace. By the third loop, I push harder, every muscle firing. The fourth feels easy and I'm all warmed up.

"Done?" Coach rises from the metal bleachers, clipboard in hand.

"Yes, sir." I lift my shirt, wiping the sweat from my face. Thunder Creek's about ten times hotter than Chicago and I'm out of practice dealing with the heat.

"First thing we'll work on is your cuts. Yesterday, I watched some footage from a few of your games last season. Looked like you struggled a bit with explosiveness and direction change."

He's one hundred percent right, even if I don't want to admit it. I got beat more than once last year and I sure as hell won't get picked up by another team if I can't outrun the competition.

"Okay, sounds good."

He points at the cones set up in the center of the field. "Remember the footwork drill? Y'all run that in the pros?"

I nod. "I remember. And yes, sometimes we do. It's been a while, though."

"I figured. Thought we'd get back to the fundamentals. I'll blow the whistle and you sprint straight toward the first cone. Maneuver around the cone, then run toward the second and cut to the right past the third. Got it?"

"Yes, sir."

"Good. Once you pass the third cone, cut hard to the

right at a ninety-degree angle and curl back to cone number four."

"Okay—"

"Then turn and sprint to the right, take another 90-degree cut, and sprint to the fifth cone. We'll finish by curling around the sixth cone."

"Got it, Coach." I roll my shoulders, shake out my calves and ankles, and get ready to run. Coach pulls his stopwatch from his pocket, thumb hovering on the start button. The whistle blows, high and shrill, and I take off toward the first cone.

The sun's bright rays shimmer on the turf as I race through the cones, running the drill I've practiced many times before. My lungs burn as I make the cut and curl back to the fourth cone.

"Good hustle, keep it up," Coach yells, his voice carrying across the empty field. I turn the burners on, forcing my legs to move faster, knees to rise higher, arms to pump harder.

"And—time!"

I lift my arms up over my head, expanding my rib cage to get more oxygen into my burning lungs.

"Decent. Ten seconds."

"Shit," I mutter under my breath, shaking my head.

"Just the opening time, son. Two minutes and we'll run it again."

I take a deep nose breath, cracking my neck to the right, then the left before lining back up at cone one.

Tweet!

The whistle blows again and I sprint off toward the first cone, repeating the drill. Once, twice, three times. I run those cones so many times, I lose track.

"Time!" Coach shouts across the field and I bend down,

hands on my knees. I'm sweaty and tired, and we're still on the first drill.

"That's better, Crawford. Eight seconds."

For the first time in weeks, I feel marginally better about my career.

"Not too shabby. We'll keep working on it. Let's move to the sit-up and catch. Grab some water—don't want you passing out on me here on day one." He tips his head at the bleachers and I glance over at the risers for the first time all morning.

There's Sloane, sitting about halfway up, long, tanned legs outstretched in front of her. She's wearing a Thunder Creek ball cap, her hair pulled back in a ponytail, and I swear I haven't seen anything near as sexy in a good, long while.

Seeing her here takes me straight back to high school, when she'd come and do homework on the bleachers during practice, waiting for her dad. Other girls would show up, but they'd all sit around giggling, flirting with the players.

Not Sloane.

She barely poked her nose out of her books—except to say hi to me.

She waves at us now and my heart pounds double-time, racing faster than it did during the cone footwork drill.

How long has she been watching? Did she see my first ten runs? Or just the last few that were actually fast?

"You coming, Crawford? Or you going to dawdle the morning away?" Coach taps at his watch and I take a big chug of water before jogging back over to him.

"I'm sure you remember this one. Take a seat." He gestures at the turf and I sink down onto the ground, knees bent. "You're going to lay down, then when I say go, do a sit-up. I'll throw the ball and you catch it as you sit up. Simple, but effective."

I nod, laying down on the hard turf. The sky's a bright blue now, the sun fully risen, and I stare up at the cloudless morning and wait.

"Go!"

I crunch up and the ball flies straight at my chest. Catching it, I toss the football back to Coach and lay back down.

"Go!"

We repeat this drill over and over, Coach sometimes throwing the ball, sometimes not, just to keep me guessing. I try to forget about Sloane watching from the bleachers and focus on catching the ball. By the time Coach calls the end of the drill, my abs are on fire, my back itchy from the turf and drenched in sweat.

"Pretty good. We'll keep working on it, but that was respectable. Your reaction time up close is fine. You have your eyes checked regularly?" He peers down at me, tossing the ball from hand to hand.

"Had an eye exam at the start of last season. Wish I could blame it on failing eyesight, but no such luck."

"Okay, then. Last drill for this morning, wall ball. Hop on up—" He extends his hand, helping me up, and I follow him over to the concession stand to the left of the bleachers.

"Stand there, good—" He points to a red taped line about five feet away from the wall, then tosses me the ball. "Throw the ball at the wall and catch it. Sounds easy, but we both know it's not. Start head-on, that's right—"

I hammer the football at the wall and it bounces off to

the left at an angle. I race to catch it, barely getting there in time.

"Good hustle. Again…"

I follow his instructions, throwing the ball at the wall at all different angles and speeds, darting to catch the football before it falls to the ground. By the time Coach calls the drill, sweat's pouring down my face, dripping into my eyes. My shirt clings to my soaked back and I'm pretty sure my antiperspirant failed me.

"Good practice today, son. You can hit the weight room later. Tomorrow's off, then Monday afternoon we'll have the boys out here. You hit the weights in the morning, then we'll run routes in the afternoons."

"Thanks, Coach. I appreciate it."

Coach pauses, waiting for me to make eye contact. "Crawford, you looked fine out there. We'll get you back up to speed in a month or two, tops. You've got this." He pats my arm and a tiny fragment of anxiety chips away.

If Coach believes in me, that's saying a lot. He's not one to mince words or blow smoke up people's asses just to make them feel good. There's a reason he's the winningest high school football coach in the entire state of Georgia.

"Hey, Daddy, Cam." Sloane skips down the bleachers, her dark ponytail swishing behind her. She leans over and hugs her dad, shooting me a wide, pretty smile.

"Hey, baby. Thought you'd still be asleep." Coach picks up his clipboard, tucking the stopwatch back into his pocket.

"No. I'm so used to getting up early. Habit, you know?"

"Always good to seize the day. Listen, I need to swing by Mack's house and work on a few last-minute summer roster changes. You think you could give Cam a ride home?"

"Sure," Sloane says. "No problem."

"Thanks, baby. Good practice today, Cam. Go eat some breakfast, refuel."

"Will do. Thanks, Coach."

Coach shoots us a two-finger salute, then heads out to the parking lot, whistling.

"You ready?" Sloane tips her head, adjusting her sunglasses on the bridge of her nose.

"Sure."

We walk out to the almost-empty parking lot together at an easy pace, Sloane keeping step with me even though she's much shorter.

"You looked good out there," she says, sliding into the driver's seat of her Volvo. "Sorry, let me move that stuff."

Reaching across the console into the passenger seat, she grabs a thick stack of files, chucking them unceremoniously into the cluttered backseat.

"You probably need to adjust the seat."

I kick a few empty water bottles out of the way and fold myself down into the leather, jamming the plastic button on the side of the seat to move it back. The motor groans as it slides backward, relieving the pressure in my knees.

"Wow, I didn't realize the seat went back that far." Sloane peers over the rim of her sunglasses, one brow arched high on her forehead. "Who knew?"

She presses the start button and the engine roars to life. Gunning out of the parking spot, she does a quick one-eighty, heading back toward the house. Instinctively, my fingers grip the door handle as she flies down the residential street. At this rate, we're going to be home in half the time it took to get here.

"You always drive this fast?" I ask, glancing over at her. Her small hands grip the wheel and at least she's staring straight ahead and not fiddling with the radio or something.

"You think this is fast?" She cuts her eyes at me for a quick second before turning back to the road.

"Yeah, for Thunder Creek. Maybe not in Chicago."

"I'll slow down for you, how about that?" Her voice is light and teasing, the mood between us easy. I always appreciated that about her. Where other girls made things tense and weird, with Sloane I could always just be me.

"Thanks. Can't afford an injury."

"Oh, true." She eases off the gas, slowing way down. Now we're practically crawling and her knuckles turn white from gripping the wheel.

"How long have you been back?" I ask.

"A few months."

"Where were you before?"

"New Orleans."

She drums on the steering wheel as we idle at the stoplight. AC blasts from the air vents, freezing the beads of sweat on my face, and Taylor Swift belts out something about being an anti-hero.

"You working now?" I notice the corners of her mouth tense, her lips pressing together tight.

"Not at the moment. I was working at a law firm in New Orleans, but I hated it."

"Gotcha."

"I had a job as a paralegal, but honestly, it was boring. I didn't love New Orleans all that much, either. And I was engaged."

The words tumble out of her, then she pauses and bites down on her lip. Her teeth dig into the flesh so hard, I'm worried she might break the skin.

"Engaged, huh? Wow."

"Yeah, turns out he was a ratface. Cheated on me with his secretary. Like how fucking cliché can you get, ya know?" She glances over at me, her cheeks turning pink, and I'm shocked.

She was engaged?

My chest tightens, knowing she promised herself to someone else. Was presumably in love with someone else.

And then the asshole cheated on her?

In what wild, unhinged universe does a guy cheat on a woman like Sloane? A person so kind, so genuine, so honest, loyal, and true?

I clear my throat. "I'm sorry, that really sucks."

"Yeah, well, better to find out before the wedding, I guess. Really would have been great if he decided to bang her before I paid all those down payments, though. Asshole."

"That is a dick move."

"Yeah, the actual, literal definition of a dick move. So, when you feel bad about your life, slide on over and talk to me. That should cheer you up." She shoots me a wan smile and I search for something—anything—to say that might make her feel better.

"I heard one of the Jonas brothers is single again."

Really, Crawford? That's all you can come up with? A stupid joke about the Jonas brothers?

"Haha, funny. Doubt I'd have much luck with a Jonas brother at this stage of my life. Besides, I think I may have evolved from there."

"Really? You're out of your boy band phase then?" I cock a brow.

"Firmly." She pauses for a minute. "What about you? I'm sure you've had tons of girlfriends since you left Thunder Creek. Did you leave anyone special back in Chicago?"

"Me? No, definitely not." I smooth my hands down my shorts. "There's been no one special. Casual stuff here and there. But my focus has been on football. Doesn't leave time for much else."

"Yeah, I'm sure that's tricky."

She pulls into the driveway, inching her car up next to mine. Cutting the engine, she turns to face me. Her face is flushed from the sun, the cinnamon freckles across her nose a touch darker. The scent of sunscreen fills the car and I can't stop staring at her glossy lips, wondering what she'd taste like. Her tongue darts out, licking at her lower lip, and a tense silence stretches between us.

I swallow hard, pulling my gaze up and away from her shiny pink mouth. "Thanks for the ride. I'm gonna hit the shower." I nod toward the house.

"Sure, anytime."

Before I say or do anything stupid, I hop out of the car and jog inside, putting plenty of space between me and the coach's way-too-good-for-me daughter.

CHAPTER 7
SLOANE

Well, cat's out of the bag now. Cam knows I was engaged and got unceremoniously dumped.

Super. Nothing like putting your best foot forward.

There is one bright spot, though. He can't have read the World's Most Embarrassing Email because he acted surprised. Either that or he's a damn good actor, but I kinda doubt it.

So at least he's still in the dark about my feelings for him.

Besides, he's bound to find out about my broken engagement in this tiny town. May as well hear the story straight from the source. I'd rather he get the facts from me and not some wild spin on the truth.

Buzz, buzz.

My cell vibrates in my hand as I walk into the house, the conditioned air chilly on my heated skin.

Bestie: What's going on? Can you talk?

> Sloane: Just got back from the football field

> Bestie: CALL ME. Better yet, meet me at Java Jolt

> Sloane: Ok, see you in five

I hesitate at the corner of the sofa for a second and debate checking in with Cam. The shower's already on in the bathroom—he's probably naked right now. Much as I'd like to bust in, that would be highly inappropriate.

Amazing, but inappropriate.

I settle for knocking on the door.

"Hey, Cam. I'm heading over to Java Jolt to meet Gracelyn. You want anything?"

I pause, waiting for his response.

"I'm good. Thanks." His deep voice is muffled through the door.

"Okay. If you change your mind, shoot me a text. Or you can meet us up there if you want." I cringe as soon as the words leave my mouth. Probably being too forward. I'm sure he has better things to do than hang out with me and my best friend.

"Cool, thanks for the invite."

I relax a little, seeing as he doesn't seem bothered. I'm just being friendly is all.

Yeah, right. No ulterior motive at all. Has absolutely nothing to do with the rippling muscles clearly outlined beneath his shirt or that sexy smirk.

"I'll be back." I wave at the closed door before trotting down the hall and heading out.

Java Jolt is in downtown Thunder Creek, about a five-minute drive from the house in the opposite direction of the school. The downtown's historic, all red-brick buildings with white awnings over the storefront windows for shade. A narrow sidewalk runs alongside the shops, outlining the town square, a large open lawn in the center for gatherings.

Mid-morning on a Saturday the town square is pretty packed, but I manage to find a parking spot a block away from the coffee shop.

Walking down the street, I pass by places I've known my entire life. I do my best to be friendly, waving at people I've known since I was in pigtails.

"Hey, Ms. Tilly, how are you?" I shout at the florist sweeping the sidewalk outside her shop. The same flower boxes still decorate the front windows, the blooms rotating seasonally. Pink and white peonies are the special of the day, exploding out of the wooden boxes. She glances up from the broom, tucking a loose strand of hair behind her ear.

"Good, Sloane. You?"

"Can't complain."

"Tell your dad hi for us."

"Will do."

"Sloane!" Mr. Anderson bellows at me from the hardware store across the street. "How's the team gonna do next year?" He's a big supporter of the football program and hasn't missed a game in fifteen years.

"Not sure, Mr. Anderson. But I'll report back as soon as I hear anything."

"'Atta, girl. Go Mustangs!" Pumping his fist in the air, he swings back into the air-conditioned store.

I dodge a runner and a young couple with a stroller

before finally hitting Java Jolt. The outside tables sit empty, probably because they're in direct morning sun and no one wants to sweat this early in the day. I head in and immediately spot Gracelyn sitting at a high top in the corner. She's already sipping an iced latte and waves a second through the air.

Bestie got me a beverage. Honestly, she's an amazing friend and I don't think I'd survive without her.

"Hey, girl, hey!" Gracelyn jumps up from her seat the minute I'm close enough to the table to touch, wrapping her arms around me in a tight hug. "You look fab. Must be love…" She waggles her eyebrows and I punch her in the arm.

"Stop! Sit down, everyone's staring," I hiss, slinking onto the stool.

"No, they're not. And even if they were, you know I wouldn't give a hoot."

"Yes, but I do. Sit…" I motion at her empty seat and fan my face, cheeks flaming.

"So…how's Cam? Did he come with you?" She whips her head around, glancing over both her shoulders, sending her golden curls flying.

"No, he's back home taking a shower." I sip my latte, enjoying the instant hit of caffeine and sugar.

"Ohhh, a shower. Sexy." She leans in, her nose almost touching mine. "I'm disappointed you didn't join him."

"Stop! It's my dad's house, I can't do that!"

"Wait—what? Cam Crawford's taking a shower at your house?"

"Correction: my DAD'S house. I just happen to be living there temporarily."

"Fine, whatever. That's not the interesting part of that

sentence. Let's circle back to Cam." She draws a tight loop in the air with her finger.

"Cam's staying with us for a while."

"Oh my god, spill. Right now." Gracelyn clutches my forearm, literally sitting on the edge of her seat. I swear, she's my best audience.

I take another sip of my drink, debating how much to say. I don't want to break his confidence and share details he'd rather not be made public. But Gracelyn is my best friend and word about Cam's bound to spread through town fast as wildfire.

"He got cut from his team. He needs help with his game, so he came back home to work with my dad."

"Of course he did." She rolls her eyes, annoyed on my behalf.

And that's why we're best friends. She gets it—the feeling of being an afterthought, outshined by your own father.

"So—this has nothing to do with the email you sent then?" Grace narrows her eyes.

"No." I fold the edge of the napkin beneath my drink into a perfect white triangle, then unfold it again. "I don't think he even read it."

"What? How do you know?"

"I had an overshare moment this morning. I told him I was engaged and then Ratface cheated on me and I broke it off. He acted like that was news to him."

"Oh."

"Honestly, I wish I could unsend the damn thing. Tequila's the sole reason that email's out in the universe."

"No, uh-uh. The universe knows you've been in love with Cam Crawford practically your entire life. Breaking up with Ratface was a huge blessing—look who was delivered to your doorstep! It's fate, Sloane."

"Ssh," I tsk, urging her to lower her voice at least two decibels. She gets high-pitched when she's excited and that sound carries like you wouldn't believe. "I agree that breaking up with Ratface was a blessing in disguise. However, Cam showing up is a coincidence. And he's not interested, anyway. Did you miss the part about how he's here to work with my dad, his coach?"

"Pish-posh. I'm sure he thinks you're hot and would be more than happy to date you."

"Highly doubt it, but thanks for the vote of confidence." I sit back, checking my cell for any missed texts. Nothing.

"What's the game plan? You going to ask about the email? Or just come right out and tell him how you feel?"

"No and no." I tick both options off in the air with my index finger.

"What? C'mon, Sloane! You can't piss away this golden opportunity. It's your chance to get the guy!"

"Grace, you watch too many rom-coms. That doesn't happen in real life. In real life, your ratface fiancé screws the secretary on his desk. In real life, a boring girl like me does not get the pro football player, the homecoming king, the town golden boy."

"And why not?"

"Because I'm average. A plain Jane. Nothing special. Once you see Cam again, you'll get it. He's a ten and I'm about a five."

"You're selling yourself way short, Sloane. You're at least an eight. Could be a ten with the glow-up we talked about last night at Mustang's."

"I love you, but you're delulu. Fake lashes and blonde highlights will not make me a ten."

"You're wrong. Let me do it, please?" She folds her hands, begging. "Come into the salon and I'll fix you up."

"Maybe." I twirl my ponytail, doubting Gracelyn's assessment of the situation. "But back to the Cam thing—besides the fact that he dates beyond-gorgeous models, he's really focused on football right now. He's trying to get picked up by a new team—I don't want to be a distraction."

"Cam's a big boy. He can decide if he wants to be distracted or not." She folds her arms over her ample chest, head bobbing.

Grace does have a point. Although I'd feel awful if professional football didn't work out for Cam. I know how much he wants it—has always wanted it—and there's no way I would stand between him and the sport he loves.

"It's Saturday. Invite him out tonight. There's a bonfire at the lake. You two should come—unless you'd rather sit at home with your dad and talk running routes."

Shoving the straw up and down in my cup, the plastic lid shrieks as I contemplate. I shake what's left of the ice and it rattles against the plastic.

Damn, she has a bunch of good points today.

"Fine. I'll ask if he wants to go. Fifty-fifty chance he'll stay home with my dad, but I'm willing to take that risk."

"Yes!" She raises her hand for a high-five and I humor her, slapping her open palm.

"Want me to give you a blowout for the occasion? I am a professional, after all. I think I have some lashes left over from last weekend's prom, too."

Gracelyn works with her mom at the only salon in town. She's been doing my hair since we were little girls, but now she has a shiny beauty school diploma hanging on her wall declaring her state-licensed ability to do so.

"I'll handle my hair, but thanks."

"You know where I live if you change your mind." Her cell buzzes, vibrating on the tabletop, and she quickly reads the text. "Sorry, babe, but I have to jet. Much as I'd love to sit around and chat about Cam all day, I promised my mom I'd help her with the Field wedding this afternoon. See you later?"

"Absolutely. Eight?"

"Yep, eight at the lake."

She gives me another quick hug, then sashays out the door. I check my own cell one more time, but still nothing.

Standing, I decide to hit the restroom before heading home. I toss my cup into the trash and make my way down the narrow hallway to the lone bathroom. Knocking, I try the door, but it's locked.

"Just a sec," a voice calls out and I slump back against the wall, waiting. I stare at the bulletin board directly in front of me, taking up most of the wall space. A flyer for summer camp's pinned to the board next to another advertising a new dog-walking service. A poster for the local art show next week hangs in the corner and next to it is a bright yellow sheet of paper.

Love to read? Have book recs you want to share? Come join the team at the library! We're looking for part-time help this summer at the Thunder Creek branch. Position available immediately.

A fringe of identical phone numbers hangs off the ad, begging to be pulled.

What the hell. I've been sitting around my dad's house moping for far too long. I do love the library–reading's totally my jam–and there aren't a ton of job prospects available within a fifty-mile radius. Maybe this is exactly the type of thing I need right now. Low-stress but fulfilling and also kind of fun. Plus, I'm not exactly dying to leave Thunder Creek, given the current Cam situation. Gracelyn got that part right, at least.

Tearing off a sunshiney rectangle with the number to the local library, I shove the paper in my pocket.

CHAPTER 8
CAM

I haven't been to a bonfire out at the lake in years, probably since the summer after graduation. When Sloane asked me to go with her tonight, my gut response was 'Pass.' The last thing I want to do is go hang out with my old buddies and shoot the breeze, answering a million and one questions about my career that's teetering on the line. But she looked so hopeful and enthusiastic about the damn thing, I didn't have it in me to let her down.

So now we're bumping along the red dirt road that leads to the lake in my Rover, rust-colored dust swirling in tiny cyclones even though I'm barely hitting twenty miles per hour. Sloane's window is rolled down, one arm slung out the window, and she's singing at the top of her lungs to some shitty pop song I've never heard. If it were anyone else, I would veto the terrible music selection, but she's so cute sitting in the passenger seat with her head thrown back, not a care in the world.

I wonder what that's like, not caring. The only time I

ever have that sensation is right after a win. The rest of the time, I'm wound tight with anxiety, like one of those rubber band balls people keep on their desks. Worry wrapped around worry, pressure and tension holding everything together.

Not Sloane.

Her face is relaxed, fingers tapping on her thigh to the quick beat of the song. Her hair's blowing in the breeze, dark strands flying around her tanned, bare shoulders. She glances over at me, the corners of her pink lips tipping into a slow smile.

"What?" she asks, a slight blush coloring her cheeks.

"Nothing. I was just thinking about the last time I was out here. Had to be the summer after graduation."

"Probably. The night Nick swam across the lake naked?"

I chuckle, picturing my buddy Nick's ghost-white ass bobbing in the dark water.

"Then Brayden shouted at him about gators and he totally freaked." Sloane shakes her head. "That was a dick move. Nick almost had a panic attack. I don't think the guy's been back in the lake since."

"I mean, Brayden probably wasn't wrong. I'm sure there are gators in the lake. Not the brightest idea to swim across at midnight buck naked. Especially drunk."

"Yeah, we were dumb kids back then." Sloane's gaze drifts out the window as the water comes into view, golden rays of the sunset shimmering on the flat surface of the lake.

I pull the Rover up next to a black pickup and throw the vehicle into park, joining the neat line of cars—at least twenty so far and counting.

The knot of anxiety in my gut tightens as I take in the gathering crowd and I inhale a deep breath.

I can do this.

So what if I got cut. I'm between teams right now, waiting to hear back on the next great opportunity.

What that opportunity will be and where it will take place, I'm not sure, but that's the line I'm running with all night.

"Hey, you okay?" Sloane squeezes my forearm and I relax my grip on the wheel, focus on the touch of her delicate fingers against my skin.

"Yeah, I'm fine." I inhale, long and slow, then exhale a tiny bit of anxiety.

Thump, thump, thump.

The entire vehicle shakes and I scowl, glancing out the windshield at Nick's sunburned face pressed against the glass. He's grinning at us, screwing up his mouth and sticking out his tongue. Classic Nick. Clearly hasn't matured much in the last decade.

"What's up, big man?" Nick pounds his huge hands on the windshield and I hop out, eager to get him and his body off my car. He's no longer a seventeen-year-old athlete at the top of his game; now he's tiptoeing into his thirties with a few extra pounds on his already-large defensive back frame.

"What's up, Nick?" I smack my palm against his and we bro hug. A few seconds later, Sloane swings around to meet us.

"Hey, sugar." Nick bends down, wrapping Sloane in a tight squeeze and lifting her off the ground, and a sharp twinge of jealousy pings through me.

Stop it, Crawford. You have no hold on her; it's not like you can call dibs.

Nick drops Sloane's feet back to the ground and I relax, shoving a hand in my pocket.

"Guys, look who Sloane brought with her!" He spins around to the group, announcing my presence and every muscle in my body contracts.

So much for relaxation.

Immediately, almost everyone sitting around the bonfire jumps up and runs over, swarming Sloane and me. There's a flurry of hugs and hellos and how-you-beens and I'm already over it, wondering how soon I can leave.

"Give the guy some breathing room. C'mon, y'all, let's grab a beverage." Nick grabs my arm and I instinctively take Sloane's hand, pulling us out of the overwhelming circle of people.

Her hand is soft and warm in mine, grounding me in this moment. She smiles over at me and the knot loosens a touch more as we head over to the bonfire already roaring near the lake.

The sun's almost all the way down now, sinking into the water, the last few lingering rays of light swallowed up by the night. Cicadas hum in the distance over the rhythmic splash of water lapping against the shore. Without the blaze of the sun, the air temp drops a degree or two, but it's still muggy as hell. No-see-ums buzz around my head and I swat at my neck, trying to bat them away.

Nick reaches into a cooler and tosses a beer in my direction. I gratefully pop the top and take a long chug while he runs through the various drink options with Sloane. Someone cranks up the music on a portable speaker, the bass so loud the ground vibrates. Clumps of people stand around in circles, some at the edge of the lake, others clustered around the fire. Orange and red flames flicker against the darkening sky, the heavy scent of woodsmoke tickling my nose.

"How ya been, Crawford? Long time, no see." Nick elbows me before plopping down in a folding chair and crossing one leg over his knee, ready to hold court.

"Fine, man. Good." I let Sloane take the seat next to Nick before sinking down into the chair beside her. She sips at her drink, totally at home out here, with these people. Basically, the exact opposite of me, all wound up and edgy. I've been gone for so long, I don't know how to fit in anymore. Sloane's always been more at ease and it seems like she hasn't skipped a beat.

"When did you get to town? I'm kinda hurt you didn't call." Nick gives me his best sad puppy dog expression and my apprehension rockets up. I fiddle with the aluminum pop top on my beer; I don't particularly feel like playing Twenty Questions.

"Only yesterday. I figured I'd be seeing everyone out here tonight. Of course I was going to call. But hey—now I don't have to, right?" I shoot him a sideways glance and his face breaks into a grin.

"Right! You still up in Chicago?" He tips his beer back, shooting the rest of the drink.

"Nah. I'm a free agent right now."

"Wow. Well, shit. That sucks."

I shrug. "Should be fine. My agent's working on negotiations with a few teams." I let the half-truth roll off my tongue, smooth as whiskey. "What've you been up to?"

Changing the topic of conversation, I nod in all the right places at Nick's long-winded resume, trying to seem invested. I fully lose interest once he starts talking about the various types of insurance he sells, my attention drifting to Sloane instead. The glow from the fire highlights her high cheekbones, the cinnamon freckles splashed across her nose, and I wish we were alone right now.

I've thought of her off and on over the year—what she was up to, where she was and who she was with. But there was never a right time to reach out and try to reconnect. I was always busy—playing, training, traveling. I had no time for anything outside of football. And definitely not pursuing any kind of romantic relationship.

You have nothing but time now.

The thought's unsettling, yet somehow sort of appealing.

Now that I'm back here in her orbit, I wonder what she's like as a woman. Is she the same sweet, funny girl, with the goofy sense of humor that had me laughing so hard my abs cramped? Does she still eat Skittles sorted by color, unceremoniously chucking all the purple ones into the trash because she thinks they taste like allergy medicine? Is she still the good girl she was back in high school? So innocent that when Nick asked her what a 69 was, she immediately checked the grading scale posted on the classroom wall and said a 'D'?

I want to find out.

Would love to touch her, taste her, feel her body beneath me.

"Crawford, you in?"

"Huh?" I snap back to reality, Nick nudging my knee.

"All of us going out on the lake tomorrow. I've got a sweet boat, a Pathfinder. And of course, it's insured out the wazoo." He chuckles at his dumb joke. "We can do some fishing, the ladies can float out at the sandbar. It'll be real fun."

"Uh—" I glance over at Sloane, the default social planner, and she shrugs.

"Sure. Let's do it."

"Great. Hey—Frisco! Over here!" Nick shoots his arm up in the air and another high school buddy and ball player from our class waves before heading over with a bunch of people.

There must be at least fifteen of them and soon everyone's jammed around us, pinning me in. The air's hot and stifling and my chest tightens. I stand to get more oxygen into my lungs as faces I vaguely recognize stop to chat me up, ask about playing pro ball. A petite brunette requests a selfie with me and inwardly I wince. But she pushes her hip against mine and leans in close, arm outstretched to take the photo, so I grin and bear it. The bright flash blinds me for a second, and when my eyes adjust to the darkness the group's somehow multiplied.

I'm surrounded by a flock of women, all asking for photos. I nod and smile, taking pictures with each of them. Nick's nearby, chatting one of the ladies up, and I overhear him inviting her and her friends out on the boat tomorrow.

Where's Sloane? I swivel around, searching for her, but she's nowhere to be found.

"Hey, Camden." I turn toward the sultry voice. "It's me, Jamie."

I do a double take as I stare at the tall redhead standing in front of me, hand on hip. She seems familiar, but I can't quite place her.

"Tenth-grade homecoming date. Remember?"

"Oh hey, how are you?" I nod in her direction, but she comes in for a hug, pressing her large breasts against my torso. I pat her awkwardly on her back, right between her prominent shoulder blades.

"I'm great. Better now that you're here. You back in

town for good?" She pulls away slightly, batting her long fringe of lashes at me.

"No, only for the summer."

"Aww, too bad." Popping her lips out in a glossy pout, I wonder how much filler she's pumped into them.

"Guess we'll have to make the most of it." She splays her palm wide on my chest, running her hand over my pecs. The gesture's so intimate, so bold and brash from someone I haven't seen in over a decade. My jaw locks tight, every muscle in my body clenching, and I desperately want to get out of here. I have no interest in rekindling a relationship with a woman I haven't thought about since high school.

"Yeah, sure. Listen—I need to find someone. Great to see you, Jamie." I inch away from her and a flash of disappointment crosses her face, her brows furrowing as much as they're able.

"Let me guess. Sloane?"

"Yeah. I'm her ride."

Jamie rolls her eyes. "Of course you are."

I don't bother diving into the dig, giving it more airtime than it deserves. "Catch you around."

Spinning on my heel, I rush away from her and the rest of the gang huddled around the bonfire. The music pumps louder, and my temples throb. Sweat beads on my lower back and I long for air-conditioned peace and quiet.

Unfortunately, I can't cut and run just yet. Not without Sloane.

CHAPTER 9
SLOANE

I back away from the huge crowd circling Cam and head to the edge of the lake alone. The waves lap at the sand as I stare out into the darkness.

I should have expected this. Of course everyone's going to swarm Cam. He's a gorgeous professional football player living every small-town boy's dream. Like I told Gracelyn at Java Jolt, he's a regular ole' hometown hero. Guys want to be him and women want to be with him.

Why did I think coming out here would be a good idea?

I would much rather be sitting at home, watching a made-for-TV movie on the sofa with my dad wedged between us, than out here with all these people.

"Hey."

The low, gravelly voice drifts on the wind, a light tickle on my skin. I spin and face Cam.

"Hey. Thought you'd still be busy snapping selfies with your adoring fans." I tip my head in the direction of the bonfire and he grimaces.

"Nah. I've done all the PR I'm doing tonight. Why are you out here all alone? No Gracelyn?"

"I couldn't find her. Too many people. I just needed to get away for a minute. Being back home is kind of a lot—I'm out of practice."

"Agreed. I thought it was just me."

"Nope."

"You think the swing's still out there?" Cam squints at the massive oak tree in the distance.

I follow his gaze. "I don't know. Want to find out?"

His deep blue eyes slide to mine and my heart thunders harder in my chest.

"I'd like that."

Cam and I move side by side in the darkness, with just enough space between us to keep me guessing.

"Careful, Trouble," he warns, offering me his large hand as we cross over the flat but slippery rocks lodged in a tiny stream. His skin's rough against mine, his fingers strong.

He doesn't let go.

I try not to freak out or dissect the meaning of it all. Frogs croak off to the left, probably hanging out in the tall grasses near the lake or sitting on the lily pads at the edge. A light breeze blows, ruffling my hair and cooling the heated skin on my neck, my shoulders.

Finally, we're near the tree.

"Oh my gosh, Cam—it's still here!" I can't keep the excitement out of my voice. "After all this time…"

"Guess some things never change." He locks eyes with me, squeezing my fingers lightly, so lightly I may be imagining it. A warmth blooms in my chest and I'm happy. Genuinely happy, here in this moment.

"Wanna swing?" Cam asks and I give him a slow smile.

"Absolutely."

We make our way over to the towering tree and Cam gives the ropes a good, hard tug, checking the stability.

"Should be good."

I sit gingerly on the wooden swing, testing the board under my weight. I'd hate to go crashing to the ground and bust my ass right in front of Cam.

"You're fine, Trouble. Relax." He moves behind me, his massive hands covering mine on the ropes, the heat from his body soaking into my back. I lift my feet and he gives me a light push, the limb of the tree creaking.

I'm instantly transported back in time, the wind cooling my cheeks as I float through the air. All the anxiety and frustration of the past few months melt away as Cam pushes me, higher and higher. I suck in, the fresh air filling my lungs, and I can breathe again.

Really breathe.

And Cam's right here with me.

Even though all this time has passed, it doesn't feel that way. Being with Cam feels easy, simple.

So many mistakes have been made—on my end, at least—but all of that blows away on the summer breeze. I tilt my head up at the white glittering stars and marvel at the perfect night, this absolutely magical moment.

"You happy, Trouble?" Cam asks as the swing gradually slows, my feet dragging across the dirt.

"Right now? Yes."

His chest rests against my back, a solid wall of muscle, the scent of his cologne winding around me.

"Not just now. Like, in general."

Cam's breath rises and falls behind me, the swing swaying slightly as I press my tongue to the inside of my cheek, contemplating.

"I'm happier now than I was in New Orleans—" My stomach flip-flops thinking about my broken engagement, a hot flush creeping into my cheeks. "I'm glad I didn't make a huge mistake."

In one quick move, Cam's standing in front of me. His marine eyes meet mine, and he fixes me with a smoldering gaze. The tip of his tongue darts out, licking along his bottom lip, and I'm frozen in the sultry southern heat.

"Me too."

My breath hitches and I'm vaguely concerned I might pass out. I force air in, then out, then back in again.

"What about you? Were you happy in Chicago? Playing pro football?"

He presses his lips together, his gaze dropping down to the red clay. "Yes and no. I love playing ball, don't get me wrong. Always have. But it wasn't what I expected."

I study his face, trying to read his expression. Cam's never been an easy one to figure out, and he's more guarded now than ever. Probably serves him well with the press, but the attribute's not making my life any easier.

"Oh? How so?"

His jaw tenses, and I know I hit a nerve.

"It's nothing. Stupid, really." He shoves a hand in his pocket, shuffles his feet.

I drop my voice lower. "You can tell me, Cam. It's just me—I won't drop any sound bites to the media, promise."

Blowing out a heavy breath, he sighs. "The pressure was intense. Not the pressure of performance, or the game. I know how to handle that, been practicing for years. But the interviews, the media, all the constant noise. Not to sound like an asshole, but some of the fans were too much, getting rowdy and handsy after games. Like I said—it was a lot. I didn't realize how private I am until that wasn't an option."

"I don't have the experience like you do—" I chew at my lip, tossing around for the right words. "But I think there's an option. You keep a part of yourself private, hidden and tucked away. You save it. For the people you trust."

He lifts his eyes to mine and I'm struck by the dark shadows haunting his face. Making him no less handsome, but giving him a sharp edge. Some of his shine's dulled, the glint in his eyes dimmed.

"You're right. I'll have to try that."

"You want to go back to the pros, right?"

"Yes. Football's my life—" His voice trails off and he glances away toward the lake, the moon shining bright over the water.

A long beat passes, the croaking louder, leaves rustling overhead.

I take a big, scary risk, rising from the swing until I'm face to face with Cam. Stepping in close enough to feel the warmth radiating from his body, to count the tiny dark hairs shading his square jaw.

Lifting my hand to his chest—daring to touch his steely pecs—I rest my palm over his heart, feel the dull thudding with each passing second.

"You're more than football, Cam. You always have been."

He blinks, pupils wide beneath his dark lashes. His jaw tics and I worry for a second that I overstepped, acting like one of the fangirls he dislikes.

"Thanks, Trouble. I needed to hear that, more than you know." He swallows hard, Adam's apple bobbing in his thick neck, and I'm glad I took the risk.

A loud whoop rises from the direction of the bonfire and I drop my hand, stepping back into my own space.

"Wanna get outta here?" he asks and I nod.

"I'd love to."

Together, we make our way back toward the gathering, the space between us smaller now.

"I should text Gracelyn and let her know I'm cutting out. Gimmee a sec," I say, already punching out the message. Cam waits, hands shoved in his pockets as he stares out across the lake.

"Ugh—she asked me to meet her real quick. Do you mind?"

"No, that's fine. I'll wait."

I tell Gracelyn to head over toward the parking lot and Cam and I start walking that direction. He's hunched forward, shoulders slumping, a marked difference from his earlier confident swagger.

Cam really doesn't like crowds.

"Crawford? Is it really you? The prodigal son returned home?" a voice booms from behind us and Cam spins around.

"Nash. What's up?" Cam grins and high-fives, then bro hugs Nash, another high school football buddy.

"Not much. You home for a visit?"

"Sort of a longish visit. I'm in town for the summer, training. What's good?"

"Everything, brother. Yo, Nate! Look who's here!" Nash bellows to his twin brother across the field and within minutes Cam's swarmed by people again. At least this time they're mostly his friends, so he seems more comfortable.

I lean in, touching his arm. "I'm going to find Gracelyn real quick. I'll meet you at the car."

He shoots me a thumbs-up, and I jog away to find Gracelyn.

"Hey, sorry I'm so late." Grace hugs me, the scent of bleach and her heavy floral perfume kicking me in the nose. "My last client was an hour late, but it didn't feel right to cancel on her since it was the babysitter's fault. Anyway—what did I miss? Where's Cam?" Gracelyn waggles her brows at me before swiveling her head around like an owl, searching for Cam.

"Not much. The usual stuff—Nick draining Mich Ultras like it's his job, bragging about his boat and his big insurance job. Everyone going wild over Cam and his career."

"Like that?" Gracelyn grabs my shoulders, spinning me around toward the bonfire. Sure enough, there's a large group of women gathered around Cam, cell phones out, cameras flashing.

"For fuck's sake, the guy can't get a break," I mutter, feeling guilty for leaving Cam's side. A tall redhead strokes his forearm, rubbing on him like he's a genie in a bottle, ready to grant her three X-rated wishes, and my gut twists.

"That snake—" Gracelyn hisses, her fists balled.

"Who is that? I don't recognize her."

"Oh, you know her. That's Jamie Ware, the girl who tripped me in the ninth grade when I was getting on the bus. I splatted face-first in front of Nash and Nate, busted up both my knees. I bled the whole way home, mortified. Bitch," Gracelyn scowls. "She dyed her hair and her eyebrows finally grew back from the horrendous wax job she got over in Lightning Ridge. You know—because she wouldn't come to our salon. Said it was 'too country' for her." Gracelyn air quotes the last part, her frown deep.

"Oh, right. Now I remember." I stare at the scene as she

fawns over Cam, inching in closer. She is beautiful and I wouldn't blame him if he was interested.

He backs away, but she throws her head back, laughing. Then she spreads her hands over his chest, stroking him, and bile rises in my throat.

Nobody should have to endure groping like that, not even a professional football star.

Fire licking inside me, I grab Gracelyn's elbow and stalk over to the group crowding around Cam.

"Hey, Cam. You ready to go?" I jostle my way in next to him and he visibly relaxes, fingers uncurling at his side.

Jamie glares at me, puffing out her ample chest.

"Oh hey, Sloane. I heard you were back in town, living with your daddy." Her tone's saccharine-sweet as she smirks at me with deep red lips.

"I am. I'm kind of between places right now. What have you been up to?" I work hard to infuse the same sweetness into my voice. Damn, the struggle is real.

Jamie flips her long, scarlet hair over her shoulder. "I've been away most of the spring. Modeling in Europe."

Of course she has.

"Awesome. Good on you. Ready, Cam?"

"Yeah."

I try to drag us out of the uncomfortable conversation, but Gracelyn keeps going, stirring the pot.

"Where in Europe?" she asks, folding her arms over her chest.

"Mainly Paris. I did do a photoshoot in Milan, though, and that was amazing." Jamie somehow draws the word 'amazing' out to a full six syllables.

"What were you modeling?" Gracelyn presses, and I swear I hear my bestie murmur *'Besides your tits'* under her breath.

"Perfume. Sunglasses. I did a lingerie shoot." Jamie pins her eyes on Cam as she mentions the lingerie and Cam shifts uncomfortably.

"Catalog stuff. Nice. Maybe we'll catch your photos in the Dollar Depot flyer this weekend," Grace quips and Jamie blanches.

"Hardly, Gracelyn," Jamie fires back. "You having as much luck in the love department as your bestie here?"

"Fuck off, Jamie," Gracelyn spats and I interject, taking Grace by the elbow.

"Oh-kay. Have a great night!" I wave at Jamie and the growing crowd, people now fully invested in the catfight between Jamie and Gracelyn. Jamie waggles her fingers, the corners of her lips tipping up into a sly smile, knowing she got under Grace's skin.

"Bye, Cam!" she trills as we retreat.

We head to the parking lot, Gracelyn cursing Jamie under her breath and stomping her feet the whole way. Cam stays silent as I try to calm Grace down.

"Don't worry about her, Grace. She's probably had a rough time or something, we don't know."

"Oh, I do know. She's always been a bitch. Good to see things haven't changed."

I pop Gracelyn into her car and we say our good-byes.

"I don't think I'm up for the boat day, Sloane. Not if *she's* going." Grace stares at the crowd, her nose scrunched up as if she's smelling garbage that's baked out in the blazing sun for a week.

"Fine by me." Cam shrugs. "I'm pretty beat and could use a rest day."

"Okay, it's decided. No to the boat day."

Truth be told, I'm a little bummed because I would have loved seeing Cam in a swimsuit. But I'd also love having him all to myself—and I'd rather avoid Jamie too. I didn't like her pawing at Cam, and I definitely didn't like the snarky tone she took with me and Gracelyn.

"See you kids, later!" Grace waves through the window as she peels out of the lot, dust circling behind her.

"C'mon, Trouble. Let's get out of here." Cam grabs my hand and breath hitches in my throat as I sneak a glance at the spot where our fingers join.

The motion's so easy, so natural—almost instinctual—and I wonder if Cam knows the effect his touch is having on my pounding heart.

CHAPTER 10
CAM

*S*loane came to my rescue back there.

Between the crushing crowd of people and Jamie's touchy-feely hands, I couldn't wait to escape the bonfire.

I'm already breathing easier the further we get from the lake.

I turn the volume on the radio down, lowering the Red Hot Chili Peppers to a more acceptable decibel level.

"Thanks for the save." Taking my eyes off the dark road for a split second, I slide to meet her gaze.

"No problem. Those big group things sometimes get overwhelming, ya know?" She smooths her dress down over her lap, the lights from the dash highlighting her high cheekbones.

God, she's gorgeous.

"I'm kind of hungry and still pretty keyed up. You want to get something to eat? Maybe grab food at The Burger Basket?"

"Sure."

Relaxing into the comfortable leather seat, the muscles in my low back loosen as we drive toward town. Sloane hums along with the music, content to sit back and take in the scenery.

It's nice being with someone I don't have to be 'on' for. For the first time in a long time, I'm not worried about saying something stupid or trying to impress. With Sloane, I can relax. She knows me, we don't have any secrets.

Well, I have the one secret. The dumb mistake I made that got me and two of my buddies cut from the team. That and my shitty scoring record this year.

But there's already been too much drama tonight, what with the crowd at the bonfire and the little dust-up between Gracelyn and Jamie.

No need to dredge up the video right now. Besides, if all goes well here and I'm picked up by another team, no one has to know about it anyway.

"Cam? You passed The Burger Basket."

"Oh shit, I did." I spin the wheel and make a hard left turn, popping a quick one-eighty.

"You okay? You really zoned out there."

I check the side mirror, pulling into an empty spot. "Yeah, all good."

Locking the car—although that's more out of habit than necessity in Thunder Creek—we head into the restaurant, the one and only late-night spot in town.

"Good to see nothing's changed," I say, holding the glass door open for her. "Same linoleum, same pink stools and metal counter."

"Same great service too," Sloane whispers, leaning in close to my ear. She smells nice, like soft florals mixed with bonfire smoke, and I wonder what she'd taste like. I follow behind her through the almost-empty dining room—we're kind of between popular times, dinner having passed and the late-night crowd still out partying.

"This work?" She waves her hand at an empty turquoise booth in the back and I nod.

"Sure."

We sink into the pleather seats and Sloane plucks a menu from behind the silver napkin dispenser, handing it to me.

"You still get the usual?" I ask, perusing the choices. Doesn't seem like they've updated the menu since I left, either.

"You know it. Chocolate milkshake, double cherries, with a side of fries. Hits the spot every time."

"That does sound tempting—" I glance over the plastic menu and the pink tip of her tongue darts out, licking her lip.

"Don't go ordering something healthy, like the cottage cheese on lettuce," she teases, flicking the back of my menu, and I chuckle.

"Wouldn't dream of it. Your dad worked me hard today—I'm entitled to a cheeseburger every now and then."

"Hiya, kids." Angela, a waitress who's worked here as long as I can remember, slides over to take our order. She pulls a pencil from behind her ear, hovers it over the order pad. "Great to see you two, just like old times. What'll ya have?"

I motion at Sloane and she places her order, then I make mine and Angela shuffles away to grab us waters.

"I think she changed her hair color since last week. Last time I saw her, it was definitely pink." Sloane rips the wrapper from her straw, wadding the paper into a tiny white ball.

"The lilac suits her. Matches the décor here nicely."

Sloane grins as Angela deposits two glasses of water and the chocolate shake on the table.

"Food'll be out in a sec, kids." Then she hustles away again, a table at the opposite side of the dining room signaling for their check.

"So—you have any big plans for the summer?" I ask.

Sloane pops a cherry off the blob of whipped cream in her shake.

"I think I might apply for a job at the library. Could be fun for a while." She sucks the cherry into her mouth, pulling the fruit from the stem, and I try not to stare at the perfect pink circle of her lips.

I wipe my palms down my jeans, stretch my legs out under the table, trying to get comfortable in the increasingly tight denim.

"You always loved to read. Sounds like a good fit."

"I thought so." She pops a second cherry in her mouth, rolling it around with her tongue, and now I have a rapidly growing stiffy. Good thing I'm covered by the table.

"How's your family? They moved out to Colorado, right?"

"Yeah. My sister Jessica has two kids now, and she and her husband have big jobs. They're both lawyers and were struggling with childcare, so my parents decided to move closer and help out."

"Wow—that was nice of them."

I shrug. "My sister might have a different opinion. I think my mom was tired of traveling out there all the time to see her grandkids. She's practically living with them now."

Sloane giggles, a soft, tinkly sound that bounces off the

hard surface of the table, her face glowing under the pendant light.

"And Ansley? Where's she now?"

"Ans is out there now, too. She was in Manhattan for a while, but she said the city was bad for her chi. Blocked her chakras or something, I don't know. She yaps so much about all that stuff, and I only understand like a quarter of it."

Sloane sips at her milkshake, smiling. "Ansley was always entertaining. Do you get out there to visit much?"

"I've gone out a couple times. Jessica has a nice house in the 'burbs. Last time I was relegated to the basement rec room because Ans had the guestroom, but it was fine. At least I had my own space."

Angela bustles up to the table, lifting the baskets of food from a black tray and setting them down in front of Sloane and me.

"Here's the burger and fries, kids. Enjoy." She shuffles off without asking if we need anything else.

"Best fries in town." Sloane salts the golden pile of crinkled potatoes and my stomach growls. Reaching for the ketchup, I squirt a healthy blob on the bun before taking a big bite.

"Mmmm—best burger too. I missed the burgers."

"Dude—Chicago has great food! The pizza, the beef sandwiches, the sausages—"

"The food was good. But nothing's better than Southern cuisine." I swallow hard, realizing how much I missed Thunder Creek.

And Sloane.

I should have reached out sooner.

But now's not the time for regrets. There are plenty of those to go around at the moment.

"Remember when we came here after y'all won the State Championship?" She swirls her straw around in the melting chocolate shake.

"Yeah, that was a great night. Free food for the whole team and we doused your dad in lemonade, like we won the big game or something."

She laughs, shaking her head, dark hair spilling over her shoulders. "He did not love that. I do believe he grumbled about the lemonade ruining his shoes for a solid month afterwards."

"Sounds about right."

"And we got full access to the juke box and even the usuals didn't mind listening to 'Hey Jude' on repeat."

I chuckle. "Yeah, we were pretty obnoxious, in retrospect."

Sloane's hand darts out, squeezing my forearm. "But we beat Lighting Ridge! Y'all earned jukebox rights."

"That was a great night. One of the best." My gaze slides up to hers, the gold flecks in her wide hazel eyes glittering, and all the feelings come roaring back—from that night and all the other nights we spent together.

Hundreds of nights. The two of us talking and laughing, sharing the very best parts of ourselves with each other. But also the scary parts—the worries, the fears, anxiety about the future.

Sloane was the girl I let in, the one I trusted.

Why did I ever let that go? Let her slip through my fingers, like a grain of sand on the beach? As if she wasn't special.

Because damn, she absolutely is.

You let her go to protect her. To give her a shot at a normal life. One without the pressure, the fear of failure, the uncertainty.

I didn't drag her into the weeds then, and I shouldn't now. No matter how badly I want to.

It's not right.

She deserves more, better.

Sloane Carter deserves the fucking world—and I'm not the guy who can give it to her.

"Cam? You okay?" Her soft voice jolts me out of my thoughts.

"Yeah. You save me any fries, Trouble?"

Shoving the basket toward me, I shoot her a laid-back grin and steal a fry. I need to stay superficial, need to be the fun version of myself.

It'll be better—safer—for both of us.

CHAPTER 11
SLOANE

Cam and I spend the next two weeks hanging out together practically non-stop, cocooned in our safe little bubble, just the two of us.

I put off applying for the job at the library to spend time with him, sprawled on the sofa in the middle of the day. We binge watch *Bridgerton* (my pick, but he's lying when he says he didn't like it) and all four thousand *Star Wars* movies (obvs, his pick).

Scouring TikTok videos, we try out a bunch of recipes. Quick thirty-minute dinners, fancy gourmet meals, some gluten-free desserts. Most of the sweet treats end up in the trash, but a few of the thirty-minute recipes turn out great, a real bonus.

I drag him to the bi-weekly farmer's market to visit my grandmother, Mimi, and check out the goat products she's selling. We sample the cheese and milk and I convince Cam to buy a bar of goat milk soap—great for exfoliation.

In return, I spend time quizzing him on the Thunder

Creek playbook, drawing the routes out on the whiteboard my dad installed in the kitchen. You know—for when lightning strikes while you're in the middle of making a grilled cheese sandwich.

The only time we're apart is when Cam's at practice or the gym.

It's the best two weeks of my adult life.

Everything I loved about him in high school is still there. That quick, easy smile, the dimple in his right cheek that winks at you when he's happy. His deep belly laugh when I say or do something silly. The intensity in his marine eyes when he's concentrating, a furrow etched in his brow. The absolute passion the man has for football. The only person I know with as much love for the game is my dad. I sit back enraptured every night at the dinner table, the two of them going back and forth about this play or that play. Cam will make a great coach someday, after he retires from the pros.

We're as close now as we ever were and everything feels so right between us.

Everything except for the fact that we haven't kissed.

I'm still deep in the friend zone. There's been some long, lingering gazes, a flirtatious arm stroke here or there.

But that's it. Nothing more and I'm beginning to wonder if I'm reading the room all wrong. Maybe this thing between us is all one-sided and I'm only seeing what I want to see, what I hope is there.

Gracelyn keeps telling me to open up to him and confess my feelings, but I can't bring myself to do it. The fear of rejection, of hearing Cam say the word 'no' out loud, silences me. The words dry and wither on my tongue every time I try, and I swallow them back down, bitter little pills.

Cam and I are in the middle of a cheesy made-for-TV thriller when my phone buzzes with a text.

"Cam, Gracelyn got invited out on Nick's boat again and wants us to go with her. For moral support."

"You want to go?" he asks.

"Well, here's her text." I read the text out loud in my best Gracelyn voice.

> Bestie: Sloane—please, please, please come out on the boat with me. You and Cam both. I cannot go out there alone
>
> Bestie: PLEASE!

"That's in all caps by the way," I say, waving the screen close to his face so he can see.

"A shouty text. She must be desperate," Cam teases, chuckling.

> Bestie: If Jamie's there, she may throw me overboard and leave me to the gators

"Gracelyn's so dramatic." I roll my eyes at the phone. "Well, what do you think? Want to go? I know tomorrow's your rest day."

I'm not too thrilled about having to share Cam with the world on one of our last full days together before the summer schedule starts. But Gracelyn's having a mini-crisis, so I figure I need to show up for her. I would've been lost without her this spring, so a boat day with the gang's the least I can do.

"Do you want to go, Trouble?" He squints at me over his shoulder, the TV screen casting shadows on his face in the dim light of the living room.

"We can. I mean, I feel like I need to go. For Gracelyn."

"Okay. Tell her to count us in."

I tap out the message before settling back onto the sofa, scooting as close to Cam as I dare with my dad home in the other room.

———

Cam drives us out to the lake for the boat day, giving me ample time to field Gracelyn's litany of texts.

> Bestie: You excited about boat day? Cam in a bathing suit, am I right?

I can't help but giggle at my friend.

> Sloane: Yes, should be fun

> Bestie: Sexy fun, yessss!

> Bestie: You guys almost here? Lots of people already

> Bestie: Where ARE you?

> Bestie: SLOANE! Are you almost here?

> Sloane: Relax. We're parking

"Sloane! Cam! So glad you two could finally make it!" Nick taps the face of his watch as we walk over to the boat launch, a white captain's hat slightly askew on his shaggy hair. "Okay, guys—everyone's here now so we're good to go! Hop aboard."

At his command, a crush of people scrambles onto the boat.

"Hey, beautiful." Nick extends his hand out to me, helping me up, and I smile at him.

"Hey, yourself. Thanks for inviting us."

"You're welcome, anytime. Drinks are in the cooler, along with some snacky-snacks."

Cam follows right behind me and Nick shouts toward the back of the boat. "Crank up the tunes, boys—let's get ready to party!"

Nick takes his place at the helm, easing the boat away from the dock as the music ratchets up. The fiberglass deck thrums with the beat of the bass and the vibration of the motor. Cam and I take a seat, wedging in between Gracelyn and Frisco.

The boat idles slowly through the no-wake zone, then we pick up speed as we move into deeper water. The wind whips my ponytail around behind me and I'm acutely aware of Cam next to me. Our thighs touching, warmth radiates from his skin, his clean scent winding around me and mixing with the humid marine air. I sneak a quick glance over at him and a hot blush creeps into my cheeks when we lock eyes. His pinky brushes mine and I fight the urge to wrap my finger around his, instead clasping my hands together.

The music's loud, and coupled with the wind, it's impossible to hold a conversation, so I don't even try. Instead, I relax back into the seat and enjoy the ride out to the sandbar. It's a trip I've made hundreds, if not thousands, of times, but today feels different, more charged— and I have a sneaking suspicion I know why. He's tall, dark, and impossibly gorgeous. Also so far out of my league I'm not sure we're even in the same galaxy, but it doesn't stop me from wanting him.

Nick pulls back the speed as the water lightens,

signaling that we're nearing the sandbar. People start chatting and Frisco kicks up a conversation about football with Cam, talking salary caps and contracts. Finally, we get to the sandbar and Nick cuts the motor.

"Anchor's down and the bar is open!" He flips the lid on the cooler and a loud cheer rises from the crowd at the back of the boat. Hands dip into the cooler, beers cracking open, and two people jump into the water.

"Come on in, the water's fine!" A guy I vaguely recognize waves at us and several people strip off their T-shirts and shorts, diving in.

"You two going in?" Gracelyn asks me and Cam as she shimmies out of her cover-up.

"Sure." Cam's deep voice sends a thrill through me, straight to my core. "I need to put some sunblock on first—haven't seen sun as strong as this in a while. Sloane, would you mind doing my back?"

"Uh, not at all," I stammer, taking the blue tube of lotion from his outstretched hand as he lifts his shirt over his head. Grace waggles her eyebrows at me and I shoo her away before Cam catches her antics.

Uncapping the sunblock, I squeeze the white cream into my hands, my heart thudding so loud I'm afraid Cam might hear.

Relax, Sloane. Of course he's going to ask you. You're friends and you're sitting next to him. Makes you the logical choice.

Lathering the lotion in my hands, I reach up, tentatively smoothing my hand across the broad area between his shoulder blades. His skin's warm, cords of strong muscle rippling beneath the surface. I work the white sunblock in, careful not to miss any spots. My fingers glide between his shoulder blades over his shoulders. Heat curls in my belly and I'm lightheaded. I keep rubbing, working the lotion in, pausing to squirt more into my palm. Sliding over the entire surface of his back, my fingers dance up and down his muscular torso.

"Thanks." The rumble of his voice vibrates against my palms, every inch of my body on fire.

"Sure, no problem." The words come out breathy, as if I've been jogging for miles instead of sitting and applying sunscreen on a boat.

"You need some?" Cam glances back at me, seemingly unfazed, and I nod.

"Yeah, I do, actually."

"I got you." He reaches around, taking the sunblock from my hand, and electricity zips straight up my arm. "You're gonna have to take your shirt off." He gestures at my tank top.

"Oh, right."

Yanking my shirt over my head quickly, I toss it into my bag before offering my back to Cam.

"All over, right?" His eyes travel downward and my face burns.

"Yes, please."

Cam's large palms land on my back, the cool lotion a balm to my overly heated skin. His touch is gentle as he works the cream over my flesh, tiny chill bumps rising in the wake of his calloused fingertips. He skates up and down my spine, over the shoulder blades, across my shoulders, then down the sides of my body. Dampness pools between my thighs as he rubs my skin.

"All good." The click of the sunblock lid snapping into place jolts me back to reality and I ease away from him.

Tucking a loose hair behind my ear, I smile over my shoulder. "Thanks."

"No problem."

We gaze at each other for a long second, everyone around us fading away. All I see is Cam—his strong jaw, full lips, the small, jagged scar above his right eye he got during a game in the tenth grade.

"You two coming in or what?" Gracelyn interrupts the moment, splashing water up at us.

"Yeah, yeah. Hang on." Standing, I kick out of my sandals and shorts before walking to the back of the boat and snagging the last inner tube, throwing the pink plastic float over the side.

I tuck my legs up beneath me and jump overboard, feet-first into the cool water. Sinking down into the blue-green water of the lake, I relish the sensation of weightlessness, the relief from the heat.

After a long second, I swim back up to the surface, swiping to clear my eyes.

"Hey." Cam's low voice startles me, bubbly anticipation fizzing in my chest. He's treading next to me and the small ripples swirl around my calves.

We're so close our legs brush beneath the surface. Shiny water droplets glisten in his dark hair beneath the rays of the bright sun. A flash of heat rushes through me and my cheeks flame, and it's not from the beating rays beaming down on us.

"Want to swim out further?" Cam tilts his head toward a sandbar a ways out, far from the crowd.

"Sure."

"Hop on." He pats the pink tube and I duck under, trying to lift myself up through the center as gracefully as possible. Pushing up and over the top, I flip over and kick my legs out in front of me, toes barely touching the water, fingers trailing along the glassy surface.

"You think you can make it all the way out there—" I

point into the distance at the furthest sandbar. "Pushing me on this tube?"

"You doubt my swimming skills?" he teases me, already moving around to the front of the tube and grabbing the rubber handle. His fingers brush mine and my breath catches in my throat.

"No—" I lick at my lower lip, the brine from the lake salty on my tongue.

"Good. Trust me, Trouble. I got you." Cam gives a hard kick beneath the water and we're moving out toward the sandbar faster than anticipated. I try to help, reaching down and paddling with my hands, but I don't make much of a difference. Most of the forward momentum comes from Cam.

His back is to me, one arm outstretched as he moves us away from the crowd. I marvel at the muscles rippling beneath the flesh, long cords of strength, flexing and bunching. Hot desire unfurls low in my belly and everything in me coils, tightening.

The sounds from the boat fade as we get further out into the lake, with only the occasional peal of laughter cutting through the quiet. A slight breeze cools my skin, waves lapping against the tube. Finally, Cam glides us onto the golden sand of the sandbar.

"We've arrived." He eases the tube onto the edge, flashing a white, cheeky grin at me, the dimple in his right cheek popping.

He's gorgeous. Even better grown-up, all sharp edges and chiseled physique. Gone is the boy—no more scrawny, awkward adolescence remains. Any insecurity's been replaced by muscle, strength, confidence. Masculinity rolls off Cam in waves, like a force field humming over his taut skin. Every move lithe and athletic and my mind flashes to what that would be like in bed, his huge body hovering over mine. I want to reach out and run my fingers down his chest, over each pronounced abdominal muscle, all the way down to that deep-V that leads to…

"Sloane?" Cam's voice startles me out of my fantasy. He inches closer to me, the raft squeaking as his body rubs against the plastic.

"Yeah?"

"Do you have any regrets?" He peers over his shoulder, marine eyes lasered on mine.

"Sure. Doesn't everybody?"

"I mean, like, big regrets. Things that you did or said—or didn't say—that haunt you."

The question feels dark and deep out here in the bright sunlight. I ponder for a second, rolling over all the things I could say.

Instead of answering, I kick the question back to him. "Do you?"

Cam leans back on his elbows, tipping his head up to the sky, his Adam's apple defined in his long neck. I watch as his chest rises and falls, waiting. We sit still for a long minute, the waves lapping against the sandbar, the din of music from the boat pulsing over the surface of the water. Finally, Cam looks over at me again.

"I do. I've done some stuff I'm not proud of. Things I wish I could take back. But I can't." He bites at his lower lip, staring out over the blue of the lake. His jaw tics and I wonder what he's talking about.

"We all have, Cam. You know and I know there's no such thing as a perfect game. Life's the same way." I shrug, my wet ponytail flopping on my back.

"I know. It's—some things change you. And now everything's different, Trouble. I'm different." He sits up, brushing his hand over my calf dangling in the water. Shock waves of excitement ripple through me at his gentle touch as I try to figure out what he means.

Another long beat passes before I respond.

"I think we're all different now, Cam. Well, maybe all of us but Nick. He seems to be permanently stuck in high school."

Cam chuckles, the corners of his lips tipping up into a smile. "I agree on Nick. But you don't seem all that different." His fingertips glide up and down my calf and I'm struggling to make sense of anything right now. "You're still the fun, easygoing girl you always were, with the same sense of humor, the wit."

I let out a half-laugh. "If by easygoing you mean floating along, still trying to figure shit out, then yeah."

"We're in the same place then." Cam picks his hand up out of the water, sliding his fingers through mine. A light wind blows, the sun warm on my skin, as I stare at our fingers intertwined on the pink float. His much larger and thicker than mine, his grip strong yet tender.

Everything about this moment—about us here together—feels right.

Lifting my gaze to meet his, my entire body trembles as he leans forward, his face inches from mine. We're so close I feel his breath on my face, the scent of the coconut sunscreen strong.

Crack!

A loud clap of thunder rings out and the sun's rapidly eclipsed by dark, almost black, clouds. Cam peers up at the sky as the wind picks up, whipping away every remaining water droplet on my skin.

"We better get back. Looks like they're heading in." He

gestures at the boat, everyone scrambling to climb aboard as more thunder rumbles in the distance.

"Yeah, we better hustle." I slip off the float, dropping down into the water. "I'm helping this time. We don't want to get stuck out here."

"Fine. Let's go."

Together, Cam and I swim back to the boat in silence. My mind's racing, replaying the last few minutes on loop.

Was Cam about to kiss me or was that my imagination running wild?

The first large raindrops plop into the lake and I kick harder and faster. Then the rain really starts, moving quickly from a few drops to hard sheets sloshing down, blurring my vision.

"Come on, Trouble, we're almost back. We've got this," Cam says, taking over the float fully. I don't argue with him about the tube, panic starting to creep in. I didn't realize how far out we were and the motor's already cranked on the boat. I know Gracelyn won't let them leave us behind, but I'm still worried.

"Just a few more yards, you've got it." Cam's calm, soothing voice coaches me along and I relax a teensy bit. "Almost there—"

Finally, we're within arm's reach of the boat and I can catch my breath. My legs ache from kicking so fast and cold rain's pounding down all around us, the water sluicing down my face into my eyes.

"Good girl," Cam murmurs into my ear, the low rumble of his words barely audible over the storm. He grips my waist, helping me onto the ladder and I scramble onto the boat, endorphins pumping through me. From the swim, the storm.

But mostly from Cam.

"Well, that came out of nowhere," Gracelyn shouts over the roar of the motor as Cam and I squish down onto the seat next to her. She throws us a towel and Cam catches it, spreading it over my shoulders first, then his. We huddle together under the towel, wind whipping cold rain into our faces as we speed back to Thunder Creek and reality.

CHAPTER 12
CAM

That was a close one.

If the storm hadn't kicked up out of nowhere, I definitely would have kissed Sloane out there on the sandbar.

Another mistake to add to my increasingly long list of fuck-ups.

No matter how badly I want to feel her lips on mine, taste her, breathe her in, deep down I know I shouldn't go there.

Besides being Coach's daughter, she's too good for me, too pure. I've done things I'm not proud of. Things I don't want her to know about, let alone get dragged into.

Sloane shouldn't get involved with me and all my screw ups. She has marriage and babies and white picket fences written all over her. I want to play football and stay out of the headlines.

Even if her hand fits perfectly in mine.

Her smile lights me up from the inside out.

And being in a room with her makes it easier to breathe.

It's not enough.

I'll never be enough.

I'd be selfish to make her mine.

No matter how badly I want her.

I need to keep my distance. Get my life back on track, then get the hell out of Thunder Creek for good.

As soon as we're back at the house, I cut the engine and unlock the doors, darting from the car to the safety of my room. I can't trust myself sitting in such close proximity to her, the intoxicating scent of her filling the air, wrapping around me and making it hard to think.

Nope.

Focus on football, Crawford. Keep your eyes on the prize—and off of Sloane's tits.

I slam the door to the bedroom shut, lean back against the flimsy wood door, my chest heaving hard from the mad dash. I'm rock fucking hard, my dick bulging in my swimsuit. I peel the wet fabric off my skin, the shorts slipping to the floor in a soggy pile.

Fisting myself, I slide my hand up and down the hard shaft, stifling a groan. I squeeze my eyes shut and work on picturing any female other than Sloane Carter.

But there she is, gazing up at me through a thick fringe of dark lashes. Her eyes wide, the golden flecks in her irises glimmering as she licks her full bottom lip. Seductive, enticing.

I dip my head, smashing my mouth against hers. She tastes delicious, like sweet nectar from a ripe fruit plucked straight from the forbidden vine.

I work my dick harder, faster, growing longer and bigger by the second. Imagining my cock driving into her,

her pussy hot and wet as our flesh slaps together. Her nails claw at my back, digging into the skin she slathered with sunblock. Every muscle in my body's tense as I drill into her, over and over and over again.

Faster, Cam.

Harder.

Fuck me, Cam.

The base of my spine tingles, my balls tightening, and I'm close, so fucking close to release. I squeeze harder, picturing the two of us joining together, her tight pussy milking my cock.

"Sloane—" I hiss, catching the long rope of cum with my T-shirt. "Fuck…"

Collapsing back against the door, my muscles relax as the tension I held onto all day leaks from my body.

Knock, knock, knock.

"Cam? You okay?"

I freeze, my heart rate rocketing back up as Sloane's voice carries through the door.

"Yeah, fine. Just wanted to get out of my wet clothes."

"Oh, right. Okay." Her voice wavers and she sounds disappointed.

"I'm jumping in the shower, but I'll be quick."

"Take your time," I yell back, covering my naked dick even though I realize she can't see me through the door. Still, hot embarrassment flames through me.

I really, really hope she didn't hear anything.

No way could she have heard that, I'm sure I was quiet.

I clean up as best I can, the close call further solidifying the plan. The sooner I get picked up by another team, the sooner I can get out of Thunder Creek. And that will be best for everyone involved.

———

I lay low the rest of the night, doing my best to avoid Sloane. Finally Monday rolls around and I sneak out early, hanging around town until it's time for practice. I head over to the high school, a mix of nerves and excitement pinging through me.

Apparently, it doesn't matter if I'm playing in the pros or with teenagers at my high school alma mater because I'm as nervous walking onto the Thunder Creek High field as I would be jogging into any bigger stadium in the nation.

Probably because I have as much—if not more—to prove here right now.

Dumb? Yes.

Irrational? Yes.

Still fucking feeling all the things? Hell, yes.

Pulse racing, I hustle over to Coach. He's heads-down, staring at the clipboard and planning out practice.

"Crawford!" He barks my name, and there's a totally different vibe on the field than we had on Saturday when it was just the two of us. It's as if he's setting the standard for the team, the entire upcoming season, which I can appreciate.

"Yes, Coach."

"You'll be running drills with one of the quarterbacks, Langley. He's a sophomore and this would be his rookie season playing QB. But Rex graduated, so we need someone to take his place."

Coach drops his voice low, so only I can hear. "Between you and me, Langley is my top choice. But there's a junior, Dalton, who thinks he should get the nod to step up. I have to be fair about it and do what's best for the team. Work with Langley and see what you think."

I suck in a breath, the wheel of anxiety starting to churn deep in my gut. *Coach wants me to help vet the QBs?*

"You got it, Coach. Any particular thing you want me to work on with him?"

"He needs to be able to read the field. But he's also gotta be able to get it into your hands. So let's run some routes, see how he does."

"No problem." I toss my bag onto a bleacher and start my stretching routine, reaching to the sky and opening up my lungs. Sucking in a deep breath, I close my eyes and try to focus on football. But my mind's still swimming from yesterday, at least half of my thoughts coming back to Sloane.

Get your shit together, Crawford. You have a job to do.

"Afternoon, boys!" Coach's voice booms over the field, echoing off the empty bleachers. "Welcome to the unofficial start of football boot camp. We're going to work hard, learn the plays, and condition all summer so we can be the winningest team in Georgia. Got it?"

"Yes, Coach!" Thirty-six voices belt out the familiar phrase and I'm transported straight back to my own high school football days, back when I was still trying to make it. Everything inside me is jumpy, amped, and I'm ready to play ball.

"We have a week left of school and afternoon practice. Once summer officially begins, we'll run practice every morning, Monday through Friday. First we'll have conditioning, then we'll run drills. Saturdays are optional practices, but I hope you'll be able to make at least some of them. Those will be the scrimmage practices. Afternoons are reserved for lifting and meeting with the trainer."

Heads nod as the boys dial in, absorbing Coach's words as if they're gospel. Which—let's be honest—they kind of are.

"Next year will be a transition year, with a bunch of the seniors graduating. That doesn't mean I don't expect us to take home the title. Just means we need to practice harder and longer to figure things out and gel as a team. Some of you may have noticed this guy—" Coach slaps me on the back. "Cam Crawford, one of my former star players. He's been in the pros the last few years and he'll be here at practice, helping me out."

All eyes swivel to me and I stand taller, straighter, a part of me wanting to impress these kids.

"That's enough chitchat for now. Everybody run four laps around the track and then we'll break into teams for drills."

Groups form, players building alliances as we all take off around the track. I jog at a nice, easy pace alone, warming up my body. The afternoon sun's beating down, hot and strong, and the humidity's so thick my skin's sticky with a light sheen of sweat after only one lap.

I finish in the middle of the pack and head over to the bleachers to hydrate while the stragglers limp in.

"What are you doing back here, in Thunder Creek?" A kid about five inches shorter than me with tightly buzzed hair stares over at me. He kicks his leg up on the bleacher and bends toward his toes, stretching out his hamstring.

"Like Coach said, I'm here training with him. Getting back to basics."

"I heard you got cut."

Word travels fast. This kid is up on his football intel.

"I'm in between teams right now is all. What's your name?"

"Dalton. I'm the new QB for this team. You play wide receiver, right? So you're gonna be my man for the summer or something?"

"Maybe. We'll see what Coach says. He'll probably try you out with a few different players, since I obviously won't be here during the season. Fresh out of eligibility." I shoot him a wry smile, but he doesn't return it.

"Right." Dalton draws the word out, giving me a cold stare.

"Drill time, boys!" Coach blows his whistle, waving everyone over to the center of the field. I'm not torn up about cutting the conversation short.

"Dalton, you'll be working with Stevens. Langley, you're with Crawford. My O-line will be running the Over the Middle drill with Coach Baker. The D-line is working on the forty-five degree drill with Coach Mack. Any questions?" Coach glances around, but no one raises their hand. "Alright, then. Let's get to work."

The huddle breaks and players group up according to the assignments. Dalton, Stevens, Langley, and I follow Coach to the far end of the field. Coach stoops down and picks up two footballs, tossing one to Dalton and the other to Langley.

"With Rex gone, we'll be needing a new quarterback this season. One of the two of you will get the starting position; the other will be back-up. This is your chance to practice your skills. You boys are lucky to have a pro in town to show you how it's done." Coach tips his ball cap at me and my chest tightens, nerves firing.

I'm not sure how lucky they are to have me, but it's nice to hear Coach say so.

"Baker and I will be watching you both all summer.

We'll make the decision at the end of camp, before school starts. Got it?"

"Yes, Coach." All four of us respond in unison and then Coach pulls out the playbook, reviewing the list of plays. Langley listens intently, drawing the various routes on his hand with his index finger while Coach talks. Dalton stares off into the distance and looks bored.

"Hit it, boys. Dalton on the left, Langley on the right." Coach points the two quarterbacks to their respective spots and then blows his whistle, the sharp tweet signaling the beginning of the first play.

I jog to mid-field and spin, ready to receive the pass. Langley rockets the ball in my direction, but overshoots by at least ten yards.

"Shit," I mutter, landing on the turf empty-handed. Kid definitely has some work to do.

"Again!" Coach shouts. The whistle blows and the ball flies in my direction. I jump into the air, the ball slamming into my hands this time.

"Nice one, Crawford." Coach shoots me a thumbs-up and Langley grins.

"Next play! Corner route, go!"

The whistle shrieks and I take off, running straight before cutting forty-five degrees toward the sideline. Spinning around, I spot the ball but can't get there before it tumbles to the ground.

"Again!" Coach screams and I jog back to mid-field and repeat. Then repeat again and again, Langley overthrowing or underthrowing every damn time.

"Son, respectfully, what the hell are you doing out there?" Coach calls out to Langley.

Langley drops his head, staring down at the turf and shaking out his throwing arm.

"Take five, boys. Get a drink of water and regroup."

I take the opportunity to head over to the bleachers and grab my water bottle, squirting the cool liquid into my mouth before swiping at the sweat dripping off my face. I forgot how freaking hot it is here.

"Lang, that the best you got?" Dalton calls out to Langley. The poor kid's standing near me, his lanky arms folded across his sweaty chest.

"Piss off, Dalton," Langley hisses, brows scrunching together.

I watch for a second as Dalton grins before ducking his head and chatting with his receiver. I'm impressed Langley doesn't flip Dalton the bird—guess that's one of the main differences between the pros and high school. That and the fact that Langley didn't just deck him, I suppose.

"Ignore him, Langley. We'll get it figured out. Come on." I motion him back onto the field, then hustle to take my position. We run the drill five more times, and I only fumble it once.

"See? You got this!" I shout, pumping my fist high in the air as I make the completion.

"Time!" Coach calls, waving his arms in the air. "Good practice today, boys. Go home and rest up. I'll see you back here tomorrow."

The team grabs their gear and heads toward the locker room. Langley lags behind, chucking his stuff into his duffel bag one item at a time.

"Hey—" I call out, shuffling up to him. "Keep your chin up. You'll get better."

The kid shrugs, his shoulders rising and falling, defeat etched on his face. "Sure."

I reach out, squeezing his shoulder. "Trust the process.

If Coach thinks you can do it, you can. He picks winners. Consistently, year after year."

"Yeah. But he didn't pick me yet for a reason." Langley zips up his bag, avoiding my gaze.

"But he thinks you have it in you. That's what matters right now."

"Sure. Dalton's gonna get the spot, I know it. He's bigger than me, throws harder and farther. He's a sure thing."

"With that kind of attitude, yeah."

Langley stands, wiping sweat from his brow with the hem of his Thunder Creek T-shirt.

"That's easy for you to say, coming from the pros. You don't know what it's like being here, not getting picked."

I huff out a breath, my gut squeezing. "Sure. Believe it or not, I have a pretty good idea of what that feels like."

"Bro, you're in the league."

"*Was* in the league. Trying to get back there. Everyone has ups and downs, man. Even once you go pro. The good news for you is you're a rising star. I'll take that any damn day of the week."

Langley peers off into the distance, up at the blank scoreboard. A long minute passes and I stoop to grab my gear.

"Thanks. It was cool of you to stick around and give me a pep talk." His voice is quiet and warmth spreads through me, from my gut up through my chest. I rise to face him.

"No problem. Keep your head in the game."

Langley nods and waves, trotting off to the locker room and I pray that I can heed my own advice, keeping my mind on football and off the coach's daughter.

CHAPTER 13
SLOANE

Cam's been avoiding me since the boat trip and our maybe-almost kiss. I'm not sure what happened between the lake and the house, but he's been acting strange ever since. Aloof and like he can't wait to get away from me, out of Thunder Creek.

Well, fuck that noise.

I've had about all I can take in the guys-and-games department.

Deciding the best offense is a good defense, I do my own thing and try fervently not to worry about him. Easier said than done, but I can certainly try.

My first order of business on Monday is applying for the job I saw posted at Java Jolt. I pop through the doors of the Thunder Creek library wearing my brightest smile and my cutest yellow sundress. I could use this job—both for the money and the distraction—and what better gig is there than helping people find a good book? Nothing quite beats the blues like getting lost in a book.

Walking through the main lobby area, I pass tall

shelves of books on display: the New Release section, the Librarian's Choice picks. Off to the left is the Children's Department, filled with toddlers eager for story time, bouncing around on the colorful carpet tiles. The same cozy bean bags sit in the corner beneath the window, the exact spot where I'd sit for hours devouring every chapter book I could get my hands on.

I sashay through the Reference section, the distinctive scent of ink and paper hitting me as I head over to the information desk.

"Hi. I'm Sloane Carter and I'm here to apply for the part-time job y'all have advertised."

The clerk glances up at me from her computer, her fingers hovering on the keyboard. She's probably in her early forties, with brunette hair cut in a stylish lob. Her name tag reads 'Megan.'

"Did you say Carter? As in Coach Carter?"

"Yes, ma'am. That's my dad."

"My son, Langley, plays football for the team. Your dad's quite the coach. Langley adores him." She beams up at me and I smile and nod politely, used to people having a strong opinion of my dad, one way or the other.

To everyone in town, my dad's Coach Carter, football coach extraordinaire. To me, he's just dad. The man who scrambled my eggs in the morning before school and learned how to French braid for Picture Day, taught me to ride a bike and kissed my skinned knees when I inevitably crashed.

"Mabel! Coach Carter's daughter's here, applying for the job!" she whisper-shouts over her shoulder at the woman transferring books from the rolling cart to the bookshelves behind the desk.

"Sloane?" Ms. Mabel spins around and peers over at

me. "I knew you were back in town, but I thought you were just visiting."

Ms. Mabel swishes over to the desk, reaching over and squeezing me in a hug. "So grown. I remember when you used to come in for the summer reading program. Won the grand prize when you were only seven years old, if I recall."

I smile, a hot blush creeping from my chest up my neck. "Yes, the summer before third grade. I got a huge teddy bear and a gift certificate to Swirly-Q. I always loved the summer reading program."

"So, are you back in Thunder Creek for good then?" Ms. Mabel asks, scrunching her nose.

"I'm not exactly sure at the moment, to be honest. But I could use a summer job and you know I love this library."

"Yes, dear, I do know that. But I'm afraid the pay isn't great, not like a city salary you're probably accustomed to. There've been a bunch of budget cuts, but we're hanging in."

"That's fine. I mostly want to keep myself busy and get out of the house."

"Well, in that case, you're hired. Monday through Friday, from two to six p.m. You can help shelve books, work the desk with Meg. And you'll be in charge of the Children's Department—including the summer reading program."

Ms. Mabel reaches into the desk, pulling out a single sheet of paper. "Fill this out and you can start as soon as the county scoots you through Human Resources."

"Wonderful." I beam at both ladies, genuine excitement bubbling inside me.

Taking the paper, I complete the form before handing it back to Ms. Mabel along with my driver's license. She makes a photocopy of both, then returns my license and the copy of the application.

"It's great to see you back in town, Sloane. I'll let you know as soon as I hear anything back from the county. Your cell number's on here, right?" Ms. Mabel scans the form for my phone number.

"Yes, ma'am. And thank you, Ms. Mabel. I look forward to working here!"

"Anytime, dear. Tell your daddy hi from me."

"Will do."

I wave and skip out of the library, feeling lighter and more content than I have in a long while.

———

"How'd practice go, Dad?"

"It went fine. Team could be real good. They're pretty green—we're losing a bunch of our seniors—but there's some talent there."

"Nice." I dry the last dinner dish, then stack the plate in the cabinet with its buddies. "Great news—I got a job today."

"You did? That's fantastic, baby. Where? With Gracelyn at the salon?"

"Nope. Better. At the library."

"That's perfect for you."

"I know. It's only part-time, but I get to run the summer reading program, which is cool. Ms. Mabel's still working there, so I was a shoo-in for the job. Hey—I met one of your player's mom's too. Langley or something like that?" I frown, trying to remember.

"Yeah. Good kid. He's one of the two up for the quarterback spot next year."

"Well, apparently he adores you. Sounds like his mom's a big fan too," I tease, grinning as his cheeks turn bright pink beneath his tan.

My dad hates when I mention women around him. He's practically taken a vow of chastity at this point, which I don't get. I mean, yeah, when I was a kid, sure. It made sense then. He had me straight out of high school and I know he struggled during those early years, with my mom totally out of the picture. We lived with Mimi and Poppa the first few years of my life when money was tight, his plans for a professional football career shattered. The man didn't exactly have a whole lot of time to date.

But now I'm almost thirty freaking years old. He doesn't need to take care of me anymore—not much, anyway. I'm grown, I'd be fine with my dad dating. Honestly, maybe it would take some of the pressure off me if he got a life of his own outside of football and Thunder Creek High.

Plus, objectively, he's the most eligible bachelor in town. Not that I love thinking about him like that or anything, but I get it. There aren't that many single guys hanging around Thunder Creek, especially ones as good-looking and accomplished as my dad. I've seen more than one woman throw herself at him, hoping to catch his eye.

But the man has a one-track mind, I swear. And that track is football.

I can't recall him going on even a single date. And believe you me, I would remember something that earth-shattering.

"Kid's got real talent. I paired him up with Cam today. I'm interested to see what he thinks."

My ears perk up at the mention of Cam. "Cam went to

practice then?" I keep my eyes on the silverware, drying each individual tine of the fork I'm holding meticulously.

"Yeah. You didn't see him before practice?"

"Nope. Haven't seen him all day."

"Huh."

I hold my breath, waiting for more information, but nothing comes. My dad's never been big on chitchat.

"How'd he look out there?" I ask, mining for any nugget I can get.

"Cam? He looked good. I'm surprised he got cut from his team, truth be told. I don't see a ton of weaknesses in his game. Sure, he could be more explosive at times. But his accuracy and speed are both good, his endurance seems fine."

A gnawing sensation grinds deep in my belly as I remember the convo Cam and I had right here in this kitchen.

Attitude problem.

Bad reputation.

What the hell did he do to warrant getting axed from the team? I may not understand all the ins and outs of being in the league, but seems like you'd have to do something pretty awful to get fired. I mean, guys end up in jail before that happens sometimes.

"Dad—did Cam tell you anything about why he got cut? When you had your heart-to-heart out on the porch?" I set the fork down, glancing over my shoulder at my dad.

He shrugs. "Not really. He's not in trouble with the law or anything like that. That's always a big thing with the league. So I'm not really sure. And it's none of my business, either."

I bite the inside of my cheek and hold my eye roll in check. Of course that would be my dad's perspective.

Always staying above the fray of town gossip. So aggravating.

He's worthless in that department, I swear.

"Listen—" He drops his voice lower, his green eyes serious. "I know you and Cam have always been friends. And he seems like he could use a friend. Now more than ever."

"Yeah, okay—" I sense a big-ass 'but' coming on, judging by the tight line of his lips.

"It's fine for you to be a shoulder to cry on. You've always been a good listener, a good friend. But be careful getting involved."

The knot in my stomach tightens and my face heats. *Am I that obvious?*

"I imagine you might be reeling from the break-up with that fella in New Orleans. Never liked him, by the way. I mean, you brought home a Dallas fan. Really?"

I force out a strained laugh, even as my chest squeezes tight and my palms slick with sweat.

"I thought I raised you better than that." He shakes his head, scrubbing a hand over the back of his neck. "Anyway, what I'm trying to say is, I think Cam's in a bad spot. Be his friend, but leave it at that."

I suck in a deep breath, nodding. I'm not entirely surprised we're having this conversation—he's never been too keen on me dating anyone—but I am a little shocked.

Because it's Cam.

He loves Cam.

His golden boy. The player who made it out of Thunder Creek, all the way to the pros.

If Cam's not good enough for me, who the hell is?

"Sure, Daddy. Got it. Be a good friend. Just like they taught me in Sunday School. But keep my clothes on."

My dad turns beet-red and slams his hands into the pockets of his cargo shorts. "You get what I'm saying, Sloane."

I shoot him a sassy grin. "I do. You're fun to tease, though."

"Night, baby girl." He steps forward and presses a kiss to my forehead. "See you tomorrow."

He heads to his bedroom for the night, leaving me alone in the kitchen. I doubt my dad needs to worry about anything happening between me and Cam, considering Cam's done an excellent job of avoiding me since the incident on the sandbar.

So close, yet so far.

I probably misread the whole damn situation. Between me and Gracelyn, you'd think we were starring in our own rom-com or something. Except the romance bit seems to be entirely one-sided—and that realization is more depressing than breaking off my engagement with Ratface.

I should listen to my dad and leave Cam alone. But what my head knows and my heart wants seem to be two entirely different things.

CHAPTER 14
CAM

I'm getting way too attached to Sloane. I need to steer clear of here, keep my distance. But that's almost impossible while we're both living under the same roof. I join the only gym in town just to have somewhere to go. Somewhere to hide from her glittering smile, those full, pink lips taunting me.

Every time the tip of her tongue darts out, gliding along the glossy surface, all I can think about is dropping my mouth to hers. Tasting her, sliding in and making her mine.

When she glances at me from across the table, mossy hazel eyes wide and innocent, I instantly see her sprawled naked across my bed, her luscious breasts on display. How I'd love to tease the rosy tips into sharp points until she's panting for me. Rub up and down her thighs, then sink my fingers into her pussy, stretching her, getting her ready to take all of me. Bringing her pleasure, over and over again.

I've jacked off in the gym shower every day and still leave here with a woody.

I need to find a hobby or something before I rub my poor dick raw. I'm also tired of eating take-out in an effort to avoid dinner with her and Coach—there's only so many options in Thunder Creek and I've exhausted all of them.

Or you could grow a pair and tell her how you feel.

I squeeze my eyes shut tight, heavy tension sitting at the base of my neck.

Terrible idea, Crawford. What you fucking need to do is find a new team and get out of town before you screw things up worse.

Taking my own advice, I tap out a text to my agent.

> Cam: Practice going great here. Any word on a new team yet?

I sink down onto the wooden locker room bench and wait for his response. Troy, my agent, always has his phone and typically responds within minutes.

True to form, my cell pings.

> Agent Man: Had a few nibbles. But nothing firm yet

> Cam: Which teams?

> Agent Man: Dakota was interested

I suck at my teeth. Not my first pick, given the horrible weather. But beggars can't be choosers.

> Cam: What was the deal?

> Agent Man: No deal. They pulled out

Shit.

Dakota would be better than nothing.

Cam: Did they say why?

Agent Man: They saw the video

Fuck me.

Cam: Motherfucker. They know their running back got a DUI last year, right?

Agent Man: Yeah. That's why they don't want more problems

This is so stupid. If I would have known I was being recorded, I never would have gone back to the hotel room with two of my teammates and those women from the bar. So fucking rash and naïve. I had too much to drink and made a mistake.

A fucking costly one. For me and my buddies, who also got kicked.

Not to mention my dating life, which has been non-existent since I got cut. It's pretty hard to trust anyone after a dupe like that. And it's not like I have a whole helluva lot to offer at the moment.

Cam: Bro. You can't explain it away? What if I send footage of me on the field? Running drills?

Agent Man: Send me what you've got, I can add it to the highlight reel

Cam: Okay. Any other bites?

Agent Man: Still working the angles. I'll
keep you posted

The muscles at the back of my neck tighten, tension shooting up and pulsing between my eyes. That doesn't sound too promising.

Cam: You're supposed to be the best in
the business. It was a stupid one-night
thing

Agent Man: I know, I hear ya. I'm trying.
But the league is cracking down on shit
like that. Everyone's very image-
conscious right now, what with all the
social media

Agent Man: Maybe do some charity work,
give back to the community

Cam: I am

Agent Man: Excellent. Polish that
squeaky-clean Boy Scout image to a
damn shine. Give me something good to
work with

I start to tap out *Go screw yourself,* but then remember we're on the same team. Troy's one of the good guys and he's on my side. I probably shouldn't piss him off if I want him working hard on finding me a new team.

Cam: Thanks. Let me know as soon as
you hear anything. One way or the other

Agent Man: Will do

I throw my cell into my backpack harder than necessary, a loud thud echoing through the empty locker room. Hot anger bubbles inside me and the hunger pains from a few minutes ago disappear, replaced by nausea.

I may never get back to the pros.

The realization hits me like a Mack truck. Sure, I had kind of a rocky season last year, didn't play as well as I wanted to. Had a few run-ins with the asshole tight end on my team and fought with the coach.

But reading between the lines, it seems like my biggest issue is the stupid video. I shouldn't have gone up to the hotel room with those women. It's not like I regularly engaged in random group hookups. It was a birthday bash for one of the guys and heavy drinking was involved.

Stupid fucking mistake, a set-up.

And maybe one I'll never live down.

Troy's good, but he wasn't good enough to intercept the video before it landed in my coach's inbox. And now my entire career's been reduced to a forty-five second sex video with my teammates and three random women.

A vein throbs at my temple as I regret my life choices. That video could cost me everything I've worked for. All the practices, the hard work, the dedication sliding down the drain. And for what? A night out with the boys and a few seconds of fleeting pleasure?

I've never felt more awful about anything in my entire life. But the video's out there now and I can't get it back.

What if Sloane finds out about it? She'll never look at me the same way again. I'll be just another washed-up, bad boy football player who does stupid shit in his free time.

No. I need to do whatever I can to keep that video a secret from her. Because as much as I hate to admit it, I don't think I'll survive the fall from her good graces.

I kick at the tile floor, hot embarrassment colliding with anger. I really fucked up this time—I only hope it doesn't cost me everything I love.

CHAPTER 15
SLOANE

'm lying on my bed scrolling through Instagram when the front door squeaks open. I check the time—after ten p.m. Definitely not my dad. He's been asleep for at least half an hour by now.

It's either a burglar or Cam and I don't think anyone in Thunder Creek or the surrounding counties would be stupid enough to break into Coach Carter's house. It has to be Cam.

Should I go say hi? Stay here and see what happens? Or shut my light off and avoid him altogether?

Before I make a decision, there's a knock on my door.

"Come in." My stupid, optimistic heart pounds in my chest and my stomach gets all fluttery as Cam pops his head in. His hair's damp and he has at least a day's worth of scruff peppering his jaw, making him that much sexier.

"Hey." The deep rumble of his voice sends warmth spreading through me like melted butter, oozing into every pore of my body.

I clear my throat. "Hey yourself. You okay? I haven't seen much of you since the day on the boat."

I try to keep my tone light and airy, as if seeing him—or not—doesn't matter to me.

Lies.

One large palm resting on the doorframe, his broad body fills the entire space. His right arm casually flexes, the tanned flesh taunting me, tempting me. My mouth honest-to-God waters at the sight of him leaning there, veins popping beneath the skin. His dark brows pull together, jaw tense, and I sense something's wrong.

Scrubbing a hand over the back of his neck, he crosses over the threshold into my bedroom. And I don't know why—Cam's been in my bedroom, loads of times—but this time feels different. Like the ions of the room are charged or something. Or maybe I've watched one too many rom-coms, who knows?

I inch back toward my headboard and cross my legs, patting the duvet. "You can sit—I won't bite, promise."

That not-at-all witty joke garners me a half-hearted smile, and he eases gingerly down onto the side of my bed. Heat radiates from his body, the strong alpine scent from his body wash wafting around him. He turns his marine eyes on mine, and they're darker than usual, his pupils wide.

"I've been training pretty hard. Don't want to disappoint your dad, since he's helping me out."

"Right." I bite at my bottom lip, wishing we could keep my dad out of this conversation.

A long beat of silence passes between us, and I twirl a strand of my hair round and round my finger. Anything to distract me from the absolute perfection perched on my bed right now.

"How's the hunt for a new team going?"

Cam heaves out a long, hard sigh, his chest deflating with the effort. "Nothing so far."

My hand instinctively flies out to touch his forearm, my thumb feathering over his warm skin.

"That's okay. I'm sure your agent's waiting for the right team and the best deal to come together. It will all work out."

His gaze drops to the place where our skin's making contact—I feel his stare—and now I'm self-conscious. I slide my fingers away from his arm, cheeks burning.

"I don't know, Sloane. What if I don't get picked up this season? It's almost June. Training starts at the end of July."

"You've got time."

His broad shoulders slump forward and my heart hurts for him.

"Cam—what's really going on? My dad said you're doing great at practice. But you're more down than I've ever seen you."

He cuts his eyes at the wall, boring a hole in the floral wallpaper I picked out in the tenth grade.

"He's being positive, like Coach always is."

I tsk, the noise loud in the quiet room. "My dad? Positive? No. Nuh-uh. He tells it like it is, no bullshit. And you know it. He wouldn't say you were doing great, looking good out there, if he didn't mean it."

Cam's shoulders straighten a little at that, but he still doesn't divulge any more details.

"Is this about the sandbar? Did I do something, say something, to upset you?"

"What?" He glances over, locking his eyes on mine. "No, not at all. You've done nothing wrong—it's me."

Then, with a shaky breath, he starts to talk. Like, really talk.

"I screwed up, Sloane. I made mistakes in Chicago that I regret. Deeply. If I could have a re-do of the entire season, I'd take it in a heartbeat. I got distracted—took my eye off the ball. And I blew it. Simple as that. I let my coach down, I let my team down. I let myself down." He smooths his palms over the fabric of his gym shorts and stares at the ground, his brow furrowed.

"Cam—"

Inching forward, I reach for his hand and he lifts his gaze to mine. Those deep blue eyes full of sadness, but also something else. Something I haven't seen there before, the pools of his irises dark and stormy. Interlacing his large fingers with mine, our palms touch, and still he doesn't break contact.

All the air's sucked out of the room and I can barely breathe, let alone think of anything reassuring to say. Sparks travel up my arm, straight to my pounding heart, and my entire body's on fire.

Cam leans in until we're inches away from each other, his breath warm against my lips. He touches his mouth to mine in a kiss so soft, so light that it's entirely possible I'm imagining we're touching at all.

"Cam—"

He pulls away slightly, serious eyes searching my face.

"Sloane, I—" His words vibrate against my skin, chill bumps rising on my flesh.

I shake my head, licking my lips that now taste of mint and Cam.

"Please. Kiss me again," I whisper.

He doesn't hesitate, cupping my cheeks in his large,

calloused hands. Not breaking his gaze, he presses his mouth to mine in a long, slow kiss and I melt into him.

Giving into all the feelings, all the sensations I've been waiting a lifetime for.

And damn, it's worth the wait.

His tongue teases the seam of my lips and I open to him, wanting to taste him, feel him, let him possess me. He slides in, fully in control, our tongues tangling. Gliding over one another, teasing, testing. He's delicious, better than the best dessert I've ever eaten, and I want more.

More of his touch, more of his body.

More of him.

CHAPTER 16
CAM

shouldn't be doing this.

Kissing Sloane in her childhood bedroom while Coach is asleep on the other side of the house.

It's wrong on so many levels.

Yet everything about her mouth touching mine feels so, so right.

Like she was made for me. Our lips, our hands, our bodies fit perfectly together.

The dull ache in the pit of my stomach that's been dogging me since I got axed from the team is gone, replaced with hot, burning desire.

I'm alive again.

Skin soft and smooth against my rough palms as I trace my thumb along her cheek, her shuddery exhalation vibrates my hand. She tastes sweet, like vanilla lip balm, as I lick along the seam of her full lips. Another breathy exhale and I float away on the quiet sound, getting lost in the moment.

Lost in her.

She opens her mouth to me and I dip in, my tongue seeking hers. Swirling round and round, exploring. Sloane's delicious and I'm a starving man, so damn hungry.

"Cam—" she murmurs, her delicate fingers twining in my hair. A shiver dances across the nape of my neck at her touch and every muscle flexes as her fingertips skip across my skin. My hand slides down to her lower back and I pull her across the bed, closer to me. Heat shimmers between us.

I want her.

I want to lay her down—right here, right now—and make her mine.

"Sloane—" Her name comes out half plea, half moan as I ease away from her supple body. For a long second, I wrestle with myself. "We shouldn't be doing this."

Hurt flashes across her face, but she doesn't move away, her arms still resting on my shoulders, hands wrapped behind my head.

"Why not?" Her bottom lip thrusts out in a pout and I'm rock hard for her, every single muscle in my body ready to go. I'd love nothing more than to kiss the disappointment right off her face, strip her out of those silky pj's, caress every inch of her skin until she's panting my name.

Using every ounce of self-restraint I possess, I somehow tamp all of that down.

"Because your dad's my coach. Because I'm living rent-free in his house." I run a hand through my damp hair, sighing as I crash back down to reality. "Because we're friends and I'd like to keep it that way."

Tipping her head, dark waves flow over her shoulder and her eyes sparkle in the dim lamp light.

"We could be friends with benefits?" She teases the idea, but I shake my head 'no.'

"I can't do that with you."

She blushes, her cheeks turning pink. "Why not?"

"Because you mean too much to me."

Her eyes narrow as she winces and I know I'm fumbling this entire thing.

"I'm sorry, I shouldn't have—" Her voice trails off and she glances away. "I was dumb to think there was more to this, more to us."

Reflexively, I reach out and tip her chin up, forcing her to meet my gaze. "You're not dumb, Sloane. And I meant what I said. You. Matter. To. Me." I emphasize each word, each syllable, willing her to understand just how much I mean this.

Tears shimmer in her eyes, those gold flecks glittering, and my chest squeezes tight.

"Don't." I run my thumb along her lash line, swiping away the offending moisture. She's so beautiful, her cheeks flushed a soft shade of pink.

Too beautiful. Too perfect.

Too vulnerable.

I shouldn't be here.

"I'm sorry, Sloane."

I take one last, longing look at her, memorizing every plane, every angle of her face. Wishing we could be more. Wanting to be more. But deep down, knowing I'm not the one for her.

Standing, I bend down and press my lips to the top of her head, breathing her in. All her goodness, her sweetness. Letting her scent wind around me and squeeze all the air from my lungs.

I only want *her* air, *her* breath. But I know we're not meant to be.

After a long moment, I force my legs to move. I need to get out of this bedroom. Away from temptation. Away from her.

"Do you ever check your email?" Her quiet voice rings through the room and I freeze in the doorway.

"What?" I glance back over my shoulder.

"Your team email. Do you ever check it?"

"Every once in a while. But not often. Why?"

"It's nothing. Forget I mentioned it."

"Oh-kay—" I frown, confused.

"Night, Cam."

Then she clicks the light off, leaving us both in the dark. I fumble my way out of her bedroom and down the hall to my own, shutting the door behind me. Knowing full well I may have just made another huge mistake. Possibly one of the biggest mistakes of my life.

I crash onto the bed, not even bothering to take off my clothes, and stare up at the popcorn ceiling.

What was Sloane talking about, that business about my team email?

Her melodic voice echoes in my head, over and over, and I'm wide awake. Snagging my phone from the night-stand, I tap the screen and click until I'm inside my team email. I'm surprised I still have access, but there may be some HR bullshit I still need to take care of.

Seems like I haven't checked my email in a while, judging by the 5,702 messages. Oops.

I stop scrolling when I spy a message from Sloane.

Clicking on the email, I hold my breath and read. Stopping, re-reading.

Sloane thinks I'm funny. And cool. And apparently hot.

And she's always had feelings for me.

Feelings I just exploited a few minutes ago.

With a shaky inhale, I force myself to keep reading, guilt edging in.

Sloane wanted to kiss me. Dreamed of it, in fact.

She doesn't want to live with regrets.

She put herself out there. Mustered up the courage to be authentic, be real.

She took a huge risk, a gamble, and here I am hiding out in the spare bedroom. Running away from my feelings, avoiding her because what exists between us is special and I'm scared as hell to ruin it.

Sloane Carter missed me.

And she signed off with love.

It's that last line that hits home. A strong force bubbles up inside me, pulling me out of bed and back down the hall.

I burst into her room and she sits up, startled.

"Cam?"

The room's dark, only a sliver of white moonlight shining through the blinds, outlining her silhouette. I cross to her bed, dropping down to my knees so we're face to face.

"I'm an idiot." I brush her cheek with my knuckles and she rests her face against my hand. "I shouldn't have run out on you like that and I'm sorry." My voice comes out strained and gravelly, but I push ahead.

"I'm afraid I'll hurt you, screw things up between us. I care about you, Sloane. A lot more than you know." Breath hitches in my throat, my chest tight.

She doesn't say anything. Instead, she cups my face, her delicate fingers feathering over my jaw. She touches her lips to mine and I kiss her back with everything I have, swelling with happiness.

This feels right. We feel right.

Maybe, just maybe, life is starting to turn around.

CHAPTER 17
SLOANE

Was last night a dream? Or did I finally kiss Cam Crawford in real life?

I roll over, the masculine scent of Cam drifting from my pillow. He was definitely here, in this room. And I wasn't drinking tequila this time, either. So I'm going with yes, all of last night was indeed very, very real.

Our first kiss.

Cam reading The World's Most Embarrassing Email.

Then the best part—the grand finale—and my personal favorite: him running back to my room, confessing his true feelings, and kissing me again.

It was a scene straight from the most romantic movie, complete with a Taylor Swift soundtrack playing in my head on loop. I can't stop smiling as I text Gracelyn.

Sloane: You're never going to believe what happened last pm!

Bestie: You got to watch ESPN 3 instead of 1 or 2? Lol

Sloane: MUCH better than that. Although ESPN 3 sometimes has ice skating and I do love watching the pairs

Bestie: Ratface called and apologized?

Sloane: I said you wouldn't believe it, but that's a little too far-fetched

Bestie: Does this have to do with the very hot pro football player living at your house?

Sloane: Maybe...

Bestie: OMG, y'all finally had sex!

Sloane: Ok, tone it down. We did not have sex with my dad in the house

Bestie: Damn

Sloane: But we DID kiss

Bestie: Yeah! You made it to second base!

Bestie: Just kidding. That's amazing!

Bestie: How was it? Best kiss ever? He looks like he'd be a good kisser. He's got nice, full lips

Sloane: Best. Kiss. Ever.

Bestie: I need DETAILS! Can you meet me at the salon? My appt just walked in

> Sloane: Sure. But we need to talk in private. I don't want all of Thunder Creek knowing about me and Cam by lunchtime

> Bestie: Come at 9:30. I'll throw Mrs. Slater under the dryer and we can pop outside to chat

> Sloane: Ok. See you then!

Setting the cell down, I stretch my arms over my head, my body soft and relaxed. It's the best I've felt in a very long time. Way before the engagement ended, if I'm being honest.

This could all come crashing down.

I shove the thought away, taking a deep, cleansing breath. No need to manifest anything negative. Sure, we didn't talk about the future or anything. But right now I choose to live in the moment, take things one day at a time.

Besides, getting ahead of myself is how I managed to get into the whole wedding debacle with Ratface. Instead of trusting my gut—and the whispers around the office—I turned a blind eye to his actual personality (or lack thereof) to live up to some societal expectation about marriage.

Well, not this time.

This time, I'm trusting my gut—and my heart.

And my heart's been beating for Cam since I was four-teen years old.

After one more luxurious stretch, I climb out of bed and head down the hall to the bathroom. Cam's door is open and the house is silent.

Peeking in, I note his bed is neatly made and the room

tidy. He's probably already at the gym. A twinge of disappointment hits me in the gut, but I squash it.

Relax, Sloane. Cam needs to train, not lounge around with you all morning.

I hustle through my daily routine, grabbing a breakfast bar and an iced coffee to go before heading out.

Plumb Perfect, Gracelyn's salon, is a few blocks past the town square. A cozy, lilac bungalow with white shutters, window boxes overflowing with wildflowers, and a cute porch with a swing, the Reynolds's converted the house to a salon many years ago. Practically every female in town is a client, and some of the younger males as well. Gracelyn's mom's been in business since before I was born —she gave me my first haircut, my one and only perm, and fashioned updos for every school dance. Basically, Shelby Reynolds is a Thunder Creek superstar and the first to hear any and all gossip. Of course Gracelyn's a natural, following in her mother's footsteps.

"Hey, y'all!" I push through the crickety white door, the tinkle of a chime signaling my arrival.

Grace waggles her fingers over her shoulder. "Hey! I'm almost done." Rolling the last pink plastic curler into silver hair, she secures it with a clip. "Last one, Mrs. Slater. Let's pop you under the dryer for a few and get this all set up."

Grace helps Mrs. Slater down from the salon chair, leading her across the honey-oak floors into the next room. The dull whir of the heater starts, vibrating the entire house.

"Hey, darling." Ms. Shelby gives me a quick squeeze on her way over to the chair beside Grace's. "How are you doing?" Her heavily penciled brow arches in concern. "You holding up?"

"I'm doing just fine, thanks Ms. Shelby."

"I still can't believe that no-good scoundrel. Abso-lutely gobsmacked when Gracie told me what happened."

I shrug. "It was for the best."

"Such a shame. I do love weddings." Ms. Shelby's eyes glaze over as she stares into the mirror, presumably envi-sioning a white, puffy wedding dress and the matching sleek chignon hairstyle she'd pair with it.

"Mom!" Grace hisses, running in and smacking her on the shoulder. "Stop. What did I tell you about bringing up the wedding again? Sloane does not want to keep rehashing it, I'm sure."

Ms. Shelby tsks at Grace, rubbing her arm. "What? I can't say I'm sorry?"

"No! Not again. She doesn't want to be reminded about that asshole. Excuse my French."

Ms. Shelby rolls her eyes at Grace, tsking at her younger daughter's foul language.

"Sloane, sugar, I'm sure the right one will eventually come along. In the meantime, you can keep Gracie company."

Grace sighs so hard she loses an inch of height. "Might as well say Bless Your Heart, Mama. Geez…C'mon, Sloane. I have a quick break before Mrs. Slater's done under the heat."

Grace grabs my arm, pulling me out of the salon and onto the porch, back into the stifling Georgia heat.

"Forget her, Sloane. Spill!" she hisses, patting the spot on the porch swing next to her.

I drop down into the swing, happy to be hidden from view of the street.

"Grace—it was magical." A warm, tingly feeling floods through me thinking about last night. The kiss, the way

Cam swept back into the room and admitted he was an idiot.

I particularly liked that last part, not gonna lie.

"Tell me everything—don't leave one tiny detail out! But hurry—I only have—" Grace checks the timer on her cell—"eight minutes now."

"Cam came home from the gym kind of late. I was in my room and he stopped by. He seemed upset, so I invited him in, asked what was wrong. Basically, he doesn't have a new deal yet, so he's super bummed out. But I told him I was sure things will work out, then next thing I know, we're inches apart and he leaned in and kissed me! And, ohmygod, Grace—it was the best kiss ever. Like, twelve out of ten stars."

"Worth waiting almost fifteen years for?"

"Totally."

"That's amazing, hun. Then what? How come nothing else happened?" She shoots me a pointed look, the edge of her deep red matte lips tipping up.

"Well, then he broke it off and went back to his room."

Grace waves her hand wildly through the air. "Hold up. He bailed? He didn't get you naked and tell you he's been a damn fool all this time?"

I snort. "Uh, no. Definitely not. He said something more along the lines of he shouldn't disrespect my dad and bolted."

"Weak." Grace shakes her head, a blonde curl falling loose from her top knot.

"I don't know what possessed me, but I asked him if he checked his email right before he walked out."

"No!"

"Yes! He seemed confused. Then like ten minutes later, he came back. He read the World's Most Embarrassing

Email, Grace! But he didn't think it was dumb. In fact, I think he was kinda inspired, honestly. Said he was an idiot and he's scared of screwing things up between us."

"Wow. Babe. That's a story. And this morning?"

"Um—haven't seen him. Pretty sure he went to the gym."

"Huh. Not great."

"What? Why? He's trying to get a professional football contract, Grace. He's gotta put in the work."

"Still. I would've liked a love note or something this morning."

Right on cue, my phone dings with an incoming text. I yank the cell from my pocket, reading.

Cam: Hey beautiful. Good AM

Heat blooms, rising from my chest all the way to my cheeks.

Cam called me beautiful.

"Okay, not fair. What's it say?" Grace cranes her neck, trying to read the text.

"Good morning. And he called me beautiful." I can't help it, I'm smiling so hard my cheeks hurt.

"Nice…text him back."

Sloane: Good AM!

My thumb hovers over the keypad, not sure what else to type.

"Come on, Sloane—you gotta do better than that."

"Right. I know." I frown, unsure what to say.

"Can't write to him without the help of your good buddy Jose, huh?" Gracelyn teases. "Here—let me."

Reaching over, she grabs the cell from my hand.

"Grace!" I try to get the phone back, but she holds it out of reach, tapping away like a madwoman.

"Do not hit send!" I warn her, my chest suddenly tight. I love Gracelyn, but she can be absolutely cray-cray sometimes.

"Relax—I'll let you read before I send it. Okay, here you go." She thrusts the phone at me and I stare down at the message.

> Sloane: Hey big sexy, good AM! Did you get all hot and sweaty at the gym? Why don't you wait to shower until you get home (winky face)

I groan, deleting the entire message as fast as possible. "No, definitely not."

"Sloane—you have to take a risk! Right the heck now. You don't know how much time you have together. Besides, you can't be all coy and virginal. For starters, y'all are grown-ass adults. For seconds, Cam is a professional athlete. Do you know what that means?"

I cut my eyes at her, knowing I'm not going to like her answer. "What, exactly, does that mean? To you, with your deep knowledge of professional sports?"

"It means he has women throwing themselves at him all the damn time. Remember the bonfire? And that's just here, in Thunder Creek. And sure, you have the hometown advantage. For now. But as soon as he gets a contract, he's outta here. If you want a chance with him—a real, fighting chance to be together, like you always dreamed of—then you need to seize the day, woman! Or you're going to miss your golden opportunity!"

Grace pumps her legs back and forth in an agitated

fury while I mull over her words. She's right, I suppose, but I'm not sure how to break through the friend zone Cam and I so carefully constructed over the years. I tuck my hair back behind my ear, thinking.

Finally, I text him back.

> Sloane: Good AM to my fave football player. Did you go to the gym?

Cam: Yep. Lifted a ton. Pretty tired and sore rn, not gonna lie

I smile down at the text.

"What? What's happening?" Gracelyn keeps rocking, staring at me.

"I have an idea."

"I like ideas. As long as they're sexy ideas."

"Could be. At least it would involve less clothing."

"I'm intrigued."

Holding one finger up at Gracelyn, I tap out another text.

> Sloane: You home now?

Cam: Heading there. Why?

> Sloane: Don't shower yet. I'll be home in about twenty minutes

Cam: Sounds promising

> Sloane: It'll be good for you

"You happy now?" I hand my phone to Gracelyn and she reads through the text exchange.

"Sloane, you dirty girl! You *are* going to shower with

him. That's so hot! And in your dad's house too. So naughty—I like it." She grins her approval.

"Not exactly. I gotta bolt. Thanks for the pep talk!" I hop up from the swing, waving good-bye as I dash down the stairs to my car.

"Wait—what? You're not showering together? You better call me later!"

Grace follows me to the steps, her brows knit in confusion.

I'll explain the whole thing to her later, but right now I need to get to the Walmart ASAP.

CHAPTER 18
CAM

"Cam? I'm home!" The trill of Sloane's voice carries through the quiet house, shooting edgy excitement through me. Blood immediately rushes down south and I shift, attempting to adjust myself in the mesh gym shorts. The thin fabric can't hide my rock-hard cock, though, so I shove my hand in my pocket before sauntering out to the living room.

"Hey." I pause in the doorway, taking in every inch of her body, from the high ponytail to the tight black tank top to the tiny denim shorts. She's so effortlessly gorgeous, sunglasses perched on top of her head, hand on hip. I have no idea why any guy would even think of screwing around on her, let alone actually do it.

She smiles at me as I make my way over, drawn to her like a magnet. As soon as Sloane's in the room, she's all I see. Football, my career—all the anxiety and tension—is gone. It's just the two of us and I'm back in a good head-space, a place where I can be my genuine self. None of the other bullshit matters.

Although I know I should resist temptation, I can't help myself. We moved into a new space together last night, and there's no going back now.

I lean down and press my lips to hers. The gesture feels surprisingly natural.

"Sorry for sneaking out on you this morning—I wanted to hit the weights before the gym bros showed up and hogged the equipment."

"It's okay." She rises on tiptoe, weaving her arms around my neck. "You can make up for it now."

"Deal. What did you have in mind?" I ask as my hands find their way down her back, sneaking around to cup her perfectly round ass.

"I have some stuff in my car. I could use some help carrying it around back."

"No problem. Although I was kinda hoping to deliver a different sort of favor."

The corners of her pink lips tip up as she unwinds from me. "I do like the sound of that—but it'll have to wait until later. I have a surprise first. C'mon."

Grabbing my hand, she pulls us both outside then hits the fob on her keychain. The Volvo beeps and the trunk lifts as we make our way down the driveway.

"I can get this." Sloane leans into the trunk and hoists out a large rectangular box. "You grab the rest."

I peer in at six mammoth bags of ice. "You throwing a party this afternoon?"

"Only for the two of us—no one else is invited. Follow me." She pivots and heads around to the back yard. I grab two bags of the ice and trail behind her, admiring the view.

"Just drop the ice on the deck. I'll get to work here." Sloane crooks her thumb at the wooden deck and I do as I'm told, setting the giant bags down before heading back to fetch more. I make three trips while she busies herself in the yard.

"Is that an inflatable pool?" I ask, sidling up next to her. A large plastic aqua rectangle is spread out on the grass in the center of the lawn.

"Sure is. But today it's not just a regular old pool. No, today it's your cold plunge pool. That's good for muscle recovery, right?"

A warmth spreads through my chest like gooey caramel. Sloane could have done anything she wanted this morning—gone to yoga, hit up Java Jolt for an iced coffee —but instead she went to Walmart and bought a blow-up pool and a bunch of ice to build me a makeshift cold plunge pool. She's exactly how I remembered her—kind, thoughtful—but now she's so much more. More confident, self-assured, sexy.

Don't screw this up, Crawford. She's special.

"Yes. It's great. We had one in Chicago and I used it after every game and most workouts."

"Perfect." She flips her dark ponytail, then bends over to turn on the pump. My eyes rake over her body, the long line of her back, the slight indent of her hip bones peeking out from the sliver of exposed skin.

She pops a hand on her hip as the sides of the pool begin to fill up with air, rising and quickly taking shape.

"Thanks for doing this, Sloane."

"Well, I did have an ulterior motive."

I narrow my eyes at her. "Really? And what's that?"

She shoots me a mischievous grin. "Getting you out of your clothes, of course."

"Trouble, all you had to do was ask." I hitch my thumb into the back of my shirt, yanking the fabric up and over my head, balling it up and tossing it onto the deck. Sloane watches me intently, biting at the corner of her lip. I flex my abs for full effect, then kick off my shoes and socks. Finally, I slide my gym shorts down until I'm only wearing boxer briefs.

"I'll leave my briefs on. Neighbors." I tilt my head at the fence. "Don't want to give anyone a scare."

She giggles, two bright spots of pink staining her cheeks. "Right, sure. Can you grab the hose?"

"No problem."

I head over to the side of the house and lift the green coil, carry it over to the pool. Handing the hose to Sloane, I jog back to turn on the water. Then I grab the first bag of ice and rip through the plastic, dumping the frigid contents into the water.

"Fill it all the way to the top, right?" she asks.

"Yep. As high as it can go."

The surface of the pool's dotted with tiny glaciers and I'm cold just thinking about climbing in.

She glances at me, then the pool, then back at me again, sizing up the situation. "Sorry, this is the largest pool they had at Walmart. Probably not as deep as you're used to."

I lock eyes with her. "It's perfect."

The tip of her tongue darts out, tracing along her full lip, and my heart races into overdrive. I haven't been this keyed up over a woman in a very long time—maybe ever. And the fact that the woman in question is Sloane? Yeah, that scares the hell out of me.

"You ready?" Sloane interrupts my internal mini freakout.

"As I'll ever be." I roll my shoulders up and back, mentally preparing for the cold.

"How long do you stay in? You want me to time you?"

"Sure—usually around seven or eight minutes."

She pulls out her phone as I gingerly step into the pool, easing my body down into the icy water. The chill steals my breath as I sink deeper, trying to submerge the maximum amount of surface area. I lean back against the edge of the pool and focus on my breath, anything other than the pricking of the freezing water on my skin. Chunks of ice glob together and bob along the top of the pool, hitting against my bare arms and chest.

"How much time left?" I grit out the words.

She chuckles. "Seven minutes and thirty seconds, tough guy."

I grimace. "Easy for you to say—"

"Hey, it's not all that great out here, either. I'm sweating."

"I know how you could cool off." I arch a brow, smirking.

She waves away my suggestion. "It's okay, I'll let you enjoy the cold plunge benefits solo."

"Too bad. You could warm me up." My teeth start chattering and I clamp my jaw harder, flexing and releasing my muscles. My breathing slows down as I give into the cold and relax a little.

"That's kinda the opposite effect you're going for, though. Think how rejuvenated you're gonna be for practice this afternoon. It'll be great—totally worth it!"

"Uh-huh." I rest my head on the inflated pool edge and stare at her long, toned legs. Legs I'm itching to touch, smoothing my palms all the way up the insides of her thighs.

She checks the timer. "Three minutes left! Smile!"

I force a smile as she snaps a photo. "You should send that to your agent. He'll be impressed with your commitment to training. He could use it in negotiations."

"Mm-hmm. Good idea."

It's cute, how hard she's working to help me feel better about my current status. She's so optimistic, so upbeat. Her positivity almost makes me forget how dire the situation really is, that there is no back-up plan.

Something I'd rather not dwell on at the moment.

"Your dad doesn't come home for lunch, does he?"

"No, not usually. Why?"

"Just wondering."

"Only thirty seconds left…twenty…ten."

I silently count down in my head and then the alarm buzzes, the sharp sound ricocheting off the wood fence.

"Time's up! You did it!" She silences the phone, beaming at me as I sit up, concentric waves arcing out around my biceps. The rays of the sun beat down on my icy shoulders and back, the sharp contrast of sensations raising chill bumps on my skin. A shiver races down my spine, everything tingling as I stand and climb out of the pool.

"How was that? Did it help?" Tiny wrinkles furrow Sloane's otherwise smooth brow and she's precious as hell, the cutest amateur trainer on the damn planet.

"Pretty nice, actually."

"I know it's not fancy, like you're used to—"

"It was great." I shake my arms and legs, beads of water flying off my skin. "And the company was a lot better than Chicago."

A flush colors her chest, creeping up her neck as I brush a loose tendril of hair away from her face. Wrapping my arms around her narrow hips, I pull her warm body up against mine. Water soaks through the thin cotton of her shirt, her nipples pebbling through the slip of fabric. Her hands wind around my back, fingers dancing across my traps, leaving behind a fiery wake.

She fits perfectly in my arms, our bodies pressed together. I lift her sunglasses from her face, ease her cell from the back pocket of her shorts, tossing both items onto the grass. Then I turn my attention back to her.

Dipping my head down, I brush my lips lightly against hers. She moans softly into my mouth and I swallow the sweet sound, suddenly starving.

I want to taste her, lick every last square inch of her body, lap at her juices until they coat my tongue. I want to touch her, caress her, pump my fingers into her tight pussy until she's riding my hand, screaming for more. I want to sink into her, driving hard, pounding until I feel her muscles spasm around my hard cock and I explode inside her.

I want to make Sloane Carter mine. Right here, right now.

Kissing her harder and deeper, I lick at her mouth until she opens for me. I slide in, swirling around, increasing the force, the pressure. My hands move from her hips down to her ass and I squeeze the round globes. She shimmies up against my pelvis and blood flow starts to return, my cock twitching. Her fingers feather over my back, tracing the ridges of my lats, my deltoids, and all I can think about is her.

Not training, not football, not my career.

Just Sloane and how amazing it will be to fuck her.

CHAPTER 19
SLOANE

Cam Crawford's very nearly naked in my dad's backyard in broad daylight. Even better, he's kissing me.

This would be a real bad time for Mrs. Humperdink to check on her zucchini. She's a nice enough neighbor, but the woman's nosy as hell and loves spilling tea to anyone close enough to listen.

"We should probably go inside," I murmur against Cam's lips. "The neighbors…"

"You have nine-foot neighbors?"

"No." I giggle.

"Then they can't see over the fence."

"True. But don't discount the possibility of peeping through the cracks or pulling up a ladder."

"Guess they'll have earned the show then, with that level of effort."

I laugh, fizzy happiness bubbling inside me. "C'mon, let's go inside—it's hot out here."

"I can fix that."

In one swift move, Cam sweeps me off the ground and into his strong arms. For a split second, I'm nestled up against his broad chest. Then next thing I know, I'm on top of his body in the cold pool.

"Ohmygod, Cam!" I slap at his pecs, the water still chilly enough to take my breath away. Well, that and lying on top of a gorgeous pro football player, every muscle in his body chiseled like a sculpture straight out of the Renaissance.

"What? You said you were hot and sweaty." He smirks, playing innocent. "Thought I'd help you out."

He glides a large hand down my back, resting his palm on my ass and pulling me up tight against his body. His hard cock twitches against my thigh and I love that I have this effect on him. Pressing my hips against him, I twine my legs with his, run my fingers through his damp hair. He smells clean, like some masculine shower gel as I lean in and kiss him.

Cupping my cheek with his palm, he opens his mouth to me. I slide my tongue in, running along the straight line of his teeth, tasting him. Minty and fresh, I could lay here and kiss Cam all day long.

He palms the back of my neck, winding my ponytail around his fist and tugging lightly. "You're beautiful, you know that." His marine eyes lock on mine, pupils dark. "So damn beautiful."

Hearing these words from Cam sets my pulse racing. I've dreamed of this moment since I was fourteen years old. To think it's happening—we're happening—is surreal. I've wanted him so much, for so long.

Gazing up at him, nerves and desire commingle, stealing my words. Now that we're here, finally together like I always dreamed, I'm freezing up.

Don't blow this, Sloane.

"Thank you," I squeak out, my voice barely above a whisper. Suddenly, I'm shy and self-conscious.

He pulls harder at my hair, forcing me to look at him.

"I mean it, Sloane. You're absolutely stunning."

My face flames and it's not from the beating rays of the sun. Cam traces his calloused thumb across my cheekbone, down the side of my jaw, sending a shiver of pleasure zipping through me.

Cam thinks I'm beautiful.

A lightness fills my chest, my entire body relaxing beneath his touch as I melt into him. The water's still cool but I'm not cold, heat radiating off Cam's hard torso. He traces down my neck to my collarbone and I suck in a sharp breath as his fingers graze my breast. My nipple peaks under his touch, pebbling in the thin, wet satin of my bra. He circles the sharp point and my eyes flutter closed as I give into all the sensations. The warmth, the cold, his feathery touch, the tingle of desire dancing just beneath my skin. He brushes his lips against mine and I kiss him back softly, slowly. Cupping my breast, he squeezes.

"Cam—" I moan quietly, my core throbbing. Shimmying against him, hot need pulses through me. I'm fire and ice all at once and the feeling's delicious.

He slips his fingers under my shirt, splaying his palm across my belly, and his hand's so large it covers my entire midsection. Another moan falls from my lips as he kneads and pinches my breasts, moving between the right and the left. My thighs clench around his thick quad and the corners of his lips quirk.

"Eager beaver," he teases, then brushes a hair from my eyes. "It's cute—I dig the enthusiasm."

"In that case—" I inch away slightly before throwing one leg over his hips and straddling him. His eyes widen as he watches me try to peel my shirt off as sexily as possible—not an easy task, given the soaking wet, skintight fabric clinging to me.

"Let me help." He strips the shirt over my shoulders without issue and flings it to the ground before reaching around and unhooking my bra. The straps slip down my shoulders and he slides the satin garment away, flipping it out of the pool before palming my breasts.

"Fucking gorgeous." He flicks at my nipples with his thumbs, pinching and releasing the sharp points, and waves of pleasure roll through me.

"Ohh—" His hot tongue laves at my skin, teasing, and it's quite possible I may come just from the swirl on my nipple. He alternates between my breasts, showering attention on both sides equally as I grind against him. His dick grows longer and harder by the second, meeting my greedy thrusts in perfect rhythm.

Pulling me down deeper into the water, closer to him, he buries his face between my breasts and I'm in heaven.

Lounging in an inflatable pool on a clear summer day, Cam's breath warm on my bare skin.

Absolute bliss.

"I want you," I murmur, reaching down and stroking his hardness over the briefs.

"I want you too. Obviously." The words are muffled by my chest, his stubble rough against the tender flesh.

Lifting his head, he meets my gaze. "But we should probably take this inside. You were worried about the neighbors a few minutes ago."

"What neighbors?" I tease, the corner of my lip tipping into a grin as I rub his cock through the cotton. He lets out a groan, pushing against my hand. With deft fingers, he unbuttons my shorts and slides them down over my hips.

I roll off him, water spilling over the side as I lay back and shimmy out of the denim. Poor choice of outfit, but to be fair, I had no idea I'd end up making out in a kiddie pool this afternoon.

With much effort, I finally kick out of the restrictive clothing and chuck the sopping wet shorts onto the grass. Cam levers up on one elbow and my breath hitches as I take him all in. Thick veins pop from his forearm, every muscle pronounced, long, sharp lines beneath his tanned skin. He exudes power. Strength. Virility.

I reach out, swiping at a water droplet dripping down his pec. Tiptoe my fingers across his smooth chest, then follow the ridge of abs all the way down to the waistband of his briefs.

"Ladies first." He winks, gripping my shoulders and sliding my body down so my head's resting on the edge of the pool. Water laps at my bare breasts as Cam inches closer to me, spreading my thighs with his hand. With a shuddery breath, I hollow out my stomach like I'm in Pilates.

Cam doesn't swoop in or rush.

No, he takes his time, smoothing his palm over my thigh, his eyes serious. The water's not freezing cold anymore—the hot sun warmed it right up, melting all the ice. Yet a shiver races through me as he caresses the inside of my leg. Moving higher, inch by inch, until he comes to the apex. I hold my breath as he cups me, his thumb circling my clit through my panties.

Eyes fixed on mine, he presses down and I writhe with pleasure.

"So good…" I mumble, barely able to form a cohesive thought. I'm drunk on Cam—his body, his scent, his touch.

He drops his lips next to the shell of my ear, his breath tickling my skin.

"I've been thinking about this pussy all night and all day. How you'll taste, how tight you'll be around my cock."

The vibrations of his voice give rise to chill bumps on my skin and I want him.

Want him to taste me, touch me, fuck me.

Arching up, I crave more contact. His full lips curve into a smile, like he's stealing a cookie from the cookie jar and can't wait to take that first forbidden bite.

"I love how responsive you are." He nuzzles my neck with his nose, still caressing my pussy, and I think I might die of overstimulation. From the sun, the cool water, the teasing of his fingers on my most sensitive area.

Easing my panties to the side, he slides his fingers over my pussy and I squirm, aching for more. More friction, more pressure, more Cam.

He slips one finger, then another inside and my muscles contract around him. The fullness feels fantastic as he scissors his fingers, stretching me. Pushing in and out, I ride his hand sending water splashing over the sides of the pool.

"Such a tight little pussy."

Pressure builds, all buzzy energy, my body tensing.

"I'm close—" The words come out in a breathy rasp and Cam picks up the pace.

"That's good, baby." He thrusts harder, crooking his finger to hit my G-spot and I rocket over the edge.

"Ohmygod, Cam—" I cry out, a hot flush sweeping through me as I unravel beneath his touch.

"Such a good girl. So fucking sexy." He kisses me slow and deep, caressing my bare breasts, my belly, running his hands up and down my thighs. Touching me lightly, delicately. It's rare to see this softer side of Cam, but I love it.

"Thank you," I murmur against his lips. "That was amazing."

"Happy to deliver." He tucks a piece of hair behind my ear. "I do think we should take it inside, though. Don't want to get sunburned before practice."

"Right." The mention of football rockets me back to reality and I'm suddenly self-conscious. I fold my arms over my bare chest and sit up, trying to grab my wet tank top.

"I should have thought about towels, I guess." I cover my breasts with the black strip of fabric, holding the shirt against me like a bandeau.

"No biggie." Cam stands up, water sluicing down his legs, his bulge prominent in his wet briefs. He holds his hand out and I take it, still clutching the tank top tight to my chest. With little effort, he lifts me to standing and I tumble forward against him. Sliding his hands around my waist, he pulls me in tight and kisses me again. After a long minute, he pulls away.

"I'm gonna shower. You wanna come?"

The idea of showering with Cam in the tiny bathroom, steam billowing around us as I lather him up with yummy shower gel, does appeal.

"Sure."

We gather our discarded clothing and head into the house, Cam unfazed by his near-nakedness. I let him lead because I don't really want him staring at my ass in broad daylight, no matter how much he says he loves it.

As soon as we step into the kitchen, the front screen door screeches open.

"Ohmygod! It's probably my dad!" I whisper to Cam, hot panic seizing me.

Standing in the kitchen with Cam, dripping wet and practically naked, does not look good. There's no plausible explanation. So I do the only logical thing.

"Run!" I hiss, darting down the hall to the bathroom as fast as I can. The front door groans open, then slams shut as I duck into the hall bath.

But I'm alone. Cam didn't follow me.

Shitballs.

Pressing my ear to the door, I listen to the deep murmurs of conversation, barely able to hear over the pounding of my heart. Water drips down my legs and puddles on the floor, but I don't dare move.

What's my dad doing here in the middle of the day? He never comes home.

I hold my breath and wait. For my dad to leave, for him to discover me hiding in the bathroom, naked. Seconds tick by and I begin to wonder if I'll be waiting in here until football practice.

An eternity passes and then the front door slams again. Two seconds later, there's a rap on the bathroom door.

Opening it a tiny crack, I peer out.

Cam's standing in the hall, fully clothed, my wet lacy bra dangling from his finger.

CHAPTER 20
CAM

That was a close call.

Too close.

What would I have done if Coach walked in on me finger-fucking his daughter?

We shouldn't be so reckless. Especially me, with my entire life on the line. I can't afford to screw anything else up. And the last thing I want to do is disrespect Coach in his own home.

I tap on the bathroom door and Sloane cracks it open the teeniest bit.

"You dropped this." Her black lacy bra dangles from my finger.

"Ohmygod. My dad didn't see, right?"

"No. I scooped it before he walked in."

"He's gone now, right?"

"Yes. Coast is clear."

Sloane opens the door warily and I join her in the tight space. The bathroom's not large to begin with and with both of us in the room, I can barely turn around.

"Why'd he come home, anyway? He never does that." Her brows scrunch together.

"Forgot his playbook for practice."

"Oh."

"Listen—" I run a hand through my damp hair, debating what to say and how to say it.

"Oh boy. This isn't going to be good." She sinks down onto the toilet seat, wrapping the towel around her shoulders tighter.

"Hey—" I cup her chin, tipping her face up toward me. "Everything's fine. But we need to be more careful. I can't afford to piss off your dad."

She bites at her bottom lip, nodding. "Yeah. I get it. And trust me—I don't want my dad walking in on us, either. So cringe. No offense."

"None taken."

"He's not coming back now, though, right?"

"No, he said something about teaching a class seventh period and he was in a rush. Said he'll see me at practice later."

"Good." She reaches out and depresses the lock on the door with a loud click. "Just in case."

Then she grips my hips, hooking her thumbs in the waistband of my shorts and sliding them down my thighs.

"Sloane—" I groan as her tongue darts out, licking along the seam of her slightly swollen lips.

"Is this okay?" Her hazel eyes cut to mine, gazing up at me through a fringe of thick lashes.

"Yeah—I mean, it's great."

"Now's probably the closest we'll ever get to a safe time, so—" Her fingers tease at the band of my briefs and my muscles flex instinctively beneath her touch. She's so damn beautiful, cheeks flushed a soft pink as I run my knuckles down her jawline.

Wasting no time, she frees my cock from the wet cotton. Her eyes widen as she takes me in.

"Wow. That's—" she huffs out a breath, staring at my length. "Impressive."

"Thanks. I'll take that as a compliment."

Her high-pitched, nervous giggle bounces off the tile walls as I hustle out of my briefs, shedding the T-shirt as well. One hand runs up and down my abs, her finger tracing down the sharp V of my hip bone, all the way to the base of my cock.

Encircling the shaft with her small hand, she slides up and down my length and I'm rock-fucking-hard now, both of us breathing quick and shallow. I close my eyes and give into the sensation, balls tightening as she strokes the sensitive skin.

Then her warm tongue's on the tip of my dick, swirling around the head, licking at the drops of pre-cum already leaking.

"Fuck—" I hiss, threading my fingers through her damp, silky hair. Pulling her in closer to me, her breath warm on my skin. She licks round and round, then sucks me into her hot mouth and it feels so damn good.

The base of my spine tingles as she hollows out her cheeks, taking me in deeper. I grip the back of her neck and she holds onto my ass for leverage as she works my cock. In and out, in and out, sucking me hard. So fucking hard and it feels amazing.

So amazing, I forget everything.

Where I am. Why I'm here. And all the things that happened in between.

I'm lost in the moment. All that matters right now is her and what she's doing to my cock.

"Sloane—" I moan and the corners of her lips quirk up in a smile. "That's so good…so fucking good."

At the encouragement, she takes me in deeper still. Her teeth scrape along my length and I exhale a shuddery breath. The towel falls from her shoulders and she's an absolute vision, creamy tits on full display. I'm on the edge, heat pricking my skin as she runs her hand over my sensitive balls.

"I'm close—" Bright stars dance in my periphery, agonizing tension mounting. "If you want me to pull out, I will."

She shakes her head 'no,' instead pulling me in all the way. The tip of my cock hits the back of her throat and tears fill her eyes, but she doesn't let up. Somehow, she maintains both pressure and rhythm as I drive into her, fucking her mouth, taking me right to the edge.

"Fuck—" I grit out, hot ropes of cum erupting. She swallows quickly, throat working overtime. A few drops leak from the sides of her mouth and I swipe it away with my thumb.

"I loved the way you took my cock like that." I run my fingers over her velvety-soft cheek and she beams up at me, lashes glittering with tears. "Such a good fucking girl."

Pulling her up and pressing our bodies together, I seize her mouth in a blistering kiss. She opens to me and our tongues tangle together, both of us breathing shallow and ragged.

I want more of this, need more of this. More of her.

Fuck, I don't think I'll ever get enough. I want to taste her, eat her, drink her in until she's crying out and quivering in my arms, and then do it all over again.

Over and over, until we're so exhausted neither of us can move a muscle.

A loud buzzing at my feet interrupts the moment. Sloane pulls away slightly, stooping down to check her phone.

"Sorry, just a sec." Holding up a finger, she listens to the message, a smile spreading across her face.

"Guess what?"

I don't have a chance to guess because she answers her own question.

"I got the job!" She claps her hands together, squealing.

"Really? That's fantastic. The one at the library?" A twinge of panic hits me in my gut at the idea that Sloane could be leaving town.

"Yes, at the library. It's part-time, in the afternoons and evenings. And I get to help with the children's summer reading program!"

"Wow—that's great. Congrats." I drop my lips to hers. "You'll be super at that."

"Thanks. I hate to do this, but they need me to go through an online training before I start tonight. So I have to head over there right now."

Disappointment creeps over me, but I try to hide my feelings with another slower, gentler kiss. "Go. I should get ready for practice anyway."

Rising on tiptoes, she wraps her arms around my neck and squeezes me in a tight hug.

"Thanks—see you later tonight!"

Then she bounces down the hall to change, leaving me alone in the bathroom, wondering where the two of us go from here.

CHAPTER 21
SLOANE

The library's starting to get busy by the time I arrive, tables filling up with tutors and students preparing for exams. I hustle to the desk and Meg spots me straight away.

"Ms. Mabel's in the back office, hang on."

Two minutes later, Ms. Mabel bustles out with my login and password info. She leads me to the main room of the library, over to the bank of computers lining the far wall. A few clicks later, she has the online tutorial pulled up and I slide into a chair to begin.

"Grab me when you're finished, hun." She heads back to the Reference desk and I fly through the slides, clicking and answering questions as fast as humanly possible.

Twenty minutes later, I've completed the module and can officially begin my employment at the Thunder Creek library.

"All done?" Ms. Mabel asks when I approach the desk.

I nod. "Done."

"Great. Here's your name tag—" She hands me a shiny

metal name tag and I clip it onto my pale green blouse. "We only have a few days left to get ready for the summer reading program. I need you to cut out the decorations for the bulletin board and print the reading logs. After that, I'll walk you through the computer program we use here and show you how to check out books."

"Okay, sounds good."

I follow her to an empty conference room and she sets me up on the large wooden table, bringing me all the supplies: scissors, construction paper, the patterns for the designs, stencils, tape, and a stapler.

"Here's what the bulletin board should look like." She sets a print-out of the design on the table. "Once everything's cut out, you can go ahead and staple all of it to the bulletin board at the front."

"No problem, I can do that."

"I'll leave you to it then."

Ms. Mabel disappears and I begin the arduous process of tracing roughly five hundred storm clouds and lighting bolts onto blue, gray, and yellow construction paper. My fingers begin to cramp and my neck aches, but I keep working. A wall clock ticks loudly in the quiet and I start to question this gig.

Hopefully it gets better than this.

After an hour of tracing, I move onto cutting. This part is modestly more enjoyable and my mind wanders as I snip through the thick sheets of paper, drifting to Cam and this afternoon's activities. How we almost got caught by my dad, how freaked out Cam was.

Which could be a real issue. Because I don't want to keep our relationship a secret. And in a place as small as Thunder Creek, that task is gonna be nearly impossible anyway. All it takes is one person seeing the two of us holding hands or kissing and our whole cover's blown.

Is Cam willing to take the risk?

The topic's definitely something we need to tackle, and sooner rather than later. But my stomach knots thinking about our options. What if he decides he doesn't want to take the chance? Then what? Should I just ride it out and see where things go?

Maybe I'm overthinking the whole thing. Gracelyn told me to put myself out there and I sure did, in full technicolor glory.

And it *was* glorious.

But I don't want it to be a one-off. Surely Cam knows that—but does he feel the same way?

The only surefire way to find out is to have the conversation. But I'm not sure my heart can handle anything but a 'yes.'

———

"Hey, baby—how was the library?" My dad's gaze flicks from the TV screen to me as I walk through the door, the familiar sounds of ESPN filling the cozy room.

"It was good. But my hands are definitely tired." I massage my right palm, trying to work out the cramp that lodged there two hours ago. "Ms. Mabel put me straight to work decorating the bulletin boards for the kids."

"Bet it looks real nice. I'll have to stop by and check it out."

I smile, thinking of my dad going into the library. I bet he hasn't set foot in that building since I was ten years old.

"Thanks, Daddy. How was practice?" I crash down on the sofa next to him, kicking my feet up on the coffee table.

I don't specifically ask about Cam, but I'm dying to hear my dad's assessment.

"Good. The team's young, but they're picking things up real quick. Cam helped Langley out today, boosted his confidence."

My heart hammers harder at the mention of Cam, heat flushing through me. "Really? That's great."

"Yeah, that kid's got real talent. He's a natural, just needs to find his rhythm. Next week, I'll have Cam switch and work with Dalton, compare the two. But right now, Langley's got the top spot."

"Nice." I stare at the TV, gnawing at my lip. "How'd things go with the rest of the team?"

"Good. Mack worked with the defense and they're coming along nicely. He has some new routes he's trying out."

"Cool." I couldn't care less about Thunder Creek High's defensive routes. All I really want to know is how Cam did.

"You hungry? We waited on dinner for you."

"Oh, you didn't need to do that."

"I know. But we wanted to."

It's weird, hearing my dad use the word 'we.' It's always been the two of us, me and him. Having a third person in the house—even temporarily—feels odd.

"Cam was in the shower. He should be out any second. Go fix yourself a drink." He shoos me out of the room with a dismissive wave and I do as I'm told, standing and moving to the kitchen.

The table's set, three plates with forks, knives, and napkins all laid out, and there's an odd fluttery thing going on in my chest. All the time I was with Ratface— even engaged to the jerk—he never came home with me.

Not once. And my father was patently uninterested in inviting him, either, which I should have taken as a ginormous red waving flag.

Cam has his own damn place setting at the table, no questions asked.

Wonder if my dad would feel the same way if he knew what went down in the yard today. Or the hall bath.

I'm guessing not.

"Hey." Cam's deep voice startles me out of my thoughts and I jump about a foot in the air.

"Hey." I spin around and heat floods through me at the sight of him, his hair wet and tousled from the shower. A T-shirt clings to his broad chest, every muscle outlined beneath the tight fabric. I don't dare drop my eyes lower, knowing full well what lies beneath the mesh shorts. My panties dampen thinking about it.

"How was the library?" His eyes meet mine and the way he looks at me, he's genuinely interested in my response. A refreshing change from Ratface.

"Good. Kind of fun, although my fingers might be cramped for the next week. Ms. Mabel put me straight to work on the bulletin board and I stenciled and cut out about a thousand lightning bolts."

"Yikes. Sounds brutal." Cam reaches out, gripping my hand and pulling it toward him. His eyes flick to my palm, then back up again, his thumb massaging the sore spots. The muscles tighten, then relax beneath his calloused fingers, electricity sparking up my arm at his touch.

"There?" He presses the knot in the center of my palm hard and a low moan falls from my lips.

"Yes, that's the spot."

His strong fingers work at kneading the tightness away. Each brush of my skin makes my muscles quiver, heat blossoming low in my belly. His marine gaze is on my face the entire time he rubs my hand and I'm not even certain I'm breathing except for the fact that I'm still alive.

"You kids ready to eat?" My dad's voice booms behind us and I instantly tense, face flaming. Cam drops my hand like a hot coal straight out of a burning fire and my mouth kicks into gear.

"Yep. Looks great, Dad. Thanks for cooking." I spin toward the counter, gesturing at the grilled chicken, mashed potatoes, and green beans. Anything to avoid eye contact with my dad. Cam stays silent, racing to the table to grab his glass and get as far away from me as possible.

Maybe he didn't see anything.

I can't read my dad's expression, his face blank as he stalks across the tile floor. He brushes past me and plucks the plate of chicken breasts off the beige Formica.

"Guess you're gonna be busy at the library all summer, huh?" The chicken breasts bounce as the plate thunks down on the table.

"Sort of. The job's only part-time, in the afternoon and evenings. But it gives me something to do."

"Good." My dad's lips set in a thin, tight line and I swallow hard, throat dry as toast. The air in the kitchen's heavy, and I don't dare look at Cam.

"This summer's shaping up to be real hot. I might have to move practice up earlier. Don't want the boys getting heat stroke out there." Dad stabs a piece of chicken, sliding it onto his plate before sawing into the meat. The knife slices back and forth methodically and I try not to squirm.

He knows.

No way. He can't possibly know about anything that went down this afternoon.

Unless nosy Mrs. Humperdink saw us in the pool and

squealed on me, an action that wouldn't be totally out of character for her.

Play it cool. Innocent until proven guilty and all that.

"Besides the quarterbacks, are there any other positions up for grabs?" I ask.

The question has the desired effect, Dad launching into a long diatribe about all the openings on the team. I tune him out, happy to have diverted the spotlight from me and my summer plans—especially where Cam's concerned.

Luckily, Cam engages in the conversation and I eat my food without any further interrogation. I'm content to sit back and listen, watch as the two men discuss the high school football team and the prospects for next season. Both of them light up, their voices louder, eyes brighter as they discuss potential plays and who should take which spot. Cam's more relaxed than I've seen him, shoulders loose and his brow smooth.

Dad sets his fork down, pushing his plate away and balling up his napkin.

"I've got clean-up, Coach. Thanks for dinner." Cam stands, stacking all the plates.

"Thanks, son. I'm going to hit the hay, but I'll see you at practice tomorrow afternoon, if I don't catch you in the morning." He yawns, then drops a kiss on the top of my head. "Night, baby. See you tomorrow after work."

"Night, Daddy." I smile up at him, trying to look innocent even as my heart hammers at the thought of being alone with Cam again.

"Don't stay up too late. Cam has a tough practice ahead of him tomorrow." He wags a finger in our direction and I nod.

"Of course. I'm tucking in as soon as we clear the kitchen."

"Okay then." My dad retreats to his room and breath seeps from my lungs. I stand still for a long minute, listening. But there's nothing but quiet and I think my dad actually went to bed.

Cam watches me for a second, then turns on the sink faucet and starts rinsing dishes before loading them into the dishwasher.

"Another close call," I whisper, our arms brushing as I join him at the sink.

He nods. "I know."

His jaw tenses and a wave of anxiety washes over me, warring with the fiery desire already licking my insides.

I want to move behind Cam, wrap my arms around his broad back and rub and down his flat stomach. Feel the strength in his body, the heat. The arousal when I move my hands lower, dropping down to his hard cock. I want him to spin around, pressing his hips against mine, nuzzle his nose into the soft skin of my neck. Want him to pepper the tender spot with hot kisses, his hand finding my breast, sending ripples of pleasure rolling through me.

Instead, we do the dishes in tense silence. My mind whirs with all the things I should say, how I need to tell him what I want.

But I don't.

Water splashes in the sink, then gurgles down the drain, silverware clinking into the plastic baskets of the dishwasher as I deposit each fork, each knife, one by one into their slots. Being this close to Cam—knowing how his body feels on mine but not being able to touch him, kiss him—is an exquisite form of torture.

He cuts the water off and dries his hands on the checked dishtowel, his lips a tight line. A shuddery breath rattles his chest and my nerves thrum like the cicadas outside the window, long, low, insistent.

"Want to go outside for a minute?" He tips his head toward the deck.

"Sure."

I shut the light off, then open the door as slowly as humanly possible. Still, the old wood creaks, the sound loud in the quiet house.

"Shit," I mutter, making a mental note to WD-40 every door in the whole damn house first thing tomorrow.

Pushing through the screen door, Cam follows behind me, holding the metal handle until the door closes with a whisper.

I sink down onto the deck, kicking my feet out in front of me. Cam joins me, our shoulders rubbing and sending sparks flying through me.

"Nice night." He tips his face up to the inky sky, glittering with stars.

"Yeah. Not so humid tonight."

His fingers slide along the outside of my thigh and the knots in my stomach loosen. This afternoon wasn't a dream.

Inching closer to him, our bodies touch and I swear electricity sparks between us, sending hot pulses straight to my core. I've never wanted to be with someone more than I want to be with Cam and it takes every ounce of willpower I possess not to crawl onto his lap and straddle him, grind against his hard cock until my pussy convulses and I come in a rush of ecstasy.

He links his pinky with mine. "Sloane—" His voice is quiet, his tone serious, and I'm nervous all over again. "I like you. A lot. More than I've liked anyone in a long time."

My breath hitches in my throat, heart pounding. "I like you too. Obviously. You read the email."

His lips quirk into a smile. "I did. Nicest email I've ever gotten."

I blush, happy that it's dark and he can't see my cheeks, which I'm certain are bright red.

"But I can't make any promises to you. So if you want to stop before we take things further, I get it. My entire future's up in the air. I might not make it back to the pros, I may not have a job at all. I can't guarantee you anything right now." He swallows hard, his Adam's apple bobbing. Tension creeps back into his face, a V creasing between his brows.

"I know."

Cam runs his thumb along my jawline, moonlight bathing him in a pale light. He's so raw, so vulnerable right now, my heart aches for him as we stare into each other's eyes.

"I liked you before you were a professional football player, you know."

He sucks in a breath, licking his lips, and the deep buzz of the cicadas hum off in the distance. Leaning in, Cam touches his nose to mine and takes a deep inhale. His exhale's warm on my lips and he dips in further, his mouth hovering inches from mine. Another inhale, exhale, then our lips touch and my eyes flutter closed as I soak in this perfect moment, a moment I've longed for.

A moment I thought would only ever exist in my dreams.

But here we are, together, and I don't want to move off this deck for fear of shattering this intense feeling shimmering in the air between us.

A dog barks off in the distance and a light flickers from

my dad's room. Reluctantly, I pull away like a high schooler afraid of getting busted with her date.

"We should probably go inside. Bugs." I swat at an invisible insect buzzing around me.

"Yeah." Cam stands, extending his hand to me and helping me up. I dust off my butt and shake out my legs, my thoughts as jumbled and confused as ever.

CHAPTER 22
CAM

As much as I want to be with Sloane, I need to focus on football. I spend as much time in the gym as possible, working on strength, mobility, and flexibility. I practice in the afternoons with Coach and the high school team. He runs me hard—if not harder—than any of my coaches in the pros, not letting up even one iota. I'm hot, sore, and exhausted at the end of every practice, but I'm loving every second of it.

Then school's out for the summer and we transition to two-a-days, leaving me even less alone time with Sloane. The practice schedule's rigorous, plus Coach is home during the day, giving us fewer opportunities to escape his watchful eye.

Our only saving grace is his early bedtime and the fact that his room's on the other side of the house. Nighttime is our chance to be together without Coach staring us down.

I'm lying in bed, wide-awake in only my boxers, the ceiling fan swirling in lazy circles.

Cam: You awake?

I stare at the dark screen, willing a text to come through. She doesn't let me down.

Trouble: Yes. Can't sleep

Cam: Me neither

Trouble: You think my dad's asleep yet?

Cam: Hard to say. Probably kind of early still

Trouble: You're right—don't want to risk it

Trouble: Are you naked?

I chuckle into the darkness, cock twitching and growing harder by the second. Reaching down, I pull my length free, stroking up and down.

Fuck this. Sexting is way too much work. I hit Sloane's icon on the screen and call her.

"I am now," I say in a low voice as soon as she picks up.

"Ohh—sexy," she purrs and now my cock's a steel fucking shaft.

"Are you naked?"

"I'm wearing a silk nightie. No bra or panties," she whispers and I groan, fisting myself harder, picturing Sloane in only a tiny black nightie. Milky-white breasts spilling over the top of the lingerie, diamond-sharp nipples poking through the thin fabric.

"I'm so hard right now, thinking about you." I tighten my hand, working the length of my cock.

"What would you do if I was with you?" Her voice is quiet, seductive, and my balls tingle.

"I'd run my hands up and down your arms. Then slip the straps off your shoulders and palm your breasts."

"Keep going—" she murmurs in a breathy whisper.

"I will. But only if you follow my instructions."

She doesn't hesitate. "Deal."

"Lower your nightie down. Squeeze your nipples and tell me how it feels."

A few seconds pass and I wait, cock throbbing.

"It feels good. But it would feel better if you did it."

"Close your eyes and pretend it's me. Pinch hard," I command. Rubbing the tip of my cock, I think about Sloane pinching her rosy nipples. A few drops of pre-cum leak onto the crown of my dick and I smooth the fluid into my skin.

"How'd that feel?"

"Good. I'm wet for you." Her voice is lower, more sensual, and my body burns with desire.

Fuck me.

I stifle a groan, wishing I could escape the Jonas brothers and go to her room. Trail my fingers up and down through her juices.

"How wet? Slide your fingers up and down your slit and tell me."

There's a rustle of bedsheets, a slight creak, and I know she's adjusting into a better position. Following my directions and making herself feel good.

"I'm soaking," she whispers, and I practically feel her breath on me.

"Good girl. Rub your clit," I murmur, pumping harder and faster. Pretending I'm with her, working her clit until her body flushes.

"Ohmygod—" she pants and I smile into the dark.

"I usually go by Cam…"

She giggles, the melodic sound tickling down my spine. Every inch of me lights up and my balls ache.

"I'm so turned on right now, Cam—"

"Me too, thinking of you stroking your hot pussy."

"Now what do you want me to do?"

"Finger yourself," I command, applying tight pressure all along my shaft.

"Ahhh…."

"Are you using one or two fingers?" I ask, squeezing my dick harder.

"One."

"Use two. Stretch yourself out for me. You need to be ready to take my cock."

"I added another. I'm so hot for you right now," she whimpers.

"Same, baby girl. My dick is rock-fucking-hard. I'm pumping it, pretending I'm sliding in and out of your wet pussy."

"I'd like that. Very much."

"I can't wait to be with you." The words come out as a plea and that's all I can take of this beautiful torturous dance. I need to be with Sloane, feel her soft, warm skin on mine, our bodies pressed together. I disconnect and throw my shorts on. Then I tiptoe down the dark hallway as quietly as I possibly can, holding my breath the entire way. I'm taking a huge risk, sneaking into Sloane's room while Coach is home, but I can't resist. The temptation's too great.

I inch her door open and she pops straight up in bed, breasts spilling over the lacy top of her nightie just like I imagined. She wasn't joking—she really is wearing a nightie. I press a finger to my lips and click the door shut behind me, depressing the lock before crossing to her bed.

Her dark hair's loose and spilling over her bare shoulders, moonlight highlighting the curves of her body. She's beautiful, vulnerable, eyes wide in the darkness and I can't wait to touch her, taste her, feel her skin on mine. Leaning down, I brush my mouth against hers. Soft and gentle, she opens to me with a tiny moan and I taste the faint hint of mint from her toothpaste. Every inch of my body yearns for her as I kiss her slow and deep. Wrapping her arms around my neck, she kneads my tight muscles gently like a cat. The movement's small, but intense, sending electric shock waves rolling down my spine.

"I want to taste you." I whisper the words into her open mouth and her lips curve up into a smile.

Lifting her hand to my mouth, I suck the sticky juices from her fingers. A breathy moan hums low in her throat, her eyes wide as she watches me lick the sweetness from her skin. Pulling my lips away, I gently lower her body back against the headboard and push the silky lingerie up over her hips. Spreading her legs, I position myself between her thighs and run an open palm over her flat belly. She quivers beneath my touch as I stroke her skin, tracing light circles around her belly button.

"Play with your tits for me. Like you were doing before." I gaze up her body, watch as her eyelids flutter closed as she touches herself, her lips parting slightly.

"Keep your eyes on me."

She lifts her lids, locking her wide eyes on mine. "That's a good girl, just like that. Pinch that pretty, pink nipple."

She does as I say, squeezing the rosy bud with two fingers. Her breath hitches and my cock responds, bulging in my briefs. I ignore him, though, focusing all my efforts on Sloane.

"Beautiful, baby." I whisper the words, breathing over her sensitive skin. "Now work the other one."

She moves her hand to the other side and I drop my face lower, nuzzling her pussy with my nose. I take a deep inhale, reveling in her sweet, musky scent.

"God, Sloane, you smell so good." She wiggles her ass and arches up in response, giving me better access. "I've been dreaming of this every night for the past week."

"Me too." Threading her fingers in my hair, she scrapes lightly at my scalp. My cock twitches and throbs, straining against the cotton of my shorts.

This dance between us is so slow, so torturous. And I'm torn between wanting to draw out every single second of beautiful pain or give in and take what I want right here, right now. Fuck her in her childhood bedroom on the plain cotton sheets, the Jonas brothers poster on the wall as witness, Coach be damned.

Instead of giving in fully, I do the next best thing. I lean in and blow lightly on her clit before flattening my tongue and licking her slit from bottom to top. Her fingers tighten in my hair and she groans.

"Cam…"

"You like that, baby?"

She nods as I continue licking and sucking, tasting her for the first time.

"You're so sweet, baby." I swirl my tongue around her clit, pressing lightly against the sensitive bud. "I need more."

Gripping her hips, I lift her ass off the bed before burying my face in her hot, delicious pussy.

Then I feast.

Sloane's an all-you-can-eat buffet and I'm a starving man, lapping and sucking at her juices like she's the last meal I'll ever eat. Her thighs tremor and shake in my palms as I devour her pussy.

"Oh God, Cam—" Her voice is needy as her hips move and buck. I grip her harder, keeping her still as I apply more pressure, more friction. She's mewling for more, a high-pitched keening, and I know she's close.

I lift my head slightly, staring up at her. Her eyes are squeezed shut and her head's thrown back.

"Shh, we have to be quiet, baby. Much as I want to hear you scream my name, you can't do that tonight."

She nods, biting her bottom lip, and I dip back down. Sucking her clit into my mouth, I flick at the bud with my tongue, once, twice, three times. That's all it takes for Sloane to unravel, her body shuddering against my face, thighs trembling in my hands. Her muscles contract against my mouth and I ease off the pressure, holding her up and supporting her as she rides the waves of her release.

"Ohmygod, Cam—" she whispers, her nails digging into my traps. "That was the most intense orgasm of my life."

I smile in the darkness, wiping my mouth before shimmying up the bed to lay next to her. Tracing soft circles around her breasts, skin warm and flushed, she curls into me. Her head rests on my bare chest, the silky strands of her hair tickling me. With a deep breath, I inhale the heady floral scent of shampoo, the musk of her sex still in my nostrils. The scent's signature Sloane and if I could bottle it up as a perfume, I'd sniff it every single day.

I want this woman—need this woman—every day.

My dick throbs and aches and I'd love to bury myself in her tight, wet pussy right now.

But we can't take the risk. Being with her now, like this, is already too much. No way am I going to get balls-deep in Coach's daughter while he's here, less than a few hundred feet away on the other side of the house.

No fucking way.

"Glad I could deliver." I smooth my hand over her hair, drop a kiss to the top of her head. I hold back on telling her everything I'm thinking. It's too soon and I don't want to get ahead of myself.

Her breathing evens out, feather-soft exhales a whisper on my skin. I hold her close, so close the beat of her heart vibrates against my chest, the cicadas humming outside. Finally, she's asleep and I tiptoe back down the hall to take care of business.

I need to find somewhere else to live before my balls explode.

CHAPTER 23
SLOANE

Working at the library is the job I didn't know I needed. I freaking love it. The kids, the books, even the older ladies who come in purely to socialize and spill the tea on all things Thunder Creek. I've only been working here a few weeks, but everything about the gig is perfect, the absolute dream job.

"Sloane, honey, I have a proposition for you." Ms. Mabel corners me in the Children's Department as I'm reshelving the entire Wimpy Kid series.

"Oh-kay." I hesitate, my hand frozen mid-air. I'm afraid to commit to anything before hearing the entire scenario. What if she wants me to take over restroom duty or something?

"So, a few patrons have been asking about a book club for quite some time now. But we never had anyone who could run it. We've been understaffed for so long, and no one wanted to take it on. But now that you're here, we were hoping you'd be on board with the idea." Her voice lifts along with her eyebrows as she stares me down, awaiting my response.

"Ummm…" I gnaw at my lip, wondering what exactly I'm getting myself into here. "I suppose I could do that. Like, meet once a month or something and lead a discussion on the book?"

"Sure, we could start there and see how it goes."

"What kind of books are they interested in? A cute cozy mystery? Maybe a good thriller?"

"Romance, mostly." She adjusts her sparkly blue readers, her voice deadpan.

"Oh! A romance book club. Okay then." I swallow down my surprise. "Do you know if they have any book in particular they're considering?"

"Well, I'm pretty sure they've already read the entire *50 Shades* series."

My face heats at the image of me leading an animated book club discussion with Ms. Mabel and her friends about various fetishes and what exactly goes down in the Red Room.

"Maybe pick something beachy, since it's summer. Elin Hildebrand has a new one coming out. Or we could go small town and read Melanie Harlow, I know they all love her work."

"Gotcha. I can find something, I'm sure. Let me finish reshelving these books," I motion at the books on the rolling metal cart, "and then I'll go check the catalogue and make a selection."

"Wonderful. Once you choose the book, we can make up a flyer and post it here and online, maybe around town in a few places." Ms. Mabel claps her hands together, the apples of her cheeks turning rosy. "The gals will be so pleased. Let's schedule the meeting two weeks from today.

That will give us enough time to spread the word, but also squeeze in at least three book clubs this summer."

"Wow, aggressive. But okay, I can get it done. Guess I have some reading homework to do."

Ms. Mabel grins, clearly pleased with her powers of persuasion, before spinning and sashaying back to the Reference desk. I hustle through the reshelving, a little stressed about this whole romance book club thing. I've never led a book club before. But it can't be that tough, right? I'm sure I can come up with a few questions about a romance book and keep a discussion going. I mean, I went to college. This won't be nearly as tough as Calculus or Chemistry.

Buzz, buzz.

Cam: You busy?

> Sloane: Reshelving books. How was practice?

Cam: Tough. That kid Dalton is a real piece of work. But I think I taught Langley some good routes

> Sloane: Nice. I'm sure you were fantastic out there

Cam: Hope so. Don't want to let your dad down

Cam: You have time for a quick break this afternoon?

> Sloane: Story Time's at three, then I can duck out for a minute. Why? What's up?

Cam: I need to see you

My stomach goes all swirly, fizzy excitement bubbling inside me at his words.

Sloane: I'd love to see you too. Maybe come around four—I should be done by then

Cam: Okay. See you soon

Staring down at my phone screen, I debate for a solid minute before quickly tapping out:

Sloane: XOXO

Then I wait, doing my best not to hyperventilate or let the cell slip through my sweaty fingers and clatter to the ground.

Cam: xoxo

Lightness fills my chest as I beam down at the four letters like a lovestruck idiot.

Cam's as serious about us as I am. This thing between us could actually work.

Maybe Gracelyn is onto something with this whole manifestation thing. Maybe I need to start lighting candles, journaling, and dreaming of a wedding and babies.

Imagine me being Mrs. Cam Crawford, after all these years of wanting him.

Wild.

Smiling to myself, I get back to work slotting paperbacks in their rightful position on the shelf. But my mind's definitely elsewhere.

I know that after everything that happened with Ratface, I should be more cautious, guarded. My heart's barely healed from that trauma and here I am falling in love all over again.

But this is Cam. He's the lone exception to the rule, I feel it deep down. We've been friends forever and I know he's different. Funny and driven, smart and athletic, plus he cares about other people. He'd never do me like Ratface did.

Never.

I silence the negative Nancy voice urging me to be careful. If I listen to that bitch, I'll be single forever, leading the Thunder Creek Library Romance Book Club with only Ms. Mabel by my side, and that is *not* a position I want to be in.

No offense to Ms. Mabel, but I much prefer my romances to be real. A book boyfriend is cute and all, but nothing replaces the actual feeling of being with someone.

Especially if that someone is Cam. His lips on mine, large, strong hands caressing my skin, heat shimmering between us, all the delicious tension.

"Excuse me, Miss Sloane?" A quiet voice interrupts my daydream and I feel a slight tug on my skirt.

"Oh, hey, Abigail. What's up?" I smile down at the cute little girl, her brown hair in two braids tied with purple ribbon.

"Is Story Time happening soon?"

I check my watch. "Oh yes, it is. Sorry, I lost track of time. Let me grab the book. You can head over to the cozy corner and grab a bean bag."

Abigail makes a beeline for the bean bags while I hustle over to the desk and fetch the book of the day, a story about a family of dogs taking a trip to the beach. I head over to the cozy corner and wave at the group already assembled, waiting patiently for me to take my seat.

"Hey, y'all. Thanks for coming to Story Time today!" I slide down into the old wooden chair that's probably been at the library longer than I've been alive.

"Today we have a fun story about a dog family going on a summer trip to the beach. Have any of you been to the beach?"

At least ten hands shoot up into the air and several kids start chattering to their friends about their beach trips.

"I'm glad to see you've all had so much fun at the beach! We'll share our stories later, after I read the book. Right now it's listening time. So I'm going to need y'all to zip your lips—" I motion across my face, pretending like I'm zipping my mouth closed. "And turn your listening ears all the way up." I cup my ear and a few of the younger kids mimic me.

That's the moment Cam saunters in, flashing me his most devastating smile before sinking down onto the floor with the rest of the kids. Except he's a solid foot and a half taller than most of them, his broad torso towering over everyone. My mouth goes dry and I can't remember what I was even saying as I stare out at the group.

"Miss Sloane, are you going to read the story now?" One of the boys sitting on the front row nudges my knee and I jerk back to reality.

"Yes, yes I am, now that everyone's good and quiet. *A Rottie Family Adventure: Summer Beach Days.*" I flip to the first page of the story and begin to read aloud, comprehending exactly zero words.

Luckily, it's an early reader picture book, so at least I don't stumble over the simple prose. But all I can think about is Cam, sitting at the back of the audience. Every once in a while, my eyes slide over to his and I can't catch my breath. The way he's staring at me, listening to the story as if he's enraptured with the Rottie family—and with me—is almost more than I can handle.

I've never felt like this before. So appreciated. Seen. Adored.

Not even the day Ratface proposed, which I suppose should have been a big freaking red flag. But I guess you don't know what you don't know.

"The Rottie family pulled into their driveway as the sun set. Daddy Rottie turned to Mommy Rottie. 'That was a wonderful adventure, Mama. Pawsitively wonderful.'"

"Mommy Rottie said, 'Thank you, Papa. I thought so too. Next time we'll go camping!' The End."

A round of applause breaks out as I close the book and a few of the children hop up, their attention spans expired.

"What did y'all think of the story? Did you like it?" I ask, setting the book down on my lap.

"Yes!" Several of the kids shout and I smile out at the crowd, pretending to smooth my skirt but really drying my clammy palms. "Great! Now it's time for y'all to share your beach stories. Who wants to go first?"

At least ten excited hands shoot into the air and I listen to all the stories and chatter from the kids about their beach days. Checking my watch, I notice the hour's almost up, though.

"Okay, y'all. I set paper and crayons out on the tables. You're welcome to draw a picture of your own day at the beach and we'll display them on the bulletin board behind the desk. And remember to get your stamp for coming to the program today. It counts toward the Summer Reading Challenge!"

At that, a bunch of the kids jump up and run over to the tables. A flurry of paper and crayons fly across the table as they fight over their favorite colors. A few of the older kids stay behind, though, eyeing Cam as he rises from the colorful carpet.

"You're really tall. Are you Cam Crawford, the football player?" A blonde boy stares up at Cam, his eyes narrowed.

Cam nods. "Sure am."

"Wow. So cool. Can I have your autograph?" He swipes a sheet of paper off the table, handing Cam a green crayon. "Please? I want to give it to my dad."

"No prob." Cam takes the crayon and bends over, scrawling his signature across the sheet of paper. "Here you go."

Another kid sees the exchange and suddenly there's a line of people waiting to talk to Cam, get his autograph, or take a photo with him.

"Sorry," he mouths before bending down and throwing his arm across a kid's shoulders, grinning at the camera.

I wave him off. "It's fine."

Twenty minutes later, Cam's signed tons of autographs and chatted with every child and most of the parents. Abigail wanders over and taps Cam's arm.

"Are you Miss Sloane's boyfriend?"

My face flames, heat creeping all the way up my neck and I know without even checking that my chest is red and splotchy. I low-key want to melt into the carpet tiles, dying right here on the spot.

Abigail and the remaining kids all stare at Cam, waiting for his answer. He shoves a hand in his pocket and lifts his marine eyes to mine.

"Yes. I think I am."

Abigail's face breaks into a smile and a few of the kids cheer excitedly, fists pumping in the air. The warmth in my face dissipates a little, spreading through my whole body.

Until I remember where I am.

That this is Thunder Creek and my dad's definitely going to hear about this turn of events by dinnertime.

Fuckity, fuck, fuck.

Oh well. I guess he was bound to find out sooner or later. Guess it'll be sooner.

"Hey there, Cam." Ms. Mabel slides up to us, wrapping her arm around Cam's tapered waist and squeezing. "Fancy seeing you here. Did Sloane ask you to come in and help pick out the next book club read?"

Cam's brow creases, one eyebrow rising. "Don't think I'm the right man for the job, Ms. Mabel. Unless book club wants to read about football."

Ms. Mabel laughs, a high-pitched nasally giggle. "They're more into romance. Seems like the two of you might have a suggestion or two in that department." She shoots both of us an exaggerated wink. "You should come to the book club in two weeks. It'll be loads of fun."

"Oh, I'm sure Cam will be way too busy to make it to book club," I say at the exact same time Cam replies, "I'd love to come. Sounds like fun."

Ms. Mabel chuckles again before patting Cam's forearm. "We'll see you again soon then, Cam. And in the meantime, if you need any help with book recommendations, I'm sure Sloane can help you find some great football reads."

With that, she sidles away, leaving me beet-red and mortified in the Children's Department.

"Well, that was embarrassing," I mutter, low enough so only Cam hears.

"I didn't mean to put you on the spot like that." He reaches for my hand, linking his fingers with mine. "I hope I didn't overstep, making a claim on you like that."

My heart flutters, literally skipping a beat, which I thought was only an expression until this very moment.

I peer up at him, wishing we were alone so I could run my thumb over his stubbled cheeks, brush his full lips against mine.

"No, I love that you made a claim. The only thing is—" My chest squeezes tight, hot anxiety swirling in my gut. "My dad. He's definitely going to hear about this. 100% guarantee."

"That's actually why I needed to see you."

"C'mon. Let's go somewhere a little more private." I drag Cam away from all the little ears, back into the much-less-traveled reference stacks.

"Hey." He leans me back against the sturdy shelves of books, caging me in between his arms. Then he leans down and presses his lips to mine in a hot, possessive kiss.

"Hey." I smile even as my mind whirs with apprehension, wondering what exactly he needs to tell me that's so urgent he couldn't wait until tonight. "What's up?"

Cam traces my cheekbone, trailing his thumb down my jawline and over the curve of my chin before meeting my gaze.

"I'm moving out."

"What? Why?" Red-hot panic flares inside me and my jaw tenses.

"Relax. It's not a bad thing. It's just—" He runs the rough pad of his thumb over my lips and I taste the salt on his skin, the gesture sending a pulse of desire straight to my core.

"I can't be with you—really be with you—while I'm

living in your dad's house. He's my coach and I can't disrespect him like that."

"Oh." I swallow hard over the lump in my throat, trying to make sense of all this.

"You understand, right?" He cuts his eyes to mine and I take a shallow breath.

"I guess. I mean, I feel like we've already crossed the line, but—"

"Sloane, trust me. You have no idea the lines I want to cross with you." He rests his forehead against mine, his breath warm on my skin. "You make me crazy. I need you like I need air to breathe. Maybe more. But I can't do those things, be with you like that, under your dad's roof. It's just not right."

"Ah—" I suck in another breath, dampness flooding my panties beneath his heated stare.

"Are you ready for all this?" His voice is low, almost desperate, as he presses his body against mine.

"Yes." The word comes out in a breathy whisper.

Cam heaves out a breath of relief. "Good. Because I don't know what I'd do if you said no. Die of blue balls, maybe."

I giggle, sliding my hand over the hard bulge of his shorts.

"One question, though—who's going to tell my dad?"

CHAPTER 24
CAM

will." I clear my throat, swallowing hard over the lump lodged above my Adam's apple.

The last thing I want to do is talk to Coach about dating his daughter, but I know it's the right thing to do. Man up and be honest with him.

It's gonna suck, much like burpees and wind sprints, but what doesn't kill you makes you stronger, right?

And hopefully Coach Carter won't kill me.

"Really? You sure?" Sloane's eyes widen. "You want me to be there? Or is this gonna be a man-to-man sort of thing?"

"The latter, I'm thinking. I'll talk to him after practice tonight." I cup her chin and press my lips to hers, kissing her softly but wanting more. So much fucking more.

After a few seconds, she pulls away. "When are you moving out?"

"Tomorrow. Or maybe tonight, if your dad's pissed at me."

She frowns, tiny creases forming in between her brows. I smooth them away with my fingertip.

"It'll be okay, promise."

"I know. I like having you there, though."

"I'm planning on seeing a lot more of you now." My hand skims the side of her breast and her lips curve into a shy smile. I lean forward, seizing her mouth in a long, hungry kiss before reluctantly pulling away.

"I'll see you tonight, either way." Tucking a loose strand of hair behind her ear, I gently tug on her earlobe. "Promise."

She rises on tiptoe and presses a soft kiss to my lips. "You've got this. Text me afterwards and let me know how it goes. So I can be prepared, either way."

"I will."

"Good luck and Godspeed."

"Thanks, Trouble."

I have a feeling I'm gonna need it.

I debate the best time to talk to Coach the rest of the afternoon. Ideally, I'd love to get the conversation over with. But that's probably not the smartest approach here. He's doing me a solid, letting me practice with the team, coaching me through my crisis. It'd be uncool of me to bust in and blow up his afternoon session, distract him from the task at hand. I decide to wait until practice is over to have our chat.

"Crawford! Don't just stand there, get going!" Coach yells at me from across the field, twirling his finger in the air to indicate the laps I'm supposed to be running.

Immediately, I break into a jog, already lagging behind

the rest of the team. Sloane has me good and distracted, which is far from ideal. I need to get my head back in the game or I'll be proving Coach's point before he even gets a chance to make it.

The blazing summer sun beats down on the track and I'm dripping in sweat by the time I finish running the warm-up. At least I caught up to the team—it wouldn't do for me to come in dead last, even at practice.

Coach blows his whistle and we all huddle around him, waiting for instructions.

"Defense—you're running drills with Coach Mack. Special teams, head over to the bleachers to work with Coach McGilly. Offense, you'll be working with Coach Baker this afternoon. I'm taking Dalton, Langley, Stevens, and Crawford." Coach blows the whistle again, breaking the huddle. Then he motions for the four of us to follow him to the far end of the field.

We dutifully trail behind him. Dalton chats with the other kid, while Langley and I stay silent. I'm trying to keep my attention on football and Langley's tense, his jaw tight.

"Alright, y'all. Tonight we're mixing it up. Dalton, you're with Crawford. Langley, you'll be with Stevens. Same drills we've been doing, different partners. Any questions?" Coach looks to each of us, but none of us speak up. "Okay, then. Let's get going."

He tosses Dalton and Langley each a football and we pair off, heading into our respective positions. Stevens and I jog across the field, lining up opposite each other. Langley and Dalton take their spots and we start the drills.

I miss the first ball by a solid ten yards.

"What the—?" Dalton throws his arms up in exasperation, frowning so hard I can see it all the way down here.

"Sorry, man," I apologize weakly.

Get it together, Crawford.

Dalton shakes his head before firing a perfect spiral in my direction. I jump for it, mercifully making contact. Coach scribbles something on his clipboard before feeding Dalton another ball.

Three more passes, each one perfect, and I catch them all. Out of the corner of my eye, I see Langley bobble his next throw and my gut clenches. I shouldn't have favorites, but I really don't like this Dalton kid. I want Langley to get the starting QB position.

"Yo, Crawford! You ready or what?" Dalton hollers at me, bringing my focus back to him and the drills we're supposed to be running.

"Ready!" I shout, running my sweaty palms down my shorts.

My mind drifts to Sloane and how I'm about to tell Coach I want to date his daughter. I sincerely hope he leaves it at that and doesn't ask any follow-up questions.

Will he? If he does, what am I going to say? Yes, Coach, I want to drill your daughter, fast and hard until she screams my name.

SMACK.

The ball hits me square in the chest, knocking the air from my lungs. Coach tweets his whistle as I clutch at my pec and try to rub the pain away.

"Take five and get some water, boys! Crawford, you okay?" He adjusts his ball cap, turning it backwards on his head. I nod.

"Fine. Just a little dehydrated is all." I amble over to the bleachers and chug water from the gallon jug I brought with me.

"You trying to throw the stats, Crawford?" Dalton

scowls at me over his water bottle. "Or do you just suck this bad?"

Hot anger rolls through me. This kid and his piss-poor attitude's really starting to grate on my nerves. That, and the fact that I'm taking my eye off the ball – literally – with thoughts of Sloane muddling my brain. The exact thing I promised myself I wouldn't do.

"How about you worry about your throws instead of my ability to catch them?" I grab my towel and wipe the dripping sweat from my brow, trying to keep my cool with this little shit.

"I would, if I thought you were playing fair." He takes two big steps forward until he's crowding me, his teenage chest invading my personal space. "Know what I think?"

I couldn't care less what this high school twit thinks, but I humor him.

"No. Not a clue."

"I think you got cut because you're over the hill. Your career is over. Done-so. I mean, you can't catch a high schooler's passes. How are you going to go back and play with the big boys, old man?"

Now my hackles are up, fiery anger surging through me. I'd love nothing more than to shove this kid away from me, take him down a notch or seven.

But that wouldn't be very mature. And the last thing I need is any negative social media attention, with this sorry little punk ass whining all over TikTok about how I beat him up at his high school football practice.

Instead, I take a deep breath, pushing all that aggression away. "We'll see about that. How about you bring your A-game now, huh?"

Dalton shakes his head, glaring at me. "Whatever, geezer."

Throwing his empty water bottle down on the grass, he swaggers away down the field. I inhale again, breathing in calming air and exhaling all the pent-up negative energy. A hot tip from my woo-woo sister Ansley, and I'll never admit to her that it actually works. But my muscles relax, tension seeping from the knotty ropes in my traps. Rolling my shoulders a few times, I run back out to the field.

I don't drop another pass the rest of practice.

"Time!" Coach shouts. The sun's sinking and the temperature's finally dropping, although the humidity's still thick as pudding. "Huddle up, boys."

I stride over to the bleachers, joining Coach and the rest of the team.

"Great practice today, boys. I'm happy with the effort most of y'all are putting in." Coach glances around the circle. "If we keep it up, I feel real good about our chances next season. Make sure to drink lots of water when you get home, eat right, and get some sleep. Don't be staying up all night watching videos on YouTube or any of the other apps y'all are into these days. I'll see you boys in the weight room tomorrow, bright and early."

"Yes, sir, yes, Coach!" A chorus of male voices sounds out and I'm transported back to my own high school days, a wave of nostalgia washing over me.

Playing in the pros is great, don't get me wrong. But there's something special about your high school team that can never be replicated. Maybe it's the innocence of youth, maybe it's the fact that everyone's intentions are pure — not yet tainted by money and sponsorships and real adult responsibilities. Or maybe it's Coach Carter and how he runs his team like a family, treats you like one of his own.

"Hands in and Thunder Creek on three."

Everyone thrusts their hands into the circle and chants,

"Thunder Creek, Thunder Creek, Thunder Creek, go-o-o Mustangs!" before breaking the huddle and dispersing.

"Crawford." Coach pats me on the back, getting my attention as I'm gathering my gear and shoving it into my bag.

"Yes, Coach?" I glance over my shoulder, tension creeping back into my body.

"You okay? That ball hit you pretty hard out there." His eyes crinkle in concern and guilt gnaws at me as I meet his gaze. He and Sloane have the same eyes, and the resemblance makes me feel even worse about the conversation I'm about to have with the man I so deeply respect and admire.

"I'm fine. The pass wasn't that hard." I swallow, clearing my throat. "But I, um, need to talk to you about something."

"Yeah?" He shoves his stopwatch into his pocket, leaning down to grab a mesh bag of footballs.

"In private. If that's okay."

He shrugs, slinging the bag over his shoulder. "Come with me to the office then. You can carry the cones."

I do as I'm told, lifting up the stack of orange cones. Coach waves to Mack and the other coaches, wishing them good-night before we trudge off the field toward the offices. Dusk is upon us, the air still as the sun sinks lower in the sky. Coach doesn't speak, doesn't bother trying to kick up any small talk. Instead, we move in synchronized silence, the only sound our footsteps on the pavement.

He unlocks the metal door leading into the school and reaches inside, clicking on the bright fluorescent lights. We trudge down the long hallway, passing by the line of empty blue lockers, doors opened wide to air out for the summer. My sneakers squeak on the linoleum and I feel sixteen all over again.

Coach kicks open the door to his office, tossing the mesh bag to the floor before crashing into the rolling chair behind his county-issued faux wood-and-metal desk. Likely the same one he had a decade ago, when I was officially his athlete.

"What's going on, Cam?" He leans forward, elbows resting on the desk, fingers steepled, hazel eyes boring into me.

I do my best not to squirm.

No, I'm going to be a man about this.

I shuffle my feet and gesture at the empty chair in front of his desk. "May I?"

"Of course."

Sliding into the seat, I swallow hard over the gigantic rock in my throat. I take a deep breath and try to figure out the best way to say I want to date his one and only daughter.

Coach waits while I debate with myself, blood roaring loud in my ears.

"I want to date your daughter, sir."

Wow. Okay. That was really fucking direct.

Coach blinks, once, twice, but says nothing. His lips thin, he's pressing them together so tight. Probably to keep from saying whatever it is he's thinking. Which may very well be something along the lines of *Go fuck yourself.*

After a long, long moment, he breaks. "You sure about that, son?"

Not one-hundred percent certain what he means by that comment, I nod. "Yes."

"Because I know you're trying to get back to the pros. And that takes time. And focus. And commitment. Sloane could be—will be—a distraction." He cracks his knuckles and the crunching sound bounces off the cinder block walls, echoing around the small room.

"She's worth it, sir."

Coach leans back in his creaky chair and contemplates me. Like he's seeing me for the first time. Maybe not as a player, but as a man.

Possibly a threat, and that thought's less than comforting.

"I don't want to see you mess up your career, son. Or break Sloane's heart. One asshole's already done that. And she's tough, but twice in a row is kinda hard to deal with. Even for someone as strong as my daughter."

My chest tightens as I absorb his words, his fears. Worry's etched on his face, tension thick between us.

"I understand, sir."

And I do.

I hear what he's saying, feel his anxiety with every palpitation of my own heart.

But none of it surpasses my love for his daughter.

Shit.

I love Sloane Carter.

The thought hits me harder than Dalton's football to the chest. I've probably always loved her, I was just too caught up in my own life and football to see it.

"I'll do right by your daughter, sir, I swear. I'm going to get back to the pros. And I'll take care of her. She means the world to me. That's why I'm talking to you about it. I appreciate your hospitality, more than you'll ever know. But I found my own place and I'm moving out. And if you'd prefer me to not practice with the team, I understand." I swallow and hold my breath, waiting for him to explode. Or worse, agree with the last stupid-ass thing I said. Because I kind of still need his coaching advice.

"Sounds like you've made up your mind then. I appreciate you being forthright with me, Cam. And you know I've always treated you like a son." He leans forward again, pausing, steepling and resteepling his fingers. "But hear me when I say this—if you hurt my daughter, you'll be answering to me. Everything I've ever done has been for her. She's my entire world. And no man—even someone I like as much as you—is going to hurt her without answering to me. Are we clear?"

I straighten my shoulders, sitting up as tall as possible. "Yes, sir."

"Good. See you tomorrow."

He shoots me a salute and I take the hint, slipping out of his office and leaving him alone before he can grill me on any of the details.

CHAPTER 25
SLOANE

'm finishing up my shift at the library when I get a text from Cam.

Cam: It's done

My heart pounds hard and fast as I stare down at those two words.

It's done.

I'm assuming this means Cam talked with my dad. But he sure isn't sharing too much info about the chat.

Sloane: How'd it go? How did he seem to you?

Sloane: What was his reaction, exactly?

Cam: He was fine

Gah. I'm gonna need more than that.

Sloane: What do you mean? Define 'fine'

Cam: He took the news calmly. Doesn't seem mad or anything

Cam: I'm going to Mustang's with Nash and Nate. That'll give you and your dad some space and time to talk

Oof. Thanks for that.

Sloane: You're leaving me alone with him?!?

Cam: He's your dad

Cam: And like I said, he's fine. If anything, he's more upset with me than you

Cam: And I wouldn't say he's upset. More like worried

Sloane: About what? You not being focused enough on football? Me being a distraction?

Cam: Sort of…

Cam: Pretty sure he's more concerned about his little girl getting her heart broken again

A sharp pang radiates across my chest.

My dad's worried about me getting hurt?

I never thought of him as the sensitive type, the sort of guy who'd be concerned with inconsequential things like feelings. Any time I had an issue with a boy at school, he'd send me straight to Mimi's house. He never wanted to get involved with my love life.

Maybe I don't know him as well as I think I do.

Sloane: You want company at the bar? I can blend in with the guys

Cam: Trouble, there's zero percent chance you're blending in. You're a knockout

I blush at the compliment, although I'm not thrilled at the prospect of going home to hang with my dad. Alone, without Cam as a buffer.

Traitor.

Sloane: Nice sweet talk, Crawford

Cam: I'm just spitting facts

I send him a heart emoji and lean against the desk, grinning at my cell. The entire day feels surreal—I only wish I could avoid my dad for the next, oh, five or so years. Maybe longer.

Sloane: Are you coming home tonight? To my house?

Our house? The house? My dad's house? I'm not exactly sure how to phrase it now.

Cam: Yeah, later. I get keys to the new place tomorrow AM

Cam: Can't wait for you to see it

Sloane: Same

Although I'm a lot less excited about the actual house versus the man who'll be living in it.

I can't wait to be with Cam for real and do all the relationship-y things. Cook dinner together, cuddle while watching movies, finally have uninhibited sex. Free from the constant fear of my dad walking in and catching us in a compromising position.

> Cam: My favorite room is the bedroom, wink-wink

And—these panties are officially trashed, wetness flooding the delicate satin.

> Sloane: You're a bad boy, Crawford

> Cam: I know. That's one of the things you love about me

He does have a point.

> Sloane: I can name a few more too. Your pecs, your biceps, those abs...

> Cam: Don't stop there, babe

Fluorescent lights flicker and I glance over at the corner. The custodian's leaning on his vacuum and shooting me a pointed stare.

> Sloane: Sorry, gotta jet. Library's closing

> Sloane: Be a good boy tonight and maybe I'll tell you the rest later

> Cam: Such a tease

I giggle as the ancient vacuum cleaner roars to life, loud and rattly.

"Night." I wave at the custodian, but he ignores me, already jamming out to his music and moving back and forth across the carpet in straight lines.

I tap out one last quick text.

Sloane: See you later. XOXO

Cam: xoxo

Smiling, I toss my cell into my bag and whistle all the way to my car, trying hard to focus on the good things to come and not on the awkward-but-imminent conversation with my father.

———

"Daddy?" I call out as I push through the screen door. I'm fairly certain he's home—his truck's out front.

Silence.

He's either in the shower or out back. I move into the dark kitchen, noticing the glow of the deck light through the window. Opting for some liquid courage, I grab a beer and pop the top before heading outside.

Sure enough, my dad's sitting at the edge of the deck. His hat's flipped backward and he's leaning on his elbows, staring up at the stars. In the dim light, he could easily pass for late twenties, not middle-aged with a grown daughter.

Heavy emphasis on *grown*.

"Hey, Daddy." I sink down next to him, my legs dangling over the edge of the deck. Kicking my sandals off, grass tickles the soles of my feet.

"Hey, baby. How was work?"

His tone is neutral, his expression blank. The man's a freaking vault when it comes to his emotions. A trait that's served him well as a coach, but is low-key annoying as his daughter.

"Good. Cam dropped by during Story Time. Took photos with the kids and signed autographs. It was a real highlight of the summer for them."

His lips tip up a touch at this. "Bet they loved seeing a real-life professional football player."

"They did."

He takes a long sip of his beer, swallows. Cue the long, awkward pause. The only thing breaking the silence is crickets chirping, literally.

I clear my throat and forge ahead. "Cam said he talked to you after practice today."

"He did."

Ohmygod, this is beyond painful. Am I going to get the shortest answers possible until I have to pry it out of the man?

Okay, Sloane, just rip off the bandage. You've never been afraid to talk to your dad. Don't start now.

"And? You good?"

"With what, exactly? Cam moving out?" He lifts his shoulders, shrugging. "Sure, that's fine."

"C'mon, Dad—" I punch him lightly on the arm, surprised at how strong he is. "You know what I mean. Are you going to make me say it?"

His lips twist into a smirk. "Yep."

"Fine." My face flames and a light trickle of sweat slips down my back. "Are you good with me and Cam dating?"

He sets his beer bottle down and faces me, his expression serious. "Sloane, the two of you can do what you want. You're both adults."

"I'm sensing a huge 'but' here—"

"But I'd be lying if I said I was happy about it. Don't get me wrong—" He lifts his bottle up and picks at the edge of the label. "I like Cam. A lot. Way more than that fella you were gonna marry. But—"

"Ah, here it comes—" I press my tongue against the inside of my cheek and hold my breath, waiting for his admonishment.

"He's a professional athlete. I see the appeal, believe me. He's in good shape, handsome, makes good money, has an exciting life. Y'all are friends and always have been, so there's history there. All good things."

"So what's the problem then?" I tap my toes in the grass, agitated. My dad's not making a lick of sense right now. If Cam's not good enough for me, no other man stands a chance.

"His lifestyle isn't normal, stable. Cam's gonna get picked up by a new team and he'll be leaving Thunder Creek. Not that you're here to stay or anything, I'm sure you have bigger plans—" He takes a shuddery breath and for the first time, I realize that my dad actually likes me being back home. Here, with him. I didn't think he cared when I left for school, then moved to New Orleans with Ratface. I never considered that he might be lonely.

"Honestly, I don't know what I'm doing at the moment. I'm enjoying the job at the library, spending time with you, and Mimi and Poppa, hanging with Gracelyn. I haven't made any decisions about the future yet."

"I don't want to see you get hurt is all. And I don't think Cam would do anything purposely, but that lifestyle comes with challenges. Real, tangible challenges. You won't be number one—football will be. Are you good with that?" He cuts his eyes at me and I squirm under his questioning gaze.

"Sure." The word wobbles out of my mouth and I don't sound convincing, even to my own ears.

"And you're good with women throwing themselves at him all the time? Messaging him, sliding into his DMs—that's what people are doing these days, right?"

I laugh. "Yeah, Dad, that's what people do these days. And yeah, obviously I wouldn't love that. But I trust Cam."

"And what happens if and when you want to settle down, have a family? And he's traveling every week. That puts a strain on the relationship."

"Dad. You do know there's professional football players with families, right? Like, it's a thing. Not everyone leaves—" My dad tenses beside me and I stop, bitterness flooding my body. I kick at the lawn for a long minute. Take a deep breath.

"Not everyone's like Mom. Some people stay."

"And some people don't. It's a hard, painful lesson to learn." He peels the label all the way off the bottle and crumbles the paper into a ball, dropping it on the wood deck.

"So you're never going to give anyone a chance? Ever again? All because of Mom?" My voice tips up and I hate how shrill I sound, how defensive.

Always the stoic, my dad doesn't react. Instead, he takes a long pull from his beer. Crickets keep on chirping and for the first time in days, a slight breeze rustles the leaves in the trees.

"I don't know." His voice is low, barely above a whisper.

I shake my head, filled with sadness, disbelief, and an odd infuriation. How could this man be so stubborn, still, after all these years? Holding on to past grievances like they're a lifeline, tethering him to her forever.

"Risk is a part of life, Dad. The game you love—that's risk. Every time a player steps onto the field, they're taking a risk. You run plays. Risks, each and every one of them. I've personally seen you call an End Around. More than once. Risky. But sometimes taking a risk is worth it. Cam's worth it."

He lifts his ball cap and runs his fingers through his hair, places the hat back on his head. Reaching over, he pats my knee, keeping his eyes focused on the picket fence separating our yard from Mrs. Humperdink's.

"Long as you're happy, that's all I care about."

Then he stands and goes inside, the screen door squeaking shut behind him.

CHAPTER 26
SLOANE

'm restless all night long, thinking about everything my dad said.

How Cam's lifestyle isn't normal. How women will try to hook up with him. How traveling and long-distance will be hard.

But those aren't the points that keep me awake.

Some people stay.

And some people don't.

That's the line that plays in my head on loop, over and over again. When the sun finally sneaks through the slats of my blinds, I throw back the sheets and give up on the idea of sleep altogether.

There's only one person who can talk me through this right now and I'm sure she's up already. My grandmother rises before the sun to feed the chickens and goats, weed her vegetable garden before it gets too hot. She probably already showered and is on her second cup of coffee by now.

Throwing on a T-shirt and denim shorts, I scrape my

hair into a ponytail, brush my teeth, and slip out of the house as quietly as possible. After last night, I'd rather avoid my dad right now.

I drive the few blocks to Mimi and Poppa's house. My grandparents live at the edge of town, right where the grass starts to grow taller and the yards get bigger. The cute yellow house with the wraparound porch and the white shutters is the same one where my dad grew up. I've been coming here my whole life, and I always feel completely at home.

With a gentle knock, I push through the unlocked door. "Mimi? It's me."

"In here, sugar." Her voice carries from the kitchen, straight through to the living room. The living room's decorated in light oak wood and florals, my dad's trophy collection lining the shelves. I run my hand over his high school football picture as I walk by, my chest squeezing.

Coming here is like being sucked into a time warp, a shrine to my father's glory days. Before I came along and screwed up his life.

Not that Mimi or Poppa or my dad ever said that out loud. It's more a vibe, an undercurrent running between the three of them.

"Hi, Mimi." I bend down and give my grandmother a hug. She's poring over a crossword puzzle book, a steaming mug of coffee next to her.

"What's a seven-letter word for deli meat?" She squints up at me over her readers.

I shrug. "I dunno. Not turkey, that's only six letters."

"Hmm." Setting her pencil down, she shoves the puzzle aside. "What's cooking, good looking? You're up early."

"I know. Couldn't sleep. Where's Poppa?"

"He went to breakfast with his buddies from the men's club. What's up?" Her head bobs, platinum blonde hair swishing across her narrow shoulders. My dad got his broad build from Poppa because Mimi's tiny, barely hitting five feet. But she's a firecracker, make no mistake about it.

I slide into the seat next to her, the scent of freshly brewed coffee swirling through the air. A rooster crows in the backyard and a dog barks in the distance.

"How are Toast and Jammy? You feed them already today?"

"I did. Fed and watered the greedy little goats. Otherwise, they'd make quick work of my garden. We can wander out and say hi, though, if you want."

I shrug, then rest my elbows on the table. "It's okay. Maybe later."

"Alright."

Mimi sits quietly, waiting for me to spill the tea and tell her what's wrong. I tuck my leg up under me and gnaw on my bottom lip, focus on choosing the exact right words.

"Has Dad always been broken?"

"'Scuse me?" Mimi's eyebrows crush together. "What do you mean?"

"Before Mom. What was he like? Did he take risks?"

"You want to know if your father took risks? What are we talking about here, exactly?"

"Not like skydiving or drag racing or jumping off the roof of a boat dock. Not those kinds of risk."

"What kind then?" She tips her head, twirling the pencil in her fingers.

"Like—in love."

"Well, sugar, I think you'd best ask him. As crazy as it sounds, your father didn't tell me much about his love life."

"C'mon. He tells you everything."

"He tells me *some* things now. But back in high school, when your mother was around? No. God, no. That boy told us nothing. Good thing, too, or you might not be here." She half-chuckles at the joke and I let out a heavy sigh.

"Dad does not want to talk about Mom with me. Or his love life. Guaranteed." I pick at a loose thread fraying on my shorts.

"Your daddy's never been one for idle chatter, that's for sure." Mimi takes a sip of coffee, then sets the mug down, her finger dancing over the embossed daisy pattern. "Listen—you're almost thirty years old now, so I feel like I can finally say some things. Maybe it'll answer your question."

She sucks at her teeth and stares out the window over the kitchen sink for a long minute before speaking again.

"Your daddy was wildly in love with your mother. That was clear any time they were together. And why wouldn't he be? Every boy was crazy about her. She was beautiful and popular, a cheerleader and the homecoming queen." Mimi pauses and I hold perfectly still, afraid to move and break the spell. This is the most she's ever told me about my mom and I don't want her to stop.

"The two of them dated from sophomore year until she left town. They were the golden couple of Thunder Creek High."

The only photos I've seen of my mom are from old high school yearbooks. My dad doesn't have one picture of the two of them together, or of her with me. Three years together and there's nothing, no trace of them as a couple. Of her at all.

I shift in my chair, trying to absorb this new information. Sure, I've heard a few things here and there, through the grapevine. I knew my mom was popular, a little on the wilder side. But that's all. Everyone has the decency not to bring her up around me or my dad.

Mimi presses her lips together and I'm afraid that's all I'm going to learn, all that she'll say.

"What happened, Mimi? Really?"

"Broad strokes—your mama got pregnant senior year, but hid it real well. Easier to do when it's your first pregnancy, and it was winter. By the time graduation rolled around, she was showing. Your mama's family was Catholic and I don't think they took the news very well. They never came 'round here or talked to me or your Poppa about anything."

"Your daddy had a full-ride to Georgia to play football. But he was in love and gonna be a daddy. So he turned them down and told your mama he was staying, asked her to marry him." Mimi folds the edge of the napkin beneath her mug, unfolds the corner, then folds it again.

"I shouldn't say any more. If your daddy wanted you to know all this, he would have told you himself."

"Please, Mimi—" I reach out, grabbing her arm. "Please." My voice rises, pleading. "Daddy will never. He doesn't want to talk about her."

Mimi presses her lips together, biting at her lower lip the same way I do when I'm thinking hard about something and I silently pray she'll keep talking. I need to know.

"She turned him down. He came back with the ring— my ring I loaned to him—and that was that. She had you a month early, in August, then up and left town."

Tears spring to my eyes and I shove down the wave of grief rising out of nowhere. Stupid, because I never met the woman. My dad and his family are all I've ever known. So why am I emotional about a total stranger who abandoned me?

Mimi pats my arm, rubbing her weathered thumb across the skin. "So, yes. I'd say your daddy took risks, and big ones at that. They didn't always turn out because that's life."

I rock back in my chair and blow out a long breath. "Thanks for telling me all this. It explains a lot."

She shakes her head, long wisps of bangs falling over her eyes before she brushes the hair away.

"I probably shouldn't have. That's your daddy's story to tell. But I suppose it's your story, too. And you deserve to know. Don't be too hard on your daddy—I think he kept the details to himself for good reason. He never wanted you to hate your mother. I believe he thought it'd be easier to just carry on as if she never existed. Trouble with that is, he never moved on. Sure, he moved forward. Minute after minute, day after day. But he buried all that passion and love, tucked it down deep so no one could ever hurt him like that again. That's my guess, anyway. He never told me as much."

Mimi stands, whisking her mug off the table and pouring the last drops of coffee down the drain.

"Enough about that. Let's go say hi to Toast and Jammy." Her tone lifts and she's the upbeat Mimi again, her face cracking into a wide, easy smile. She holds her hand out to me and I take it, following her outside into the bright morning sun.

But I can't shake my dad's somber words from last night, the pain in his eyes.

Some people stay. And some people don't.

CHAPTER 27
SLOANE

When I get home, Cam's Rover is in the driveway, but there's no sign of my dad. He must still be at practice.

Despite my dad's warning about Cam last night, fizzy excitement bubbles inside me and I know I have my answer.

I'm going to go for it. Take the risk with Cam and hope for the best. Sure, Ratface did me dirty. But Cam's not him. He's never been anything other than honest with me. I can't live my life like my father, always guarding my heart and not letting anyone in because I've been burned before.

It's not who I am, not who I want to be.

"Cam!" I run into the house, shouting his name.

"Hey." He walks out from the hallway, duffel in hand. His dark hair's damp from a shower and the crisp scent of his body wash floats through the air.

"Hey." My excitement dulls and a wave of sadness rolls through me at the sight of him carrying his stuff. I know he's not moving too far and getting his own space, but the moment still feels somber somehow.

Cam must read my expression because he drops his bag and grabs my hips, pulling me in close.

"Don't be sad, Trouble. This is a good thing. For both of us." He sweeps my hair from my eyes, running his thumb across my cheek.

"I know," I whisper, my throat scratchy and tight.

"I'll still be close. And you can come over anytime you want."

"Thanks."

Cam tips my chin up, brushing his lips with mine in a slow, soft kiss. "Want to come see the new place right now?"

Happiness sparks inside me and a smile spreads across my face. "Yes, I'd love to."

"Come on, then. I'll drive." He grabs his duffel and takes my hand, and we head outside.

"Did you practice with the team this morning?"

"We had weight training. I went to the gym instead, then got the keys to the rental." He jingles a keychain in the air, grinning. "I can't wait for you to see it—I think you're going to love it."

Cam's enthusiasm is contagious. "Me neither."

Slamming my door shut, he hustles around and hops into the driver's seat. The Rover purrs to life and we back down the driveway, Pearl Jam blaring through the speakers.

"Sorry." He adjusts the volume and I steal a glance at him, appreciating the square line of his jaw, his broad shoulders, the way his T-shirt stretches across his solid chest. I don't know how I got so lucky, but I should definitely send more embarrassing emails out into the world if this is what happens.

"What?" Cam's eyes slide to mine for a second.

"Nothing. Just admiring the view."

He grins, a dimple popping in his cheek as he takes one hand off the wheel and squeezes my upper thigh.

"My view's pretty great, too." I blush as his fingers caress my upper thigh, heat pooling low in my belly.

Why the hell was I sad about Cam getting his own place? This is everything I've been waiting for.

Ten minutes later, he takes the turn out toward the lake. The road gets rougher, the trees thicker as we move away from town.

"Thought we'd have more privacy out here by the lake. It's a little longer drive, but I think it's worth it."

Cam makes another right and we bump down a long gravel driveway, finally pulling up to a modern two-story house with tons of windows. Mature trees surround the property and I catch a glimpse of the placid lake as he swings around the circular drive, parking in front of the steps.

"This is it." He cuts the engine and hops out, coming around to open my door. I take his hand and we climb the porch steps.

Cam unlocks the frosted glass door and a chime beeps, indicating the alarm. He punches in a code from his phone and the alarm disables.

"Wow." I stare out at the view, impressed. The space is huge, open and modern and airy. Floor-to-ceiling windows make up the entire back wall of the house overlooking the lake, a sprawling green lawn, and a dock. Directly to the left of the entryway is a staircase with a glass and wire handrail and all the furniture is sleek and white.

"I'm thinking no red wine here," I joke, running my hand along the buttery white leather sofa cushion.

"You can have whatever you want, Trouble. Worst case, I pay the cleaning fees. Come on—I'll give you a tour."

He links his fingers with mine and leads me through the living room to the all-white kitchen. A huge marble island stands in the center of the room and state-of-the-art stainless-steel appliances line the wall, including the biggest refrigerator I've ever seen in my life. But the best part is the lake shimmering in the background.

"I love this, it's gorgeous." I spin around, arms wide, taking everything in.

There's a built-in eating area with a table and banquette dotted with white and blue pillows. The island's flanked by white-and-blue rattan barstools and everything in the room's angled to take in the sweeping water views. A huge white fireplace covers the far right wall of the room, topped with a large flat-screen television, and there's another white leather sofa.

Cam slides open the glass door that leads to the yard and I follow him onto the patio. A slight breeze off the water feathers my hair, the sounds of waves lapping at the dock carrying across the wide lawn.

"Just wow," I whisper, my voice filled with awe. "This place must cost a fortune. It's amazing."

"I got a good deal. Promised I'd throw in a signed jersey for their kid, plus tickets and some other swag."

"Nice."

"You haven't seen the best part yet."

"No?"

"Uh-uh." Cam scoops me up in his arms and carries me back inside, through the kitchen to the stairs.

"Oh no, don't drop me," I laugh as he climbs the stairs with me firmly in his arms.

"I've got you, Trouble. Don't worry." He smiles, locking his marine eyes on mine, and I melt for this man.

Cam's got me.

I believe him, all the way to my core. He's perfect for me. Everything about us is right.

Just because my dad had a bad experience with love doesn't mean I will.

"This. This is the best part." Cam sets me down, whirling me around to face yet more floor-to-ceiling windows.

And he's right—this is the best view yet. From up here, we can see all the way across the lake, nothing but dark blue water and verdant trees. We have one-hundred percent privacy out here, a total oasis from the rest of the world.

"Amazing—" I sigh, leaning back against his muscular chest. He wraps his arms around my waist, pulling me in closer to him. His breath tickles my neck and a sense of peace engulfs me. "I love it here."

"Good. I hoped you would." He leans down and presses his lips to mine. Hot and possessive, warmth rushes through me, buzzy electricity humming below my skin.

I want this man. Now and forever.

The thought skitters through my mind and I'm on fire, every inch of me wanting more.

"Cam—"

He pulls away slightly, his brow wrinkled with concern. "Yeah?"

I lick my lips, my breath uneven and ragged. "I want you."

"Aww, Trouble." He strokes my face, his pupils wide and dark. "I want you too."

In one swift movement, he lifts my shirt over my head and spins me around to face him. His gaze rakes across my chest and I blush under his heated stare.

"Beautiful." He strokes my breasts through the pink satin of my bra, nipples poking through the flimsy fabric. A soft moan vibrates low in my throat as wetness floods my panties.

"I've wanted to do this for a very long time," he murmurs, easing the straps from my shoulders before reaching around and unhooking my bra. The lingerie falls to the ground, chill bumps rising on my skin. He palms my breasts before dipping his mouth down and sucking a rosy peak between his lips.

Swirling his tongue around the sharp point, he teases the other with his finger and thumb, making me flush hot with desire. My eyes drift closed as I give into the sensation of Cam's mouth on my skin, hot pulses zinging straight to my core. His hand moves lower still, skimming down my torso until he unbuttons my shorts and eases the zipper down. I kick out of the denim until I'm only wearing panties.

"The view just got a whole lot better." Cam grins, cupping my face. His lips capture mine, hot and needy. Then his tongue slips in and we dance. Tangling together, tasting each other, licking and sucking until I can barely catch my breath.

His hands smooth over my ass, squeezing the round globes, and I shimmy against him. He's rock-hard against my stomach, telling me everything I need to know. I spread a hand on his chest, the thud of his heart hammering beneath my palm.

Snaking beneath his shirt, I tiptoe over the ridges of his abs, one by one.

"So sexy, Crawford—" I murmur into his mouth and he groans when I dip lower, grazing his hard length. "But it's really not fair."

"What's not fair?"

"You're still fully clothed." I stick my lip out in an exaggerated pout.

"I can fix that." He grins, pulling his T-shirt over his head in a blue blur and tossing it to the ground. His shorts follow, kicked to the side unceremoniously. Now he's only in boxer briefs, his cock straining against the fabric.

"Keep going—" I shoot him a seductive smile, pointing my finger downward.

Without hesitation, he yanks the briefs off and his long, steely cock springs out. I suck in a sharp breath as he fists himself, pumping. The veins in his forearms pop and I'm mildly concerned he's not going to fit.

"Better?" Cam asks, inching toward me.

I swallow. "Yes."

"One more thing—" He grips my hip, pulling me up against him. "It's only fair if we lose these."

With one finger, Cam slides my panties down my thighs. They pool at my feet and he ducks down, flinging them away before wrapping his arms around me and bringing me in close.

"Now we're even."

Dropping his lips to mine, he kisses me long and hard and deep. Like I'm the only person in the entire world and nothing else matters outside of this room.

I fall into that kiss—into him—harder than I've ever fallen for anything in my entire life. Swept away in a wave of desire, our entire history rising up and cresting.

Cam's the one.

I was an idiot to think anyone could take his place. Ever.

He's it for me. Always has been. Always will be.

"Fuck me, Cam." I whisper the words, and he stops, staring down at me with serious eyes.

Without another word, he grabs my ass and lifts me up in one fluid motion, as if I weigh nothing. I wrap my legs around his hips and he carries us over to the massive bed, the only furniture in the room outside of a television in the corner.

Lowering me gently down onto the bed, he smooths my hair from my face before touching his lips to mine. Igniting the spark that tells me everything I need to know without saying a word.

I'm his and he's mine.

We kiss for a long time, our hands moving over each other's bodies, exploring the dips and planes, the curves and edges. His hard, mine softer, a perfect pairing. With a flattened palm, he glides up and down my thighs and I quiver for him, already on the verge of ecstasy. We have so much time, and we take it, enjoying all the sensations.

Needy.

Hungry.

Greedy.

His fingers trail through my wetness, a moan falling from my lips.

"So wet and ready—" His voice is deep and raspy as I stroke up and down his thick cock, the skin velvety-soft. He pulsates in my hand, pre-cum leaking from the crown.

"Hang on—" Cam springs off the bed and jogs into the en suite bathroom. I hear drawers opening and closing as he rummages around, then he's back, condom in hand.

"Voila," he says, ripping the packet open and rolling the condom on.

"You came prepared, huh?"

"Figured we've been waiting long enough. No need to prolong it. Besides—" He climbs back onto the bed beside me, stroking my face. "I want to feel you. Bury my cock deep inside you and give you everything I have."

"I want that, too." I wrap my arms around his neck, pulling him in closer to me. "Very much so."

Gliding my knuckles over the stubble on his jaw, I gaze up at him through lowered lashes and spread my legs, beckoning him in. I need him inside me, filling me.

His breath hitches as he glides his hand from my shoulders, down my torso, past my hip to the apex of my thighs. Locking eyes with him, I lick my lips, every inch of my body on fire as he strokes between my legs. He dips a finger in, then another, holding them still and warming up my body. Then he begins to move slowly, in and out. Scissoring and stretching and it feels so freaking good. My skin tingles, heat unfurling low in my belly as his thumb grazes my clit.

"Oh—" I moan, my eyes fluttering closed as he applies more pressure.

"Sloane, I'm going to fuck you with my hand and make you come. Okay, baby? Get you good and ready to take my cock."

I nod, panting, as his thick fingers piston in and out, in and out. Waves of pleasure roll over me as I crash over the edge, shuddering around his hand.

"Fuck. You're so responsive." Cam tickles my skin with his fingertips and I shudder.

"That was nice."

"Nice?" One dark brow raises and he frowns. "Baby

girl, *nice* is the last adjective you'll be using by the time we're done here."

I giggle as he straddles me, caging me in with his massive body. Heat shimmers between us, bright sunlight streaming through the windows casting Cam in a golden glow. He's beautiful, every line of his body sculpted and honed, the deep V of his hips even more pronounced at this angle.

Winding my legs around him, I dig my heels into his tight ass, bringing him closer to me. His scent fills my nose and I kiss his perfect lips, claiming him.

"Sloane, are you ready?" Cam's voice is deep and husky.

"God, yes. I'm yours. Fuck me."

CHAPTER 28
CAM

*F*uck.

She has no idea what she's doing to me. Those perky tits, her tight pussy, soft, smooth skin that smells like summer.

And the words. Fuck, those words.

I'm yours. Fuck me.

She's an angel, fallen from heaven, and I'm going to corrupt her. Absolutely ruin her for any other man. Ravage her body until I'm all she thinks of, all she knows or wants to know.

I shouldn't do it. Sloane's too good for me, too pure. But I can't stop myself. Hell, I don't want to stop myself.

Besides, it's too late now.

I ease the tip of my cock into her wet heat, a hiss slipping through my gritted teeth.

"Fuck, baby, you feel so good."

She rocks her hips up slightly, trying to get more of my dick.

"Greedy girl," I tease, running my thumb across her full bottom lip. She sucks in a deep breath, her tongue warm on the calloused pad of my thumb. I sink in another inch or so, then still again. She tries to move against me, but I grip her hip, stopping her.

"Relax, we have time. I don't want to break you. You're gonna be sore either way, but the slower we go, the better it'll be."

She blushes and lets out a nervous giggle, and she's so damn cute and sexy right now, I'm not sure how slow I can actually take this. I want to bury myself balls-deep inside her, watch her come undone as I spill my load.

"What?" The golden flecks in her eyes twinkle in the sunlight as she squints up at me through dark lashes.

"I was just thinking about how bad I want to fuck you."

She turns a deeper shade of pink, her chest and neck flushing as well.

"Prove it, Crawford."

I push in deeper and now I'm almost halfway there. Her tight muscles contract around my dick, thighs tense.

"Relax and breathe," I coach, caressing her breast with my fingertips. Circling around her rosy nipple, she inhales and exhales, her body loosening. I slide in deeper. "Good girl, that's a good girl, relaxing and taking my cock."

Her thighs fall further apart and I ease all the way inside her, balls flush against her ass.

"You okay?" I keep stroking her breasts, nipples peaking.

"Yes."

I stay still for a long minute, hovering over her body on my forearms, careful not to crush her. Our breathing syncs as I gaze into her eyes, pupils blown wide with desire. My cock twitches inside her, aching to move. Rocking her hips a little, she urges me on.

"You sure?" I ask, studying her face.

"Yes, Cam. I meant what I said. Fuck me. Please." Her voice is thin and needy and I can't wait any longer.

Smashing my lips to hers, I devour her. Sweet from her lip balm, her mouth opens to mine and I don't hesitate. I slide my tongue in, sweeping around and exploring. She grinds against me and I match her pace, slow at first. But we pick up speed quickly, both of us moving faster, harder, more urgently.

Her muscles clench around my cock as she lifts her ass up, meeting my every drive. I grab the round globes and squeeze, gripping her tighter, pushing in deeper until any space between us vanishes.

We're one now, joined together in this perfect moment.

Sweat slicks my skin as I pound into her, the walls of her pussy squeezing and milking my cock. Hot need pulses through my veins, dark spots pricking the corners of my eyes. Balls tightening, the base of my spine tingles with that familiar pressure.

"Fuck, Sloane. You feel so good—" I groan as I piston into her. "So fucking tight. You're perfect."

A moan vibrates the graceful column of her neck. She's close and I'm barely holding on.

"Come for me now, okay? I want to watch you shatter."

Those words push her over the edge and she cries out, her body quaking with pleasure.

"Ohmygod, Cam—" She scratches down my back as she shudders around my dick.

"Such a good girl." I don't let up, thrusting again and again, wringing every last bit of release from her body.

"Cam—" she screams, digging into my traps. That pushes me over the edge and I explode, hot cum erupting.

"Fuck—" I hiss, riding the wave, enjoying the release before pulling out and collapsing onto the bed.

Wrapping an arm around Sloane, I pull her limp body onto my chest. Her breathing's shaky and uneven, heart pounding hard against my pec as I stroke her heated skin.

"That was so good, baby," I murmur, kissing the top of her head. The floral scent of shampoo drifts from her hair, filling my nose, and I breathe her in. Wanting to remember this moment forever.

"Mm-hmm." Her head bobs on my chest, eyes closed as her breathing slows and evens out. I gaze down at her, memorizing the pattern of cinnamon freckles, the slope of her breasts, the way her slender fingers fan out over my biceps. The soft hum of happiness vibrating low in her throat, the curve of her ass cheek, the slickness of arousal on my thigh.

Heaven.

If I could stay here with her forever, I absolutely would.

No football or outside pressure. No expectations or team bullshit.

Just the two of us, together.

Sloane's always been a safe space for me, a happy place, and that hasn't changed any.

But everything else has.

Before today, I was scared. Worried that I'd somehow fuck things up and ruin everything.

Now I realize how shortsighted that line of thinking was. What just happened between us didn't ruin anything. Instead, being together—finally giving ourselves to each other—only made everything better.

Deeper, stronger, more solid.

We're no longer two people moving in a perpendicular line to each other. Now we're one unit, a team.

A force to be reckoned with.

And nothing's going to keep us apart.

CHAPTER 29
CAM

Moving out was the right choice. Now that I have my own space out at the lake, Sloane and I can be together as much as we want. Any place, any time, any way we can think of.

We've taken full advantage.

Over the past few weeks, I've had her on the kitchen island, both sofas, the dock, and of course, in the enormous clawfoot bathtub. I think that was my favorite time of all. There's something innately sexy about water—especially when you're naked with someone as gorgeous as Sloane.

"Is your new motto 'Leave no stone unturned,' Cam?" she teases, pulling the skirt of her dress back down.

"More like 'Leave no orgasm ungiven.'" I grin, glancing up from between her thighs and wiping my mouth on my sleeve. "You tasted better than the pancakes."

We finished breakfast an hour ago, but the plates and silverware still litter the dining table, the stack of leftover pancakes now cold. She giggles, pulling me up from between her legs.

"Well, you can check kitchen bench off the list." She leans back against the cushions, cheeks rosy from the pleasure I delivered. "That was amazing."

"They do say breakfast is the most important meal of the day." I wink and she shakes her head, laughing.

"You're something else, Crawford. How's everything going with the team? I haven't seen much of my dad, between working at the library, sneaking in girls' nights with Gracelyn, and spending time out here with you."

"The team's shaping up. They look decent for pre-season. Coach gave them homework—memorize the playbook over the holiday weekend. Langley will be solid on that. Could give the kid an edge."

"I'm sure that would make his mom happy. I know she's pulling for him to play QB this year."

"He's a good kid. He can absolutely win the spot, as long as he's on during tryouts."

"Speaking of tryouts—have you heard anything from your agent? Any leads on a new team?" Tucking her legs up, she twirls a dark strand of hair around her finger.

The familiar squeeze of anxiety grips me in the gut. "No. I need to reach out to Troy today, before he disconnects for the long weekend. See if he has any bites."

"I can't believe nothing's come up yet."

The squeeze turns into a squash, sour bile rising at the back of my throat.

You should tell Sloane about the video. Come clean right now, no secrets.

The edges of my vision darken and my chest's tight, like I can't get enough oxygen. Everything's buzzing and I'm suddenly nauseous as hot shame rolls through me.

I can't do it.

I don't want to hurt her and she won't get it, won't understand the pressure I was under at the time. How the stress of the season built up to that night and I made a bad choice.

That's all it was. Drunken sex with fangirls, fueled by a heady cocktail of testosterone and fame.

A dumb fucking move and now I'm paying for it.

It's better if I say nothing. Keep quiet about the incident and she'll never find out. The two of us can move forward and leave the past where it belongs—firmly in the rearview. That sordid chapter of my life's behind me now and the last thing I want to do is revisit it.

"Grace invited us to the town's Fourth of July bash tomorrow. Want to go?"

"Sure. The only thing I have on the agenda is getting you naked. As long as we can still do that, I'm game."

Her giggle floats through the kitchen, hitting me straight in the chest. She's so sweet, so innocent.

No way can I tell her about that video.

"What did you have in mind, exactly, Cam? What's your next move to get what you want?" She leans forward and places her elbows on the table, giving me a clear cleavage shot. Now I'm rock-fucking-hard for her.

"On second thought, I don't think that plan can wait until tomorrow. We have—" I glance at the clock on the built-in wall oven. "Three hours before practice. That's plenty of time for me to execute."

Her eyebrows rise in curiosity as I offer her my hand. Taking it without hesitation, she places full trust in me and my throat tightens.

Do not hurt this girl.

But telling her the truth would surely be worse?

Shoving that idea from my mind, I slide her out from the banquette and throw her over my shoulder.

"Cam!" she shrieks, slapping at my back. "Put me down!"

I chuckle. "Nope. Time to go outside. It's a beautiful, sunny day. And I'm hot. Aren't you?"

She's laughing and kicking and screaming all the way across the lawn, down to the lake.

"Cam Crawford, if you don't put me down—"

"What, Trouble? What are you going to do about it?"

"I don't know, but you're not going to like it."

I snicker. "That I doubt."

Setting her feet down on the dock, she rights herself, smoothing her dress and adjusting her ponytail.

"Not sure why you bothered with that." I fix her with a heated stare and she licks those full, pink lips, driving me wild.

In one swift motion, I lift her dress off her body.

"Cam!"

I shed all my clothes and scoop her up in my arms quickly, before she realizes what's happening.

Then the cool water pricks at my bare skin, the lake swallowing us as we sink below the waves. She thrashes about as we break the surface and she's laughing and scowling all at once, pushing any worry and doubt about the sex video from my mind.

The only thing that matters right here, right now, is me and Sloane. The sun, the wind, the water, our bodies and how good we make each other feel.

"Cam Crawford! I'm going to get you!"

I shove out of her grip, swimming away from her as fast as I can. Splashing noises sound behind me as I kick across the lake, trying to escape her playful wrath.

"Don't think so, Trouble," I tease, slowing my strokes so she'll catch me.

A few minutes later, she jumps on my back, wrapping her arms around my shoulders.

"Got ya!"

Breath warm on my neck, she presses her body against mine. "Now you're mine."

I spin around, gripping her by the waist, and she sucks in a sharp breath.

"Trouble, I've been yours."

Brushing a wet strand of hair from her eyes, I lock my gaze on hers. Trying to tell her how I feel without saying the words. Cool water laps around us, a delicate pulse fluttering in her neck.

I slide one of my hands from her waist to her ass, splaying across the round peach and pulling her up tight against my chest. Pressing my hips to hers, my cock twitches eagerly against her bare stomach. Then I touch my lips to hers lightly, like a soft, gentle breeze. She hums against my mouth and I lick along the seam, tasting the syrup from the pancake breakfast.

Opening to me, I shove in. No longer tentative or gentle, my kisses turn frantic, urgent, as my cock lengthens.

"How attached are you to these panties?" I murmur, toying with the lace edge.

"Right now? Not at all."

With a quick snap, I tear the fabric from her body and toss it toward the shoreline. The sopping pink lace flies through the air, landing close to the dock.

"We'll get it later." I cup her chin, tipping her face toward mine. Then I seize her lips in a hot, possessive kiss. Everything around us melts away, and it's just the two of us out here, alone with the wind, the sun, the water.

She wraps her legs around my hips, heels digging into my back. The heat from her core burns against me and she wriggles suggestively.

I need her. Need to feel her tight muscles wrap around my cock, need to bury myself deep inside her until I can't remember my own damn name.

"I want to fuck you. Here, right now." I kiss along her jawline, down her neck. Licking and sucking at the clear droplets of water beading on her skin. Palm her breast and rub at her nipples through the satin of her bra until she moans beneath my touch.

"Okay."

"Okay?" I suck at the tender skin of her collarbone, caressing the smooth flesh of her ass.

"Yes. I'm on the pill. And got a check-up after everything—"

"Shh, it's okay," I cut her off, not interested in having her remember anything about the last loser. "I had a physical right before I left Chicago. So we're good."

Sloane smiles up at me, a soft blush shading her cheeks. The bright sun highlights the apples of her cheeks, the golden tan of her skin. She's so damn beautiful it's almost painful being this close and not being with her, in her.

Pulling her body up against mine, I ease into her tight pussy. Her eyes flutter closed as I sink in further, her muscles clenching around my cock.

"Fuck, you feel so good." I smash my lips to hers. She's sweet and a little salty from the lake and everything's so good right now, so amazing. Rocking her hips with the rhythm of the water, I meet her thrust for thrust, our bodies slapping together in unison.

"You're so perfect, baby. So fucking tight." I piston harder, balls tightening. But somehow I hold on, waiting for her to get closer. I press against her clit with my thumb and she shimmies against my hand.

"Yes—" she moans and I rub the sensitive nub, moving in a circle, pinching until she squirms.

"That's it, baby. Let go for me, that's a good girl." The words fall from my lips and I watch as her eyes squeeze tight, then she shatters around my cock.

I don't hesitate, pummeling into her hard and exploding.

"Oh my fuck—" I hold her body tight to my chest as she shudders against me, both of us tensing and riding out the release. Rubbing her shoulders, down her back, she relaxes against me.

"Cam—" Her voice is soft and quiet and I kiss my name from her lips, swallowing whatever she's about to say.

"I love you." The words fall easily into the air between us and I pause, waiting for her to say something.

She doesn't move, says nothing.

Fuck. Too soon.

Her hand smooths over my deltoid and she sighs contentedly, resting her cheek on my chest.

"I love you, too."

Tipping her face up, I capture her lips with mine. Kissing her hard and long and deep, like she's the only woman I'll ever kiss again.

Because she's it for me.

It's taken me a while to realize, but now I see it.

Sloane's what I've been looking for. All this time she was right here, right in front of me.

Waiting.

Now that I have her, I don't plan on letting her go.

CHAPTER 30
SLOANE

love you.

The three words echo over and over in my mind and I literally pinch myself so hard I bruise.

After all these years, all the waiting and wanting, Cam said he loves me.

And of course I said it back because I'm madly in love with him. He's everything I've ever wanted and I've never been happier. Things between us are easy and fun. There's no bullshit, no lies or agenda.

I know him and he knows me. We're absolutely perfect together.

"You sure you're ready for this, Trouble?" Cam flips his baseball hat backward and squints across the bedroom at me as I slip on my sandals. "We could always hang here, swim in the lake and grill out. Catch the fireworks later tonight, just the two of us."

"That sounds lovely. But I promised Gracelyn I'd show up for the Fourth of July bash. I can't leave her hanging. But if you don't want to go, I can go by myself—"

"If you go, I'm there." Cam steps forward, wrapping his tanned, muscled arms around my waist.

I lift on tiptoe, grazing his lips with mine. "Thanks. I do want to go. This is kind of our hard launch, you know?"

He chuckles, his deep voice vibrating his chest. "I suppose."

"Pretty sure the entire town knows our business by now, though, after Story Time."

"I don't mind." Cam's fingers trail over my cheek and heat unfurls low in my belly as I stare up at him. The way he's looking at me, his marine eyes sincere and intense.

This man is my everything.

After what happened with Ratface, I swore I'd never love again. But this—this thing between me and Cam—is so different. The two can't compare.

He's the polar opposite of Ratface, caring and kind, always looking out for me.

No, this is right and good, the way love's supposed to be.

"Alright, let's do it then." Cam kisses me one last time and then we head out for Thunder Creek's Fourth of July bash in the town square.

We park at the library and walk the few blocks to the center of town. The temperature's already sizzling, careening toward the high-nineties, and there's zero breeze. Heat radiates up from the sidewalk and I'm happy I chose a light sundress with spaghetti straps.

"Mercy, it's hot," Cam grumbles, wiping sweat from his brow as we cross Main Street.

"You practice in this heat every day."

"I know. That's why I like to stay in the AC when I'm not at practice."

I elbow him. "C'mon, let's get a nice icy lemonade to cool you down."

"And maybe a burger. I see Nash over there." Cam waves at his friend, grabbing me by the hand and leading us over to the food trucks lined up on the far edge of the grassy square.

"Hey, buddy, what's up?" Nash slaps Cam on the back, bro-style, then leans in and hugs me. "Sloane, good to see you."

"Same. Is Nathan here too?" I glance around the field for Nash's twin.

"Yeah, he's hanging around here somewhere. Probably trying to escape Natalie and her girl gang."

Natalie's their younger sister and she and her friends make it a sport to torment her older brothers. She runs the dance studio in town and despite her brothers' best efforts, she often ropes them into helping with recitals, passing out programs and running the sound system. It's hilarious watching these two burly men interact with all the tiny dancers in pink tutus.

"We missed you at poker night this week. But seems like you had a good excuse." His eyes slide to me and my cheeks heat.

"I've been busy this week." Cam shrugs. "Working out with Coach Carter pretty hard, polishing up my fundamentals."

"Uh-huh. That's what we're calling it these days, huh?" Nash smirks and I try not to squirm. If this thing between me and Cam is going to work long-term, I'll deal with this type of scrutiny all the time.

Cam clears his throat, looping his arm around my waist and bringing me in close to him. The faint woodsy scent of his cologne hits me and I relax, warmth blooming in my chest.

"Something like that," Cam says, his grip tightening on my hip. "It was good running into you, Nash. Call me next time y'all go to Mustang's and maybe we'll join you."

Nash shoots Cam a two-finger wave and walks away, toward the games at the far side of the field.

We.

Cam acknowledged the relationship to his buddy, putting the two of us together in the same box.

Me and Cam.

We.

A team.

My insides turn to jelly and happiness oozes through me like sweet, gooey caramel.

"Hey!" Gracelyn jogs up. "Where have y'all been? I've been looking for you for-ev-er!"

"We got here a few minutes ago. It's hotter than blazes, so we're getting drinks. How are you?" I ask, squeezing her in a hug.

She huffs out a breath, fanning her face. "Better now that you're here. I can't take one more question about my love life, I swear. Between that and the ladies from the senior center jockeying to get on my calendar for perms, I'm dying."

"Don't worry, you're safe now." I pat her arm and she smiles gratefully at me.

"Thank goodness. Y'all hungry? I could go for some food." Gracelyn stares longingly at the brightly-colored food trucks.

"Yes, let's do it." Cam leads the way through the crowd, his large hand pressed lightly to the small of my back, Gracelyn on my other side.

Contentment flows through me, warm and fuzzy, and I cling to the feeling. I know Cam won't be here forever, but it's nice being here together again right now. Like old times, except better.

"I'm getting a hot dog and a Coke. What about you?" Grace interrupts my thoughts, shoving my arm.

"A burger for me," Cam declares, eyeing the bright red-white-and-blue truck to his left. "You want one, Trouble? Or something else?"

"Sure, I'll take a burger."

"Whoever gets the food first can snag a seat." Grace tips her head at the stand of picnic tables set up beside the trucks.

"Sounds like a plan."

Cam and I join the long line at the burger truck, his palm rubbing light circles on my back. Luke Bryan's voice booms from the speakers near the stage, urging a country girl to shake it for him. A group of teen girls in short sundresses sway to the beat, taking the lyrics to heart. Clumps of kids run around the field, waving balloon animals and shrieking with glee, and my heart is full.

"It's good to be home for the holiday." I lean back against Cam's broad chest, sighing happily.

"Yeah, it's nice," he murmurs, his breath feathering my hair. "Being here with you."

Damn. Cue the heart melt.

"Aww, thanks, babe." I tip my head back, capturing his lips in a kiss.

"Hey, Crawford. You gonna move up in line sometime soon? Or are you gonna stand around, shoving your tongue down your girl's throat all day long?"

Cam jerks away from me and whirls around to face the

dark-haired teenager scowling behind us. There's a group of them, and I bet they're all Thunder Creek High boys.

"Listen here, Dalton. I've had just about enough of you and your attitude." Cam takes a shuddery breath, trying to get a hold of his anger.

"Same, old man." The kid smashes his lips together in a tight line, folding his arms over his barrel chest. He's pretty built for a high schooler, but Cam still has him by about six inches and a good thirty pounds of pure muscle. Doesn't stop Dalton from puffing up his chest and acting like a tough guy in front of his friends, though.

Cam's fingers ball into fists at his side and his jaw tics. This Dalton kid definitely gets on his nerves.

"I wasn't sure why Coach had a washed-up pro practicing with us, but now it's all coming together for me." Dalton glances from Cam to me and back again, his eyes lingering on the low neckline of my sundress. "You're the coach's daughter, right?"

I nod. "I am."

"Huh," Dalton grunts, licking his lips.

"You don't know what you're talking about, kid." Cam waves him off dismissively and it's our turn to order. Cam rattles off the order while I shuffle from foot-to-foot, trying my best to ignore the disgruntled high schooler and his buddies whispering behind me. There's snickering and I catch the occasional curse word, along with 'Coach.'

Cam and I step out of line, moving to the side, and Dalton and his pals order their food. As soon as he pays, Dalton slides up next to us. He moves in close to Cam, clearly itching for a fight. Cam inches away, but Dalton doesn't take the hint, rubbing shoulders with him. Then he leans in, mock-whispering in a voice loud enough that anyone in the vicinity can hear.

"How is it, sleeping with the coach's daughter? Is that how you locked in your spot on the team back in the day?"

Cam's face turns red and a vein pops in his neck, pulsating. He whirls around to face Dalton, fists clenched at his side.

"Shut up. Right now. Disrespect me all you want, but don't talk about Sloane. Keep her name out of your mouth, you hear me?" Cam's voice is steely, but Dalton doesn't back down.

"Or what? What are you gonna do about it? Go tattle on me to Coach?" Dalton's brows quirk up, his lips curling in a sneer and now his friends are circling around, egging him on.

"It's fine, Cam." I touch Cam's forearm, and he shakes his head.

"It's not. This guy thinks he can say whatever he wants, act however he wants. There's consequences for actions. Remember that, Dalton."

Dalton laughs. "Yeah. Like if you suck ass at football, you get cut."

Hot anger rolls off Cam's body, the scar above his eye a fiery red. But he somehow keeps his composure and doesn't haul off and deck the kid.

"Order up for Cam!" the guy at the food truck calls out, breaking the tension.

Cam says nothing. He stalks to the window and grabs our food, not giving Dalton another glance.

"See you at practice, old man!" Dalton shouts and his friends snort and laugh.

I trail behind Cam, my stomach in tight knots. Cam sinks down onto the picnic bench across from Gracelyn, fuming. I've never seen him this angry before. He slams the food onto the table, then unwraps the foil from his burger and bites down hard, ketchup squishing out the side of the bun.

"You guys okay?" Gracelyn's brow furrows.

"Yeah, we're fine. Some high school kid was being dumb is all." I wave my hand through the air, brushing away the incident.

"That kid's such an asshole. And damn straight I'm gonna tattle on him to Coach. He doesn't deserve to be QB, acting like that," Cam mutters not all that quietly.

"Seriously? What are you going to tell my dad? That Dalton accused you of sleeping your way onto the football team in high school?" My voice tips up in hysteria and disbelief. "I'd really rather you not have that conversation, if you wouldn't mind."

Cam huffs out a heavy sigh. "Fine. Maybe I'll be vague about the whole thing."

"And then what happens when my dad goes to Dalton and asks questions? Because you know he will."

Cam frowns, his dark brows crushing together. "Dammit, you're right."

I reach across the table, laying my hand over Cam's. "It's fine, Cam. He's a dumb kid who doesn't know what he's talking about. You and I both know that's not how you got your starting position in high school. You're obviously not washed-up—I can attest to that."

Grace snickers, choking a little on her Coke. "Wow, okay—"

"And thirty isn't all that old. Just kind of old," I tease and the corners of Cam's lips curve up a touch.

"Okay, you're right. I'll let it slide this time, but he better not keep this shit up at practice. Or he's gonna get tackled really fucking hard, swear to God."

I laugh. "Yeah, I wouldn't mess with you if I were him,

but he's clearly not that bright. Can we enjoy the rest of the day now and forget about this Dalton kid?"

Cam nods. "Yes. We can and we should."

By the time we finish our lunch, Cam's chill again, happy and relaxed. Gracelyn's telling us a funny story about a woman who came to the salon with a terrible at-home dye job and I'm soaking up the holiday vibes, Cam's hand resting on my thigh.

"You want to play any games? Get your very own balloon sword?" Cam asks us and Gracelyn shakes her head 'no.'

"I can't. I have to run and help my mom with the cake-walk. I promised I'd take a shift so she could eat lunch. But I'll catch y'all later?" Gracelyn stands, flipping her curls over her shoulder.

"Yes, absolutely," I say.

"You're staying for the fireworks later, right?"

"I don't know, maybe." I shrug, catching Cam's eye. I'm pretty sure he wants to watch the fireworks out at the lake, but he may be flexible.

"I hope you do." Gracelyn gives both of us a quick hug. "Gotta jet."

She hustles away and we clear the table, collecting our trash.

"I could go for some ice cream. And maybe a game or two." I stare at a kid's colorful double-scoop cone as he walks past. "What do you think?"

"Anything you want, Trouble." He takes my hand and we navigate through the crowd, stopping and saying hi to people along the way.

Eventually, we both get double scoops of ice cream piled high in waffle cones—vanilla and chocolate chip for me, strawberry and banana for Cam. We find a patch of shade beneath a tree and talk and laugh, eating our ice cream in peace, the nasty incident with Dalton all but forgotten.

Afterwards, we play a few games. I'm pretty decent at the ring toss and Cam wins me a huge teddy bear at—surprise, surprise—the football toss.

"That was kind of unfair." I giggle as we walk away from the booth with a huge white stuffed polar bear. "You're a professional, after all."

"So?" Cam shrugs. "Doesn't mean a guaranteed win. Luck's always involved at these things."

"True. Is Mr. Chill going to sleep in between us every night now?"

"Not on my watch. But he can keep you company when I travel."

My chest tightens. Even though I know Cam's going to be away some of the time, the idea still stings.

"Hey—don't be sad, baby. I'll only be gone a night or two. And you can come with me some of the time."

"I know."

"Nothing to worry about now, anyway. I still don't have a team."

"But you will, I'm sure of it." I squeeze his hand encouragingly, but the lighthearted mood from moments ago is heavy now and I hate it.

"You want to go back to your place?" I slide my eyes to his.

"I mean, I wouldn't be opposed. But only if you do. We don't have to leave on my account or anything."

"I know. But I saw Gracelyn, we ate and played games. I think I'm good here."

A slow grin crosses his face and he loops his arm

around my shoulders, pulling me in close and kissing me on the lips.

"Hmm-hmm."

A voice I'd recognize anywhere interrupts us and I hop away from Cam faster than a caffeinated cheetah.

"Hey there, Daddy. Happy Fourth of July."

CHAPTER 31
SLOANE

t was bound to happen sometime. But I wish I could have put that awkward moment off much, much longer.

Say, oh, another half-century or so.

"Hey, baby. Cam." He hugs me and gives Cam a perfunctory nod. "Haven't seen you in a day or two. You still living at the house?"

He's joking—I think—but the delivery falls flat. My dad's a lot of things, but comedian's definitely not one of them.

"Ha ha. Yes, I'm still living at home. I've been working a lot. And so have you," I point out, deflecting. "Cam said the team's looking good."

My dad shrugs. "They're coming along. Especially with so many freshmen coming out this year. But I like our chances."

"We ran into one of your players earlier." I drop my voice so only Cam and my dad can hear. "Dalton. He's kind of a dick."

"Really. What happened?" My dad's brows knit together and he folds his arms over his chest, his stance wide.

"Nothing specific," I hedge. "Just generally kind of rude."

Cam chimes in. "It was fine. But his attitude's not great, that's for sure. Kid thinks he's real hot stuff."

"I can see that." My dad squints in concentration, a deep furrow between his brows. "I like Langley for the spot, not gonna lie. But he's gotta get more accurate. Otherwise I'll have to give it to Dalton."

Cam's fingers curl, knuckles flexing. He takes off his baseball hat, runs his fingers through his hair, puts it back on again. He doesn't give any details, but inside I'm sure he's cringing.

"Hey, Coach." A tall teenage boy with floppy brown hair sidles up to us. Meg from the library trails behind him and I put two and two together. This must be Langley. Meg's son and the kid Cam's working with, the one he really likes.

"Hey, Cam." Langley shoots Cam a friendly wave and Cam's face breaks into a grin.

"What's up, man. Happy Fourth." Cam slaps Langley on the back like he did Nash and there's a real bond there. Unlike with Dalton the dick.

"Hey, Meg." I wave to Langley's mom and she smiles brightly at us.

"Hey, y'all. Happy Fourth of July!" She catches sight of my dad and a light pink blush creeps into the apples of her cheeks.

"Mom, this is Coach. Coach, this is my mom." Langley makes the introduction and Meg blushes harder, a flush creeping up her neck.

"Nice to meet you, Mrs. Langley." My dad tips his ball cap in her direction.

"Oh, it's Ms., not Mrs. But please, call me Meg." She tucks her hair behind her ear and smiles shyly at my dad.

"Okay then, Meg." The corners of my dad's mouth tip up slightly as her name rolls off his lips and he fixes his gaze on her. Tension hangs in the air, but Langley slices right through it.

"Mom, this is Cam, the pro football player I've been telling you about. He's working with me at practice, helping me make plays."

"Great to meet you, Cam." Meg shifts her attention to Cam for a second before cutting her eyes back to my dad. "Thank you both for helping Langley. He's loved playing with y'all. Football's his passion!" Her voice rises on the word 'passion' and Langley cringes, kicking at a patch of grass with his toe.

"Um, yeah." Langley scrubs the back of his neck, the tips of his ears bright red.

"Hopefully he'll get a chance to play this year," Meg says. "Football is what keeps him going, that's for sure!"

He grabs his mom's arm. "Okay, well—good to see you, Coach. Cam. Ms. Carter." He nods at me, hair flopping over his eyes, and I've never felt so old in my life.

"Oh gosh, call me Sloane. Ms. Carter's my grandmother." I laugh.

Langley smiles at that. "Alright. Good to see you, Ms. Sloane."

I guess I'll take it.

"See you at practice next week. Memorize those plays." My dad pats Langley on the back and Langley nods.

"Will do, Coach."

"Bye, y'all." I wave to them and Langley drags his mom away, toward the food trucks.

My dad clears his throat, shoving a hand in his pocket as he watches them retreat.

"She's real nice," I say, following his gaze. "They're good people. Everyone loves her at the library." I do everything but throw in the phrase *hint, hint* here, but my dad doesn't take the bait.

"Good to know. The kid will be a great quarterback with time, I think."

Of course, he turns the conversation around to football. Everything goes back to football, I swear.

"I wasn't really talking about Langley." I elbow my dad and he grimaces. "Meg seemed to like you."

"Pshaw." My dad waves me off. "What are you doing tonight? You staying out for the fireworks?"

Conveniently changing the subject.

I shrug. "Not sure. Probably."

Much as I love my dad, I'd much rather spend the night out at the lake snuggling with Cam than back at home in my childhood bedroom.

"Alright. You two be safe out there tonight. Watch out for drunken pyros."

I shake my head, half-sighing, half-laughing. My dad's apparently always gonna dad, no matter how old I get.

"Will do, Daddy. I'm sure we'll be fine." I give him a quick hug just as Mack waves at him from across the field.

"There's Mack. I'm heading over to his place this afternoon. Gonna catch the baseball game on TV. See you kids later." He waves and strides away to meet Mack.

"Awk-ward," I trill as soon as he's out of earshot.

"A little," Cam admits, lacing his fingers in mine. "But it'll get better. He needs time to get used to the idea is all."

"Maybe...but you know what would really help?"

"What?"

"If my dad started dating someone."

Cam chuckles. "Good luck with that, Trouble. Your dad doesn't seem the least bit interested in dating."

"I don't know about that—" My eyes drift across the field, landing on Meg and Langley. "I'm not giving up on the idea just yet. Even if I have to play matchmaker."

"Oh boy. What could go wrong?" Cam shakes his head, rolling his eyes.

I slug him on the arm. "You doubt my abilities?"

"Nope. I doubt your dad's willing participation."

"Who said he has to be willing? I need to set it up— right place, right time—and then let the magic happen."

Cam laughs. "That should be easy here in Thunder Creek. Where no one ever meddles–"

I crinkle my nose up, frowning. He does have a point.

"How about we table your dad's love life for today and concentrate on ours instead?" Cam snakes his arm around my waist as we head back to the Rover and I relax into him.

"Fine. But the idea's not off the table."

"Okay. But can I make one suggestion?"

"Sure. What?"

"Wait until after football season."

I laugh out loud at this. If anyone knows my dad as well as me, it's Cam.

"Point taken. Dating the coach will be a post-season activity."

———

The rest of the day passes in a picture-perfect blur. We swim in the lake, grill out, and lounge around the house all afternoon, watching rom-coms and various sporting events. Gracelyn texts me around five asking about the fireworks, but I pass on the invite. Right now, I only want to be with Cam. Just the two of us alone together, acting as if the outside world doesn't exist.

The sun eventually sets and we walk out to the dock. Cam sits in one of the Adirondack chairs. I go to sit next to him, but he grabs my hand and pulls me down onto his lap.

"You're too far away over there, Trouble." He nuzzles my neck with his nose and electricity skitters across my skin, down my arm.

I giggle and curl back against his chest, the gentle thud of his heartbeat vibrating my back. The first sparkly firework explodes in the sky and I sigh happily.

Right now, everything is perfect.

Cam peppers the column of my neck with kisses, his tongue licking at the tender skin. Hot pulses throb in my core with each gentle lap and wetness floods my panties. Loud booms sound above us as red, white, and blue fireworks light up the sky.

I shimmy in closer to him and he caresses my calf, up my thigh. Bunching the fabric of my dress in his hands, he lifts my skirt above my hips. The breeze hits my damp panties and I shudder at the sensation, the wind caressing my pussy.

"Lift up your ass," he murmurs, his breath warm at the shell of my ear.

I do as he asks and he slips my panties down my thighs. The satin drops to the dock and now I'm bared to the night.

"Fuck, you're sexy." His fingers trail over my sensitive skin, through my wetness. I bite down on my lip as he slides two fingers into me, his thumb grazing my clit.

"You like that."

It's not a question any longer. Cam knows what I like and how to give it to me.

"Yes," I whisper as he sinks another finger inside, curling to hit my G-spot. "Yesss."

He fingers me, alternating between long and slow and fast and shallow strokes. Keeping me right on the shimmery edge of release, my breath coming in quick pants.

"Cam, I need you." My voice is high and desperate, pleasure building. But it's not enough. I want more.

"What do you need, baby? Tell me."

"I need you inside of me."

"I am inside of you." He nips at my earlobe, teasing me, as my muscles tense and coil.

"I want more."

"What do you want?"

"Your cock, Cam. I want your cock inside of me."

"Ahh. Got it." He pulls his fingers out, and they glisten in the moonlight, wet with my arousal. Sucking them into his mouth, he grins. "Delicious."

I hop out of his lap and he stands, gripping the collar of his shirt and pulling it over his head. Dropping it to the dock, he unzips his shorts and kicks those off as well.

"Commando tonight?" I eye his long, hard length, standing at full mast.

He shrugs. "Figured I might get lucky."

Then he reaches out, gripping my hips and pulling me up against his broad chest. Fireworks explode above us as we kiss on the dock, our tongues clashing and tangling, sliding over one another. One hand finds my ass, slipping beneath my dress and caressing the bare skin. He smacks me lightly, sending a hot pulse straight to my core. I press harder against him, wiggling my ass and he smacks the other side.

"Such a great ass."

His words flow over me like the rush of a waterfall, happiness filling me. I glide my fingers down his muscular chest, over the ridges of his abs and around to his firm ass and squeeze.

"It is a nice one." I smile against his lips and he kisses me hard, thrusting his tongue inside my mouth.

"You drive me wild, Trouble." He squeezes my ass, lifting my skirt. The wind blows cool on my skin.

Then he pulls away, sinking down into the chair. His dick bobs against his stomach as he stares at me with hungry eyes.

"Sit on my cock. Now." His tone is firm, urgent. I brook no argument, straddling him and sinking down onto his length. Slowly, slowly, easing him into my tightness. He groans, watching as his shaft disappears into me, inch by inch.

"Fuck—" he hisses through gritted teeth, shifting beneath me. With rough fingers, he shoves the top of my dress down until my breasts spill out.

"No bra. I like it." Cam palms each of my breasts, thumbing at the nipples until they're diamond-sharp points. He tweaks and pulls and the pain turns to hot bolts of pleasure.

My eyes close and I'm oblivious to everything around me now—the fireworks, the lake, the heat and the breeze all disappear as Cam starts to move inside me. Slow at first, then harder, he thrusts again and again. Working my breasts, my pussy clenches around his steely cock.

"Cam—" I half-moan his name, heady desire coiling in my muscles. Pressure builds inside me, hot sweat slicking my skin as we move together.

"Come for me, baby." His deep voice rumbles and pushes me over the edge. I crash, hard and fast, tingly pleasure racing through me. My body trembles as he explodes inside me, hot cum filling me.

I collapse against his chest, heart hammering as the fireworks grand finale lights up the sky. He strokes my back as I stare up at the show in a blissed-out state, buzzed on love.

"That was amazing," I whisper, tracing the sharp edges of his pecs, his biceps, the long line of his collarbone. "I love you, Cam."

"I know." He grins down at me, a cocky smirk playing on his lips.

I smack him. "I know?"

"I love you too, Sloane." Cupping my chin, he tips my head up and kisses me beneath the stars. Everything about this moment, about right now, is perfect.

CHAPTER 32
CAM

A week after the Fourth, I finally get the call I've been waiting for.

"Pack your bags. I have you booked on the five p.m. flight to Fort Lauderdale." Troy's voice is triumphant, like he won the damn championship game himself.

"What?" I rake my fingers through my hair, hope floating into my chest cavity.

"The head coach wants a meeting first thing tomorrow morning. If that goes well, he's going to have you suit up and join the recruiting camp. So let's think positive and take all our gear with us, huh?"

"Yeah, of course." I lean against the marble island and stare out at the placid lake, my mind swirling.

Fort Lauderdale might want me.

Not a great team, but good enough. Plus, the weather's decent. A little hot, maybe, but that's preferable to icy.

And it's close to Thunder Creek.

Shit. I need this to work out.

"Troy, does the coach know everything?" Tension settles at the base of my neck, my jaw tight as I wait for his answer.

"Yeah. I've been upfront with every team I've pitched. Last thing we need is you wasting your damn time, getting to the one-yard-line and then having them pull out."

Relief seeps through me and my muscles loosen a touch. If the head coach knows about the video and is still interested, I have a real shot at making the team. Especially after working with Coach Carter all summer.

"I'll shoot you the flight details."

"Sounds good, thanks."

"Crawford?"

"Yeah?"

"Don't fuck this up. No pressure, but this could be your last chance."

"Wow, thanks for the vote of confidence."

"I'm sure you'll do great. But I wouldn't be doing my job if I wasn't honest with you. I've talked to almost every team in the league. This is about as good as it's going to get."

"Got it, boss. I'll play like I already have four championship rings, how about that?"

"Perfect. And keep your pants on. Zero scandals."

"Ouch. It was a one-time thing, Troy. You know that." I don't love talking about the video and hate that he brings it up every damn time—even if it is his job.

"Let's keep it that way. Go down there, catch the football, fly like a motherfucking raptor and win yourself that spot."

"Consider it done." I disconnect, tossing the cell onto the counter with a clatter.

Anxiety churns in my gut. Coupled with the buzz of

adrenaline, I'm nauseous and I haven't even left Thunder Creek yet.

Get your shit together, Crawford. You've got this.

My phone rattles against the marble and I grab it with a sinking feeling. Troy's already calling to cancel.

"Hey, babe. It's me." Sloane's melodic voice trills down the line and I take a relieved breath. "Gracelyn wants us to get drinks with her on Friday at Mustang's. You up for it? Or do you want me to make it a girls' night?"

"I was about to call you. I just got off the phone with my agent."

"Wait, what?"

"I have an interview and possible tryout tomorrow. If it goes well, I'll have training camp with the team for at least a week."

"Cam! That's amazing!" She screams so loud the phone shakes against my ear. "Which team?"

"Fort Lauderdale."

"Oh. Well, at least that's pretty close."

"I know. This could be really good."

A long beat passes and I'm not sure what else to say. Finally, Sloane speaks.

"I'm going to miss you."

"I know, baby. Me too. But I'll be back. Either way."

She sniffles and I wonder if she's crying. My chest squeezes hard and I'm caught off guard. I never worried about traveling before, never disliked it. I kind of looked forward to the away games, seeing other stadiums and places.

This emotional stuff is new for me and I don't love it.

"When do you leave?" Her voice is soft.

"Tonight. Five p.m. flight."

"That's three hours from now. I can't even drive you to

the airport because I'm working and I'm running the book club."

"That's okay. I'll park at the airport, no big deal."

"I won't get to kiss you goodbye and good luck." She sounds so sad. The enthusiasm about the interview drains from my body and all I want to do is hold Sloane, kiss her and make it better.

But I definitely cannot do that right now. Like Troy said, I cannot fuck this up. This is my last chance to make it back.

"It's fine, Trouble. I'll be back before you know it. Good luck at book club."

"Thanks," she whispers, forlorn.

"Listen, I have to pack. I'll call you when I land."

"Okay. Cam?"

"Yeah?"

"I love you. Good luck. You'll be great, I know it."

"I love you, too. Bye, baby."

I disconnect, a sharp pang in my chest terrifyingly close to my heart. But I shove that aside and hustle up the stairs two at a time to pack.

Thirty minutes later, I'm running through my pre-game checklist in my head:

- Mouthguard: check
- Cleats: check
- Toothbrush: check
- Charger: check
- All my other shit: check

Shoving socks and underwear into my suitcase, I zip up the bag and wheel out of the bedroom without a backward glance. I grab my wallet and keys, then lock up the house behind me and race out to the Rover.

If I hurry, I can swing by the library and say bye to Sloane.

Throwing the car in reverse, I zoom out of the driveway and down the gravel road, white puffs of dust swirling behind me. I floor the gas and push the Rover as fast as I dare, all the while watching for cops.

Ten minutes later, I'm in town and let up on the speed. I make a hard right into the library parking lot and slam into the first open spot I find. I need to make this quick, but I couldn't leave town without seeing her.

I jog through the glass doors, heading straight to the Children's Department. But she's not behind the desk. Scanning the stacks, I don't see her anywhere.

Book Club.

Sloane's running the Romance Book Club right now. Obviously not in the Children's Department.

I pivot and head back to the front desk. There's a line and the woman in front of me has at least twenty books. That's gotta be the library maximum.

Abandoning this strategy, I stride through the quiet rooms, searching for the book club. Laughter spills from one of the conference rooms in the back and I follow the happy noises.

And there's Sloane, sitting at the top of a circle of women —most of them gray-haired—a slight pink flush on her dewy skin. She's absolutely radiant. I want to stand here and watch her in her element all day, but I do not have time for that.

Ms. Mabel glances up and catches sight of me and she elbows Sloane. Sloane's eyes lift to mine and widen, her mouth forming a perfect 'O.'

"Cam! Are you here for the book club?" Ms. Mabel asks, waving me over to the circle.

"I'm afraid not, ma'am. I'm headed out to the airport. May I borrow Sloane for one quick second?"

"Certainly. Ladies, let's chat about that part when he meets her family." Ms. Mabel flips through her book, searching for the part while discreetly nudging Sloane out of her chair.

Sloane doesn't hesitate, hopping up and hurrying over, taking me by the arm and leading me away from the group.

"Cam! I didn't think you'd have time to stop in." Up close, her eyes shimmer in the fluorescent lights.

"I don't. But I couldn't leave town without saying bye." I trail my finger down her jawline. "And I love you."

Dipping down, I brush my lips against hers softly. A tiny mewl sounds low in her throat and I wish we had more time.

"I love you too." She wraps her arms around my neck, kissing me deeper. I inhale her sweet scent and all her goodness, trying to memorize every curve and line.

"I'll miss you. But I'll be back soon." I swallow hard over my dry throat, run my thumb across her lower lip.

She presses her palm to my chest, resting her hand over my heart. "Promise?"

"Promise." I kiss her one last time, long and hard, before pulling away. "I'll call you."

Then I jog out of the library, praying there's no traffic, an open parking spot, and the security line moves with some semblance of speed because I cannot afford to miss this flight.

CHAPTER 33
SLOANE

Cam's gone and I miss him so much it hurts.

I miss talking to him, laughing with him.

Miss the way he smells after a shower, his smile when he rolls over and sees me first thing in the morning. Like he's pleasantly surprised to find me there.

Miss the taste of him on my lips, the touch of his hands on my skin, the way he takes me up to the highest peak and then falls over the edge with me, crashing together.

The day he leaves, Gracelyn and I hit up the Burger Basket, but all I can think about is the night Cam and I came here after the bonfire. How much fun we had together and how I wish he was with me now.

At work, a kid says something funny and my first reaction is to pick up my phone and text Cam.

But then I text Gracelyn instead. Because Cam's busy at practice and I know how badly he wants—needs—this job.

After one full day of mooning about, I can't take it any longer. I throw myself into my own life with abandon—anything to avoid the misery that is missing Cam.

I pick up extra shifts at the library, add bonus story times to the calendar, and hang out with Gracelyn every free second she has. I keep myself occupied and spend a lot of time watching ESPN with my dad.

Nights are the toughest. There are no people, no activities to distract me.

In the quiet stillness, I lay in my bedroom staring at the ceiling and wonder what Cam's doing.

He's so busy, we hardly get a chance to talk. Every morning he texts me on the way to practice, but the messages are short. He's in the zone and I know how critical that is for him right now.

Still, there are a million things I want to ask him.

How's Fort Lauderdale? Have you seen the beach?

How's the team? Did you make any friends yet?

What's the coach like?

But most of all—*do you think you'll make the team? Are you leaving Thunder Creek for good?*

That's the real question hovering on my lips every time we do get a chance to talk. But I don't say it, don't bring up the future and all the different scenarios.

Because a part of me doesn't want to know. I'm too afraid he'll say it's over. It was good while it lasted, but he's moving on.

Without me.

I should trust what he says and not worry. But the warning bell in my head—the same one I silenced with Ratface—is dinging. And that sound gets a little louder each day Cam's away.

Buzz, buzz.

My hand flies to the nightstand and I fumble around for my cell. The room's pitch dark, so it must be late.

The screen lights up with Cam's face, a cute pic of us

on the dock at sunset. An ache throbs in my chest as I tap the phone.

"Hello?" My voice is low and scratchy from being alone in the quiet.

"Did I wake you?" Cam's deep voice tickles my ear and hot desire rushes through me, every inch of me burning for him.

"No. I'm not sleeping yet."

"How are you?"

"Lonely. I miss you."

"Aww, me too, Trouble. Only a couple more days, though, and I should be back."

"Really?" I pull at a loose thread on my pj's, feeling a little lighter.

"That's what it's looking like. Can't say for sure, but that seems like the plan. I think Coach is gonna make me an offer."

"That's great." I force enthusiasm into my voice, knowing that an offer's the best thing for Cam. Football's his life.

"How do you feel about Florida?"

The back of my neck prickles and I sit up in bed. "What?"

"Florida. How do you feel about it?"

"What do you mean? Like, the beaches? Disney World? What are we talking about here?"

"Fort Lauderdale. Moving here. With me."

I suck in a breath, my heart pounding into hyperdrive. "You want me to move to Florida with you?"

"I mean, yeah. If you want to. There are a few logistics to work out when I get the contract and we'd have to find a place—"

A place. Singular.

Cam wants me to move in with him.

Every nerve in my body hums to life and I feel lighter than I have in days. "Yes! But I wouldn't have a job right away, I'd need to find one. Doubt my dad will be too thrilled about that…"

"You wouldn't need a job, not unless you want one. I make enough for both of us."

"Oh, right."

I do low-key love my job at the library. But I love Cam more.

"You don't have to decide anything right now. I didn't get offered a contract yet. But I wanted to float the idea out there."

"I love the idea."

Be careful, Sloane.

Those darn warning bells again, clanging. Always clanging.

Is this how I'm going to operate from now on? Because I hate feeling this way, torn and indecisive when I should be ecstatic.

"Good. Because I really miss you. I want to be together all the time. I want you at all my games, want you there in the morning when I wake up, want you there at night, riding my hard cock—" His voice turns husky and my body responds, chill bumps rising on my skin.

"I want that too, Cam."

"Good. I miss you so much, baby."

"Me too."

Beep, beep.

Cam has another call.

"Sloane, I'm sorry, but I gotta take this. It's Troy. Want me to call you back?"

"No, it's late. You need to get some sleep so you can be ready for practice tomorrow. I love you."

"I love you too, baby."

With that, he disconnects and I toss the cell down on the sheets.

I should be happy right now. The man I love asked me to move in with him, take the next very serious, very real step in our relationship.

Too bad all I hear is Negative Nancy, cautioning me.

You're doing the same thing you did with Ratface—and look how that turned out.

But Cam isn't Ratface.

He's not a lying, cheating, narcissist, roaming around in search of his next conquest. I'm not disposable to Cam. What we have is real and pure.

Deep down, I know he's different.

Doesn't stop me from worrying, though.

A million what-ifs race through my head:

What if I hate Florida?

What if Cam changes his mind? About me? About us?

What if my dad's right about love and people don't stay?

This last thought's the most depressing of all.

But it can't be true.

Cam loves me and I know that, feel it every time we talk, touch, kiss. Feel it when he sends me a funny meme, or lets me pick the movie even though I'm sure it's not what he would choose.

This is good.

Everything is great and I'm making the right choice.

"Alexa, play ocean waves." The sound of waves fills my bedroom and I close my eyes, picturing Cam and me walking the white, sandy beach down in Fort Lauderdale.

Finally, I drift off to sleep.

CHAPTER 34
SLOANE

"Come on, Sloane. You need to go out tonight. I know you miss Cam, but I can't in good conscience let you sit at home with your dad and Mack watching ESPN reruns on a Friday night. It's not healthy." Gracelyn crosses her arms over her chest and taps her foot on the worn library carpet, two telltale signs she isn't taking no for an answer. Not tonight.

"Fine," I sigh, giving in. "I'll go to Mustang's, but only for one drink." She does have a solid point about the ESPN reruns, which don't sound appealing. Plus, I haven't told her about Cam's proposition yet—I wanted to have the convo in person.

"Yeah!" She claps her hands, then runs her fingers through my ponytail. "Can I do your hair for you? A blowout? Maybe soft curls?"

"Don't push it." I shoot her a warning glare. "I'm getting one drink, not picking up a new man. How about we concentrate all our efforts on you?"

Gracelyn huffs out a breath. "What for? You and I both

know there's not one single guy left to date in Thunder Creek. I've lived here my whole damn life and run through most of them. Plus, you already snagged the most eligible bachelor in town."

Damn, another good point. She's full of them today.

"Fine. How about we go and enjoy each other's company then? Spend some time polishing up your online dating profile."

"Waste of time. Maybe we can convince Mike to let us take over DJ duties and play good music for once."

The chance of that happening is about as likely as me letting Gracelyn give me a makeover, but I hold back that comment.

"Sure. Meet at Mustang's at eight?"

"No, I'll pick you up. That way you for sure can't bail on me." She gives me a knowing look. "See you later!"

With a quick squeeze of my arm, she spins and sashays out of the library. The rest of my shift flies by. I restock all the books on the cart, finish rereading the next book club selection—my personal favorite, *Pride and Prejudice*—and tidy up the Reference desk for Ms. Mabel. As soon as the clock hits six p.m., I tuck in my chair and skip out of the quiet building to the parking lot.

I'd never admit it to Gracelyn, but I'm kind of glad she talked me into going out. Spending yet another night at home with my dad sounds downright depressing.

Buzz, buzz.

Cam: Hey, Trouble. You still at work?

Sloane: No, just finished. How are you?
Did you get the contract?!?

Cam: Not yet. I have a meeting with the Coach and the GM tonight

Sloane: Sounds promising. What's your agent saying?

Cam: He thinks it's good news

Sloane: YESSSS!

Cam: I know. I've been searching for rentals. What do you think about this one?

A link pops up and I click it, photos of a gorgeous high-rise overlooking the Atlantic Ocean filling my screen.

I'm in love.

Sloane: CAM—that's amazing

Cam: Good, glad you like it

Cam: If I get an offer, we can check it out

Cam: Assuming you're still in...

Sloane: Absolutely. I haven't told my dad yet

The three text bubbles swirl, then disappear, then swirl again. I stare at the screen, waiting. Finally, Cam replies.

Cam: Want me to talk to him?

Sloane: That's sweet of you, but it'll be better coming from me. Thanks though

Cam: Okay, babe. Whatever you need,
I'm there

My chest squeezes as I read his words.

Whatever you need, I'm there.

This is the Cam I know and love. He's back in his element and everything's coming together for him.

For us.

Sloane: I love you

Cam: I love you too

Cam: Ok, babe. I gotta jet and get ready
for dinner

Cam: Miss you

Sloane: Miss you too. Call me as soon as
you finish with the coach!

Cam: Will do

Sloane: XOXO

Cam: xoxo

I toss my cell into the passenger seat and drive home, belting out every word of Taylor Swift's "End Game" on the way.

Cam's my end game. I've never felt surer of anything in my life—or been happier.

————

Mustang's is bumping when Gracelyn and I stroll in. All

the high tops are taken, and the booths flanking the walls are filling up, too.

"The bar!" Gracelyn shouts over the loud country music, something by Kane Brown with a fast beat and a lot of bass.

I link fingers with her and we traverse the crowd, scooting in between tables and various groups of people waiting for a seat. We finally make it to the bar, but the scene's not much better here.

"Damn, Grace—you should have opened a bar instead of working at the salon. Seems like Thunder Creek needs another hot spot." I glance up and down the long, wood bar, trying to find at least one empty stool.

Spying an empty barstool at the far end, I drag Gracelyn hard to the left, practically jogging to grab the last two red pleather seats.

"Sit!" I pat the stool and Gracelyn slides up onto the chair, triumphant.

"Good eye, Sloane." She high-fives me before turning and squinting up at the drink menu scrawled on a chalkboard. "What are you drinking?"

"Not tequila." My stomach swirls at the mere mention of the liquor.

Gracelyn giggles. "I don't know, results recommend that drink."

"Funny. But no, thank you. I'm not sure I'll ever drink tequila again."

"What'll it be, ladies?" A young guy in a tight T-shirt and even tighter jeans saunters up to take our order.

"I'll have white wine." I point to an open bottle behind the bar. "That one works."

"Gotcha. What about you?" The bartender turns his dark eyes on Gracelyn and she gnaws at her lip, debating.

"Oh, what the hell. It's Friday night. I'll take a tequila on the rocks, with a lime." She glances over at me. "Since it worked so well for you."

"Nice." The bartender gives Grace an approving nod, his gaze lingering on her ample chest before getting to work on the drinks.

Two minutes later, he slides a tall glass of wine and the tequila across the bar on black cocktail napkins.

"Cheers." He shoots Grace a smirk and a tip of the chin before moving off to take another order.

I take a sip of wine and sneak a peek at my cell. No messages.

"You waiting on a call from Cam? That's like the thousandth time you've checked your phone tonight." Grace thumps her fingers on the bar in time with the thumping beat.

"Yeah. He's probably getting an offer tonight."

"What? That's amazing! With Fort Lauderdale?"

I nod. "Yep. Camp's been going great and the coach really likes him. Said he'll be an asset for the offense, the missing piece."

"That's super, babe!" Gracelyn smiles at me, her eyes bright beneath the neon glow of the *Drink Beer Here* sign on the wall.

"I know. I'm happy for him."

"What does that mean for y'all, though? He's leaving Thunder Creek again then, right?"

"Yes, he'll be moving down there." I take another quick sip, the sharp tang burning my throat on the way down. "And he asked me to go with him."

"Wha-what?" Gracelyn sputters on her drink, tiny droplets of clear liquid splattering the bar. She wipes the corner of her mouth, then the wooden countertop. "You're moving with him?"

I bite down on my lip, the bass shaking the stool beneath me. "I think so. I mean, we're still working out the logistics. He doesn't have a contract yet. So I haven't gotten my hopes up or anything."

"Ohmygod, Sloane! That's still huge news for you two!" She squeezes my arm and smiles, but it doesn't reach all the way to her eyes.

"Aww, babe. Don't be sad."

"I'm not. I mean, I am because I love having my bestie back home. But moving to Florida to be with your man? Understandable. I'd move too. In a freaking heartbeat."

A weight lifts off my chest, knowing she's speaking the truth. I'd be out of my mind if I turned down a chance to move in with Cam. A gorgeous professional football player who adores me? Yeah, there's only one right answer here.

"Have you told your dad?" Gracelyn rattles the ice in her almost-empty drink.

"No. You're the first person I've said anything to. I don't want to jinx it, you know? And there's no use getting into it with my dad over a possibility. I'm waiting until the offer's a reality before I go there."

"Girl, knowing you, you'll wait until the moving truck's in the driveway." She nudges my elbow and I laugh.

"True."

The bartender wanders over and leans across the bar in Grace's direction, his biceps flexing and straining the fabric of his T-shirt.

"You ladies want a refill?" He cocks his dark brow at Grace's empty glass.

"Sure, why not?" She flashes him a smile and he licks

his lips, swooping across the bar and snatching up her glass.

"What about you?" He reaches for my wine glass.

"I don't know—it's already kind of late."

"Ohmygod, Sloane, it's not even nine pm yet. Live a little! Besides, I might not have too many more nights out with my bestie."

"Fine. One more drink. But that's it."

The bartender tips the wine bottle, filling my glass almost to the tippy-top. He pours Grace another tequila and squeezes a lime into the glass, then slides the drinks over the bar and winks.

As soon as he's out of earshot, I lean over to Grace. "He's kind of cute."

She shakes her blonde curls. "He's barely out of school, Sloane. Way too young for me."

"You're the one who told me I can't be too picky, to broaden my horizons. Maybe you need to take your own advice."

"Maybe…I'm more into the older guys now anyway. Stable, established. I've had to pay for one too many dates."

"I hear that."

"At least you won't have to worry about that with Cam. Gawd, I need to head home and start randomly emailing men."

I throw my head back and laugh. "It wasn't exactly random. And I wouldn't recommend that approach. I tried to recall the email, but I am glad I couldn't figure it out."

"Hey, Sloane. Grace." Jamie slides up to the bar with a martini in hand, her assets perfectly displayed in a black satin cami and tight jeans. She jockeys for the stool next to mine, practically tapping the guy's ass as he vacates the seat.

"Hey, Jamie." Grace greets her cooly, pressing her glossy lips tight. I nod in her direction, but don't smile.

And this is why I wanted to stay home tonight.

It's nearly impossible to go out in Thunder Creek without running into someone you know. And in this case, I'm not exactly dying to sit here and shoot the breeze with one of Cam's old flings.

"Cam's not here with you?" Jamie's scarlet hair shimmers under the pendant lights as she searches around for Cam. "I heard the two of you are together now. Finally, huh?" She runs her finger around the rim of her glass, staring at me.

"We are." I clip out the words, not bothering to acknowledge the jab. "And he's not here tonight. He's out of town."

I take a sip of wine and try to stay calm. Nothing good will come from me getting in a fight with this woman. The less I engage with her, the better.

"It's so sweet how trusting you are. With him being a pro football player and all. A man that good-looking's bound to get into a little trouble every now and again." She arches a carefully penciled brow high, feigning concern for me.

"Cam? No way, Jamie. He and Sloane are serious," Gracelyn hops in, defending me.

"I'm just saying. A red-blooded guy like that, so masculine, strong, and virile. A man like that has needs, you know?" She takes a sip of her drink, leaving a dark red lipstick stain on the rim. "If it were me, I'd be worried."

Wine swirls in my stomach and nausea washes over

me. I wipe my clammy palms over the thighs of my jeans and try not to panic.

What's she talking about?

Jamie's kohl-rimmed eyes grow wide, her thick fringe of lashes fluttering at me. "Oh. Bless your heart. You don't know, do you? You haven't seen the video."

A sick, sinking feeling rolls over me and sweat beads at my hairline on the back of my neck.

"What are you talking about, Jamie?" Grace huffs out, exasperated.

Jamie slides her cell out of her leopard-print clutch, tapping the screen to life. Three quick clicks later, she's offering the phone to me. I take it with shaky hands, acid rising in my throat.

The date in the corner of the video flashes—three days ago.

Cam was in Fort Lauderdale three days ago.

The quality of the video's grainy and amateur, the angle not the best. Two women wearing lacy lingerie and heels walk across a dimly lit room with floor-to-ceiling windows and a twinkling city skyline. A bright light shines in the corner, throwing shadows across the floor. Low, deep voices rumble off-camera, directing the women to take off their clothes. Nervous giggles, then both women remove their bras and panties until they're wearing only sky-high heels. Appreciative murmurs and wolf whistles screech through the speaker of the phone and a naked man steps toward the women.

Not Cam.

A tiny shot of cool relief rushes through me. Cam's not with these women, fondling their breasts as they laugh and smile at the camera. Still, my chest tightens as I watch the scene. I feel Jamie's stare over my shoulder and I don't dare turn around.

I want to click out of this, preserve my innocent perceptions. But I can't stop watching, drawn to the images on my screen.

The women flip their long hair, rubbing against the naked man as he kisses full breasts, then motions at someone to join him. A second man comes into view, pulling his shirt over his head. He's wearing boxer briefs, his large erection bulging in the tight material. He lifts one of the women up and she straddles him, wrapping her legs around his muscular back. There's more laughter and talking, then naked guy number one chugs straight from an open champagne bottle. The blonde opens her lips wide and he spits the bubbly into her mouth, closing her jaw and tipping her head back, forcing her to swallow. She makes a big show of it, touching her breasts and swiveling her hips. The guy smacks her round ass and she squeals.

"For fuck's sake, Jamie. Cam's not on this video," Gracelyn snaps, scowling at Jamie.

"Keep watching." Jamie motions at the cell.

Guy number two backs out of view, the brunette woman kissing him as they presumably move to the bed.

Then a familiar voice sounds from off-camera, directing the blonde to get on her hands and knees.

My stomach drops, my heart sinking even as my core clenches like a freaking Pavlovian dog. Trained to respond to that deep, commanding voice. The same voice that's brought me to orgasm hundreds of times.

It's Cam's voice, although he's still not on camera. The blonde's eyes go wide, but she drops to her knees and puts her palms on the floor before licking her plump lips.

"Crawl to him." Naked guy number one gestures over

his shoulder, and I assume he's pointing to Cam. The blonde does as she's told, her narrow hips swaying back and forth, ass high in the air as she inches along the wood floor. The camera jostles as it's repositioned to face an oversized bed. The brunette and guy number two are having sex in the background and there's Cam, standing in front of the bed. The woman's crawling toward him and naked guy one saunters over, slapping the blonde's bare ass.

I stare at the screen, a bitter taste in my mouth.

No, this can't be real.

Cam wouldn't cheat on me.

And surely he wouldn't be so stupid, so naïve, to *film* something like this. To create video fucking evidence of his betrayal.

I want to erase the video, scrub the images from Jamie's phone, the web. But most of all, from my memory.

But I can't.

The blonde reaches up and pulls at Cam's pants and that's all I can handle.

I mash the pause button with a shaky hand, eyes burning, my breathing rapid and shallow. Hot tears prick behind my eyes and I slam the cell down on the bar.

I can't watch.

Can't see Cam with another woman, watch as his hands glide over her skin, his lips touch her body.

Shoving away from the bar, I push through the crowd, dodging drinks and elbows. I need to get out of here. Away from all the people, away from Jamie and the torrid sex video.

Away from the hot shame and humiliation.

"Sloane! Wait!" Gracelyn's voice carries over the

thumping bass as I run through the doors and spill out into the parking lot.

I've never been more embarrassed, more humiliated, in my entire life.

Everyone in town—hell, the world—probably knows about this besides me and Gracelyn.

How could Cam do this to me? All this time, I thought he was special, that we were special.

That we were a team.

Turns out, he's just like every other guy.

CHAPTER 35
CAM

Dinner's fantastic. The general manager and head coaches take my agent and me to a fancy five-star restaurant, wining and dining us in a swanky private room. Waiters serve course after course, so many courses I can't remember them all. Aged cheeses and Wagyu beef, vintage Cabernet Sauvignon and organic produce grown on-site. And the best part? For dessert, they present me with a three-year contract.

We seal the deal over baked Alaska and I can finally breathe again. The Chicago nightmare's over and done with, never to be spoken of again. I'm moving forward with my life and my career's back on track.

I can't wait to call Sloane.

She's the first person I want to talk to, to tell the good news. I'm grinning like a Cheshire cat all the way back to the hotel, so hard my face hurts. I'm pumped and barely make it out of the elevator before I'm dialing her number.

Ring, ring. Ring, ring. Ring, ring.

No answer.

It's only ten pm, I doubt she's sleeping.

I try again, then again. One more time, finally leaving a message.

"Babe. It's me and I have news. Call me back." I disconnect, staring out the window at the moonlit ocean.

I shoot her a text.

Cam: Where r u? Tried to call

Cam: I have great news

Cam: Call me

The messages go through, but no response. I thought for sure she'd at least respond to my texts.

A nagging feeling tugs at my gut, worry snaking through my veins. I hope she's okay.

Relax, Cam. She's in Thunder Creek, living with Coach. Nothing happened to her.

Still, I click on her icon, tracking her phone location. The map shows her blinking blue dot stationary at her house. Maybe she really is asleep.

I pace the room, debating what to do.

Should I call Coach?

Not a terrible idea, but he probably is asleep and I hate to wake him.

Gracelyn? That's a better idea.

Before I go calling every person Sloane knows, I give her one more ring.

This time, the call goes straight to voicemail.

"Dammit!" I toss the cell on the bed in frustration.

Where is she? Sloane always has her phone and answers

on the first ring or two. And she never leaves a text unanswered. That's not like her at all.

Now I really am worried.

I slip out of my blazer and toss it onto the bed, undo the top button of my shirt. I guess I'll call Gracelyn.

Blowing out a breath, I scroll through my contacts until I find her name. I hit the number and wait for Sloane's best friend to answer.

I don't have to wait long. She picks up on the second ring.

"You motherfucker!" Gracelyn shrieks, so loud the speaker of my phone rattles. "How could you do this to her?"

"Gracelyn?" I scrunch my brow, trying to make sense of her reaction.

"Yeah, it's me, Cam. You're a grade-A asshole. Worse than Ratface."

"Uh—" I falter, wondering exactly what I've done to offend her.

"Don't play dumb with me, Cam! We saw the video."

A yawning pit opens in my stomach and the five-star cuisine from earlier in the evening knots and roils into a massive, hard ball of indigestion.

Fuck.

"What? Who? What are you talking about?"

"Sloane, you jerk. Sloane saw your sex video, Cam. Even worse, Jamie's the one who showed it to her."

I can't breathe my chest's so tight. This is bad. Really fucking bad.

You should have told Sloane the truth.

"Is Sloane with you, Gracelyn? I need to talk to her."

If I can explain myself, maybe this nightmare will fade away.

There's murmuring and muffled sounds, Gracelyn covering the receiver so I can't hear the conversation.

"She is, but she's in the bathroom. Vomiting, Cam, because that video made her physically sick!" Gracelyn's voice shakes with rage and I squeeze my eyes shut, suddenly woozy.

I really fucked things up.

"Please, Gracelyn. I need to talk to her."

"No way, Cam. Maybe later. I gotta go." She disconnects, but not before I hear the distinct sound of retching in the background.

I made Sloane sick.

She's literally throwing up over what I did, how I behaved.

Hot shame rushes over me, washing away all the excitement of the contract, the fresh start. My palms itch and I'm twitchy. I want to go to Sloane right now. Hold her hand and explain. Tell her how sorry I am. About that night, about everything.

But I can't leave Fort Lauderdale tonight. I have one more meeting with the team tomorrow morning and I can't afford to miss it. Details still need to be hammered out, I's dotted and T's crossed. Too much hangs in the balance for me to leave now.

"Fuck!" I punch the fluffy stack of oversized pillows, rage surging down my arm straight into the feathers. Hitting the pillows again and again, I pound until my knuckles chafe and burn.

One night.

Too much alcohol and a stupid, rash decision. One that keeps coming back to haunt me.

I have to make Sloane understand, forgive me.

The possibility of losing football almost crushed me, hurt so bad I wasn't sure I'd survive.

But losing Sloane?

This is worse. Impossibly worse, knowing I hurt the one person who's always believed in me, no matter what.

A heavy pain settles on my chest and I sink to the floor, burying my face in my palms. *How could everything go so wrong, so fast?*

CHAPTER 36
SLOANE

Gracelyn holds my hair back while I vomit into the toilet, every morsel I ingested over the last twenty-fours emptying from my stomach.

"Breathe, Sloane. It's okay, it's okay." She repeats the mantra over and over again. Like if she keeps saying it, I'll believe her and everything will miraculously turn out fine.

Like none of this ever happened.

But I know better.

Things are not okay. I'm not okay.

Images of those women—busty and beautiful—having sex with Cam's teammates. With Cam. I can't unsee them. The mile-high stilettos, all the curves, the things they were doing with each other.

The X-rated scene out in the universe, for everyone to see.

This is worse than what happened with Ratface. At least only the office and a few mutual friends knew about that.

Cam cheated on me—and there's video evidence. Everyone in the whole wide world will know.

I'm humiliated once again and this time on a freaking global scale.

But that's not even the worst part.

The worst part is he broke my heart. Smashed it into a million pieces, then ran over it with a tank.

The first chance he got to leave town, he cheated on me. With multiple women.

He treated me like I was nothing to him. Like we were nothing.

I'm not enough for Cam. I never was.

I'm boring old good girl Sloane.

Nothing will be the same for Cam and me again.

He's not who I thought he was. *We're* not what I thought we were. Not if he could do this to me.

Jamie's trilling voice echoes in my head: *"Bless your heart."*

That smug expression, the smirk on her ruby red lips.

She sat in waiting, like a lioness stalking her prey. Waited for the chance to swoop in and ruin things.

Maybe she did you a favor.

I vomit one more time, a burning sensation from my gut all the way up through my throat.

"Sloane, you want me to stay the night?" Gracelyn rubs my back as I dry heave, the contents of my stomach now depleted.

Wiping my mouth with the back of my hand, I rise gingerly from the tile floor. My knees ache and I'm weak from puking my guts out. I clutch at the vanity and shake my head.

"You have clients in the morning. I'll be okay." My voice is raspy and unconvincing.

"I can cancel them. I feel like I shouldn't leave you alone."

She stares at me with such pity my eyes prick with tears.

"No. Go home. I'll be fine."

Throwing her arms around me, she wraps me in a tight hug. The tears well and sparkle in my lashes, threatening to fall. But I don't want to cry, not right now in front of Gracelyn. I need to be alone.

"I love you. We'll make it through this." Gracelyn squishes me harder and my nose stings as I fight back tears. "Okay, let's get you into bed before I go."

She waits while I brush my teeth, scrubbing the acid from my cottony mouth. Then she leads me to my bedroom like a child, insisting I undress and put on pj's. I protest, but she's having none of it.

Finally, she pulls back the covers on my bed and tucks me in, moonlight streaming through the slats of my blinds.

"There. Snug as a bug in a rug. I'll call you tomorrow first thing. And if you need anything—anything at all—call me. Doesn't matter the time, just call."

"Okay," I mumble.

"Promise?"

"Yes, I promise."

"Night." She pats my arm and I'm relieved it's dark because the tears finally win, spilling onto my cheeks.

Grace tiptoes out and I stare up at the popcorn ceiling, sniffling like a baby. Every inch of my body aches and I'm honestly not sure if I'm going to survive this.

Walking in on Ratface and his secretary was debasing. Calling off the wedding was mortifying.

But this?

One million times worse.

I loved Cam and he let me down so hard it's like I dove out of a jet headfirst at 14,000 feet without a parachute. Crashing to the ground and shattering. All because of him and his cheating ways.

The nightstand rattles and my cell lights up, but I don't have the strength to reach out and answer. One, two, three rings, then silence as the call goes to voicemail.

Then the ping of a text.

Still, I can't bring myself to look, frozen beneath the sheets.

I have nothing to say right now.

I just want to be alone.

Quite possibly forever.

CHAPTER 37
CAM

After calling Sloane no less than six times and sending twice that many texts, I give up and go to bed. Unfortunately, the effort is futile and I sleep a sum total of zero minutes, tossing and turning all damn night.

When dawn breaks, I lumber out and hit the hotel gym, pushing myself harder than I have in a while. I run five quick miles on the treadmill at eighty percent effort, then rep out my usual strength workout until I'm drenched in sweat.

The workout doesn't help—I still feel shitty, the endorphin rush failing to improve my mood. But I don't have a lot of time to sit around and mope. I need to lock down that contract, so at least I have a damn job.

I shower, then throw on a button-down and khakis. A quick glance at my reflection, dark circles shadowing my eyes, and I pray the coaches won't change their minds.

The meeting goes fine and Troy does what Troy does

best, working his magic and getting the new contract signed, sealed, and delivered.

"Congrats, buddy." Troy slaps me on the back and I force a smile, my empty stomach rolling.

"Welcome to Fort Lauderdale." The head coach extends his hand and I shake it, trying to focus on this moment and be present. This is what I worked for all my life, what I've been busting my ass for under the blazing south Georgia sun all summer long.

Yet a victory's never felt more hollow.

Still, I make the rounds, glad-handing all the important people, making nice with the GM. I exchange the necessary information with HR, then get fitted for my helmet and uniform. Finally, I have a schedule in hand with a start date.

I'm due back here in less than ten days.

I should spend time finding somewhere to live, scoping out the decent neighborhoods, talking to my new team-mates about traffic and the commute to the stadium.

Instead, I say my goodbyes and call an Uber as fast as humanly possible without seeming rude. I head straight to the airport and hop on the first flight back to Georgia.

Settling into my seat, I pull my ball cap low over my eyes and tap out one more text to Sloane, praying she'll respond.

> Cam: I'm on my way back. We need to talk

I stare at the screen, willing the three swirling bubbles to appear. But only my own words glare up at me, taunting me.

She hates you. She's never going to forgive you.

The flight attendant at the front of the cabin makes the announcement: "Flight 1754 is now ready for departure. Please make sure your seat back is in the upright position and turn off all large electronics, switching cell phones to airplane mode in preparation for takeoff."

Powering down my phone, I shove it into the pocket of my joggers and close my eyes. There's nothing I can do for the next hour except figure out what exactly I'm going to say to earn Sloane's forgiveness.

———

After landing, I head straight to Thunder Creek. I don't bother calling or texting Sloane again, figuring she won't respond anyway.

Instead, I track her location and drive over to the library. Her Volvo's one of the few cars still in the lot. I cut the engine and thump the leather steering wheel. She gets off work in less than twenty minutes. I don't want to risk a big scene in front of Ms. Mabel and/or Langley's mom.

So I wait, every square inch of me twitchy with nerves.

The anticipation's worse than any tryout. At least then I was sure of myself, in control. This is a whole different situation. I have no idea what Sloane's thinking, how she's feeling. For all I know, she'll tell me to go to hell.

Lights flicker in the window and it's go-time. I slump down in the leather seat, watching as Ms. Mabel shuffles to her car and drives off. A few minutes later, Sloane walks out the double-doors, arms folded across her chest.

She makes her way through the parking lot, shoulders slumped forward, waves of dark hair shielding her face. She's so small, so fragile.

I did this.

I caught the sweet ray of sunshine in my dark, twisted web and snuffed out her light. She trusted me and I took full advantage. Too afraid she'd judge me for my mistakes, I let her think the best of me. Only showed her the part of myself I wanted her to see, the best parts.

Each pulse pushes more hot shame through my body, circulating the negative energy like poison.

"Sloane!" I hop of out of the Rover and call to her as she unlocks her car door. Startled, she jumps about a foot in the air, her head whipping in my direction.

"Fuck off, Cam." She smooths her dress, her voice angry, the sparkle in her eyes gone. She doesn't move toward me. Instead, she slides into the driver's seat and slams the door shut behind her.

In three quick strides, I'm leaning against the car, rapping on her window with my chafed knuckles.

"Please. Can we talk? I can explain."

She doesn't look at me, staring straight ahead as cars whizz by on the main road. Her chest rises and falls, knuckles turning white as she grips the steering wheel.

"Please," I beg, gut churning.

The click of the doors unlocking shakes the car and I lift up a silent prayer of gratitude.

I may still have a chance.

Without hesitation, I jog around and ease myself down into the passenger seat. Heat radiates from the leather and I'm instantly sweating. I reach across the console for her hand, but she bats me away.

"Don't."

She wouldn't take my calls—of course she doesn't want to touch me.

"Sloane. I'm sorry." The words come out strained and desperate. Because I am desperate.

Desperate for her to listen, to hear me out, to forgive me.

"You're sorry?" Her voice tips up and she shakes her head. "Kind of late for that, Cam." Each syllable is clipped and laced with derision.

"What happened yesterday? Please talk to me."

"I saw the video. Rather—Jamie showed me the video. At Mustang's, while I was grabbing a drink with Gracelyn. How could you do that to me, Cam?" Tears fill her eyes, and she won't look at me.

"Sloane—"

"Don't *Sloane* me. I trusted you, Cam. Trusted that what we had was real. That I was enough." Her voice breaks and the tears spill over, splashing onto her cheeks.

"You are enough. More than enough." I want to reach over, wipe the evidence of her pain off her beautiful face. But I don't dare.

I've already done too much.

"I clearly am not. Not judging by the video, anyway." She spits the words out, her lip quivering.

"That's not true. You're my everything. Those women meant nothing."

"Stop, Cam. This isn't helping your case." She whirls at me, anger glinting in her hazel eyes. "I'm done with this. Get out. Please."

Sloane hates me.

"Get the fuck out and leave me alone. I can't do this again." Hitting the unlock button on the car door, the sound ricochets through the quiet vehicle.

"I'm sorry, Sloane. I should have told you the truth about the video." My chest squeezes in a vice grip and the awful day I got cut from the team in Chicago floods my memory, all the terrible feelings roaring back.

Embarrassment, shame, humiliation.

I'm not worthy of this woman and her love. A love so deep and so pure I thought it could wrap around my damaged life and repair all the cracks, like some kind of magical superglue.

"I'm sorry," I murmur.

"Sorry?" she snaps. "That's the best you've got? All this time we were together. I told you everything about me—my deepest wounds and insecurities, mistakes I've made. Then you turn around and stab me in my barely-healed wound *and* twist the damn knife."

I blow out a breath, rub at the scratches on my knuckles left over from my boxing match at the hotel.

A long minute goes by.

"I should have told you. Not Jamie or the internet. I never wanted you to see that."

"I bet you didn't want me to see that. You in a hotel room with multiple women and your friends." She swipes at her face, her dark hair falling over her cheeks.

There's so much I want to say to her, but nothing comes out. My throat's dry and tight, every muscle clenched.

Instead, I sit there, frozen in the steaming hot car. Wishing and hoping she'll forgive me.

"You sold me a fairytale, Cam. A happily ever after that does not exist. And I fell for it, hook, line, and sinker. I wanted to believe in love. Believe in you, in us. But I don't even know you."

That's a sucker punch straight to my gut, knocking the wind out of me. Because she's right and I know it.

I should have come clean, been forthright and honest with her. And now it's too late.

"I'm sorry," I say in a hoarse whisper. I can't look at her, can't bear the pain in her eyes, the disgust.

"I wish that was enough, Cam. But it's not. I've heard that line one too many times and it's just not good enough."

I swallow hard over the massive lump in my throat, panic clawing at my neck, my chest, threatening to pull me under.

I want to make everything right between us, put us back together again. But I'm not sure I can.

"I made the team. I'm leaving in ten days."

She sucks in a sharp breath, gnawing at her lip. "Congrats. I'm sure you'll be great."

"Thanks."

We sit in silence for another long minute. Words and phrases roll through my mind, things I should say face-to-face while I have the chance. But I don't have the courage.

I broke her and I'm not sure we can ever come back from this.

CHAPTER 38
CAM

I hit the highest of highs and the lowest of lows, all in the last twenty-four hours. I'm exhausted and feel like I'm crawling through quicksand as I trudge up the steps at the lake house. The hot summer sun's setting, vibrant pinks and oranges spilling over the white marble kitchen, but the magnificent view brings me no joy.

Not now.

Now all I want to do is collapse in a dark, cold, quiet room and sleep for the next nine days. Maybe longer.

Without Sloane, there is no point.

Two months ago, football was life. But being back home in Thunder Creek shifted my priorities.

I love football, sure.

But I love Sloane more.

And I lost her.

How am I going to survive this?

I toss my suitcase at the bottom of the staircase and make a beeline for the liquor cabinet. Pouring a healthy serving of whiskey into a rocks glass, I drain the amber liquid in one go and splash out another.

"Fuck!" I scream into the empty house, my voice echoing off all the hard surfaces.

Without Sloane here, the place feels cold and sterile. She was the warmth, the softness, the joy.

I lean against the island and stare out at the glowing orange ball over the lake, watch as it sinks down into the bluish-green abyss of the water. The light swallowed up by the darkness. I sit through that brief moment in time where there is no light—no sun, no moon—just empty sky.

Sit and think about all my mistakes. Absorb them until I'm aching. Bones, joints, tissue, and skin. It hurts to breathe and I've never felt more lonely.

I swipe the whiskey bottle from the counter and lumber through the house, up the stairs to the bedroom.

Empty.

But she's still here. Everywhere. Haunting me.

Her sparkly laugh bouncing off the windows. The scent of fresh flowers lingering in the air, winding around me. Soft, heated skin as we lay together, staring out at the stars dotting the dusky sky.

A dull ache spreads through my chest, radiating down my arms, my torso, my legs. I'm tired, so fucking tired.

Staggering to the bed, I sink down onto the white duvet and kick off my shoes. Peel off my shirt and joggers, stripping down before collapsing against the pillows.

The smell of her shampoo drifts up from the crisp cotton and I'm torn between imagining her here or trying to block the memories altogether.

Lifting the liquor bottle straight to my lips, I take a long slug and try to drown my sorrow. The whiskey burns my throat as it goes down, but does nothing to dull the pain. I tip the bottle back and drink more, hoping for relief.

None comes.

I slam the bottle down on the nightstand and stare out the windows into the dark, inky sky.

Dirty little secret.

You sold me a fairytale, Cam.

I don't even know you.

How can we come back from this? The way she looked at me, the disgust and disappointment etched over her face.

This isn't going to work. Even if she takes me back, the hurdle of my career and all the traveling, will be too much to handle. Sloane will never trust me again.

I should give up now. Leave Thunder Creek and never look back. Forget about her and what we had.

My body tenses, a dull throbbing at my temples thudding with each pulse of my heart.

I don't deserve her and I know it. I should have left well enough alone. But I couldn't stop myself from taking a bite of the forbidden fruit.

You didn't have to eat the whole damn apple.

Too late now.

I ate the apple.

Tasted it. Licked and sucked the sinfully sweet juices, bit into the ripe, tender flesh.

Swallowed the fruit down, bite after bite, making it part of me.

The whiskey's catching up, finally doing its job. My arms grow heavy and the room's starting to spin. I flop my arm out and fumble for my cell, tapping the screen and bringing the phone to life.

Sloane smiles back at me, her arms thrown around my

neck. I'm kissing her cheek and she's laughing and smiling at the camera.

We were so happy.

She's radiant, golden beams of sunlight streaming behind us, a soft halo shimmering around her.

I held absolute joy in my arms and let her slip away, dissipating like the mist over the lake on a hot morning.

Sadness washes over me and I squeeze my eyes shut tight, trying to block out the pain, the bitter disappointment.

I'm a fucking fool, a damn idiot.

I deserve to suffer.

And she deserves more—so much more—than me.

CHAPTER 39
SLOANE

"Cam's back?" Gracelyn's voice pitches up at least two octaves. "He ambushed you at the library?"

"Yes," I sigh, toying with the metal chain on the front porch swing at the salon. I drove straight here after I left work to give Gracelyn the update in person.

"And? What did he have to say for himself?"

"That he's sorry."

"Oh, great. Really fucking original. What else did he say?" Grace kicks her legs out and the wooden swing catches air.

"He made the team. Got the position in Fort Lauderdale. He's leaving in ten days." My voice is laced with sadness, an ache throbbing in my chest.

I shouldn't care that Cam's leaving, not after what he did.

But unfortunately, I do.

Dammit.

Turns out, you can't shut love off like a spigot. Even

after everything—the sex video, the lies and the half-truths —I still love him.

Sitting next to him in the car was torture. All I wanted was to touch him, feel his hands on me, to kiss his soft lips.

Which is sick and twisted and all kinds of fucked up. The man cheated on me. Lied to me and humiliated me.

I shouldn't want to be in the same room with him, let alone the same bed. I shouldn't want to feel the weight of his sculpted chest pressed against mine, his breath on my neck, the wet warmth of his tongue on my thighs, between my legs.

Yet he's all I can think about.

What the fuck is wrong with me?

"Good riddance. He'll be gone, out of your life for good." Gracelyn brushes her palms together, as if the matter's done and dusted and there's nothing left to think about.

Pursing my lips, I push off the wooden floorboards of the porch, kicking my legs out harder. The swing flies higher, creating a slight breeze from the propulsion.

In my heart, I know Gracelyn's right. I should let Cam go. Move on with my life.

He crushed me, stomping on my feelings like a creepy-crawly bug slithering along the sidewalk. I gave him all of me, every last bit, and he smashed me to pieces.

Still, he's all I can think about.

I'm a woman obsessed. Madly, deeply, sickly in love with Cam Crawford.

"Girl. Tell me you're not thinking of taking him back." Grace stares at me with wide, serious eyes.

Is she psychic?

"No. I can't. I mean—I want to. I really do. But no. I'm done. You're right. I can't trust him, will never be able to trust him. He's a cheater. And I'm clearly not enough for him. If he's into threesomes—"

"I actually think it was a sixsome," Grace points out, oh-so-helpfully.

"Whatever. Voyeuristic sex. If that's his jam, then I'm not his girl. I don't want to share him—not that he asked."

"Exactly. He screwed around on you. You cannot go there again, Sloane. You're better off without him." She twists a springy curl round and round her finger and my gut roils.

Am I better off without Cam? We were pretty damn perfect together. I never felt more loved, more understood and adored.

Until I didn't.

Gracelyn squeezes my hand. "You'll be okay, bestie. I'm here. Maybe we should get a place together—"

"You already have a place, Grace."

"Yeah, but I could move. It's really tiny."

"Makes sense, since you live alone."

"But we could move in together. It would be fun, like one long sleepover!"

The image of sharing a space with Grace pops into my mind. Her numerous make-up palettes cluttering the bathroom, non-stop reality TV playing at maximum volume, half-empty coffee cups piled high in the kitchen sink.

I love Grace, but I don't want to live with her.

"Thanks, babe. For now, I'm laying low and not making any big decisions."

"Probably wise."

My cell chimes, an alert from the Ring doorbell back at my dad's. If Cam's on my doorstep, I'm gonna fall off this swing.

But it's not Cam.

A huge bouquet of pink and white roses fills the phone screen. The delivery man sets the vase on the porch and then backs out of the frame.

"Sloane—" Grace's tone is low, a warning sound humming at the notch of her neck. "Don't fall for it. There's not enough flowers in Thunder Creek—no, Georgia. No, the world!—to make up for that sin."

I swallow hard over the lump in my throat, my jaw tight. "I know. I won't."

Grace pats my thigh. "Atta girl. Stay strong."

"I'm gonna jet. I want to get home before my dad. I don't want to have to launch into all of this with him right now."

"Okay. You're welcome to spend the night with me if you want."

"Thanks, but I'm okay." This is my new normal, this pitch black, overwhelming depression. I better get used to it because it's settled in deep already, my own personal storm cloud.

We say our goodbyes and I hustle home, determined to beat my dad there.

I pull into the driveway and my heart sinks at the sight of my dad's truck.

Dammit. Nothing's going right for me today. Maybe I can sneak in real quiet and tiptoe back to my room without him seeing or hearing me.

I click my car door closed as softly as possible and scoot up the sidewalk to the porch. The bouquet's gone.

Shit.

I'm sure my dad brought it into the house when he came home. But that won't necessarily raise any red flags. He knows I'm dating Cam.

Was dating Cam. Past tense.

Pushing through the door, I stifle a groan. My dad's sitting on the sofa, watching ESPN and drinking a beer.

"Hey, baby. Looks like you got flowers. Sure I can guess who they're from." He tips his head toward the kitchen table. "I put them in there for you. They're real pretty."

I force a smile in his direction before moving into the kitchen. My dad's correct—the roses are stunning, all four dozen of them.

I pluck the small envelope from the plastic trident, my name scrawled across the front in swirly handwriting. Holding my breath, I tear out the square card and read:

Trouble,

I'll always believe in love. Because of you.

Please forgive me.

xoxo,

Cam

My breath hitches, stuck in my chest, and hot tears blur my vision.

Damn him.

Still acting like Prince Charming, trying to sell me on the happy ending.

But not this time. There's nowhere to go from here. I can't move to Florida with him, pretend like nothing happened. Like I'll ever be enough. And I can't stay here and just blindly trust him.

Not anymore.

I slide the note into my pocket and swipe the tears from my lashes, try my best to act normal as I saunter back into the living room.

"You want dinner? There's some chicken and rice in the

fridge. I ate on the way home from practice." My dad glances up from the TV for a split second.

"Nah, I'm good." I want to duck into my room, but that will raise suspicion. So I lean against the armrest of the sofa, quickly changing the subject before he asks me about the roses.

"How was practice?"

"Good. Things are coming together. Although I need Langley to step it up. I want to give him the spot, but it's gonna be hard to justify ceding QB to a freshman if he doesn't nail every pass."

"Yeah, I know."

"You've always had good instincts about the game. Speaking of which—how's it going with Cam down in Florida? You hear anything?"

The question's loaded, the mere mention of his name shaking me to my core. Avoiding eye contact with my dad, I rub at a frayed pink embossed flower on the sofa cushion.

"Uh, good. He got the position. I'm sure he'll tell you himself tomorrow at practice—he's back in town. But he's leaving Thunder Creek in ten days."

My dad takes a swig of beer. "Is that so? He's back home and you're not together right now?"

He stares over at me and my face heats under his laser gaze, my throat tight.

I shrug, being as nonchalant as I possibly can. "We broke up."

May as well tell him the bad news, quick and dirty.

His brows raise. "Really? That's too bad."

He doesn't ask any questions and mercifully holds in his well-earned 'Told you so.'

"I know." I huff out a long breath, my insides feeling shaky. "I thought he was different."

I stare at the worn flower on the sofa. Sad, defeated. Destroyed.

Hot tears well in my eyes and I try to hold them in, but I can't. They spill out, streaming down my cheeks, and now I'm sobbing. All the pent-up emotion I've been reigning in coming out in hot, disappointed waves.

My dad sets his beer on the coffee table and stands up, wrapping his strong arms around me, holding me tight while I cry. Sadness and disappointment flow out of me, soaking his polo that smells like grass and Old Spice deodorant. He rubs my back and doesn't say a word. Doesn't ask questions or toss out stupid sayings like "What's meant to be, will be."

Just holds me in his arms, loving on me like he always has.

My dad's the only man in the entire world who's never disappointed me or let me down. Not even once.

I cry for the loss of love. The dream romance I thought Cam and I had. The happily ever after we're never going to get.

I cry for the loss of one of my best friends.

I cry until the tears run out, standing there in the living room, soaking up all my dad's quiet strength and goodness.

Finally, when I'm all cried out, my dad asks the dreaded question.

"I don't wanna pry. But what happened? I thought you two were gonna go the distance."

His gruff voice rumbles against my chest and I take a shuddery breath. I may as well tell him—he's bound to find out sooner or later.

"Cam cheated on me." My voice cracks, the chords hoarse from crying. "Down in Florida. I saw the video."

"That son of a bitch," he growls, squeezing me tighter. "After I warned him, too."

"What?" I pull away, glancing up at my dad. "What did you say to him, Daddy?"

"I told him if he did anything to hurt you, he was gonna have to answer to me." He steps away from me, snatching his ball cap off the sofa and jingling his keys in his pocket.

"Wait—what are you doing?"

"Going to see Cam and give him a piece of my mind." He starts to stalk toward the door, but I intercept him, placing a hand on his chest.

"Please, Daddy. Don't. It'll only make things worse."

He scrubs the back of his neck, a deep V between his brows as he stares down at the faded carpet, contemplating.

"Fine." He takes his hat off and runs his fingers through his sandy brown hair. "I won't talk to him tonight."

A tiny sigh of relief leaks from me.

"But I'm not making any promises about later."

My dad throws his arm around me and I rest my head on his strong shoulder. I guess no matter how old I get, I'll always be my daddy's little girl.

CHAPTER 40
CAM

wake up with a pounding headache. Wretched bright sunshine streams into the bedroom and I pull a pillow over my eyes to shield myself from the assault.

Fuck, I feel awful.

Then everything comes tumbling back: talking in the parking lot with Sloane, the hurt and distrust in her eyes. Drinking too much trying to numb the pain.

Stupid move because you always pay for it later.

Sending Sloane roses before I passed out in a whiskey coma.

I lift my cell, checking for messages. Nothing from her. Guess a secret sex video leaked on the internet calls for more than a bouquet from the neighborhood florist.

There is a message from my older sister, Jessica.

> Jessica: You better call mom. She heard about your new contract
>
> Jessica: She's crushed you didn't call

Oof. And now my mom's upset too. Lately, I cannot win.

I dial my mom and she answers on the first ring.

"Camden Crawford. You signed with a new team and didn't even call your mother. I thought I raised you better than that!"

"Sorry, Mom. I had meetings with the coaches and the GM, a helmet fitting. You know the drill. Then I caught a flight back to Thunder Creek to wrap things up and get ready for the move."

"Mm-hmm. Excuses, excuses. I had to hear about the deal online, from the League Report! And then Sandra from pickleball asked me about it and I didn't have any other details to give her."

I stare up at the alabaster ceiling and curse the liquor, my mouth dry and fuzzier than bunny slippers.

"Yeah, sorry. You and Dad gonna make it down to Florida for a game?" I change the subject.

"I will, Cam!" my woo-woo sister, Ansley, shouts out in the background. "Since I'm single and ready to mingle and all."

"Nana, do we have any more Lucky Charms?" my nephew interrupts my mom.

Must be a school break. My parents always help take care of Jessica's kids during the school breaks.

"Hang on a sec, Justin. I'll get them. Don't climb up on the counter, honey. Here—" My mom's off helping my nephew and there's clattering in the background. Ansley comes on the line.

"Cammy-poo, how are you? Congrats on the new job. You made a vision board, didn't you? I knew that would help." The words gush out of her like whitewater in the rapids.

"No. I called my agent and he got me the tryout," I say flatly.

She brushes over my lack of vision boarding, forging on. "Are you excited about Florida and the new team?"

"Yeah."

"Whoa. Hold up. You don't sound very excited."

She's real astute. Must be using her crystal freaking ball to figure that out.

"I'm fine, Ans. It's a job."

"Who are you and what have you done with my little brother? Football? A job? No way. That's not the Cam I know and love."

I huff out a sigh and dig deep to find my patience. "I'm tired is all. Long flight and lots to do in the next few days."

"What are you doing about Sloane?" Her voice ticks up and I stiffen. *How does she know about Sloane?*

"What do you mean?"

"Oh, please, bro. Thunder Creek's smaller than a postage stamp. Everybody knows you two are together."

"But you're in Colorado." I state the obvious.

"With friends still in Thunder Creek. Rosie called me weeks ago when she saw the two of you at the movie theater with your hands all over each other, sharing popcorn. Then Theo texted me after Moonlight Picnic in the Park. You think you can keep anything a secret in that town?"

Acid shoots up my esophagus, burning the back of my throat and stinging my nose.

No, nothing's a secret in Thunder Creek, that's for certain.

"Well—is it serious? Is she going to Florida with you?" Ansley doesn't let up, grilling me like a police sergeant in an interrogation.

"Check your sources, Ans. Because we broke up." My voice is gruff, tension ticking at my jaw.

"Whoa. Since when? Last I heard, you were ring shopping."

"Must have been some other guy."

"Your brother's ring shopping? Camden, what's going on?" My mom's voice tips up in the background and I regret making this call right about now.

"Ansley, please set the record straight. Or put me on speaker and I'll do it myself."

The ambient noise amplifies with a slight buzzing sound. I guess Ansley went with option number two, speaker phone.

"Camden Christopher Crawford, are you engaged?" My mom means business now, using my full given name. Not telling her about a new job is one thing; holding out on romantic relationship news? Unacceptable.

"No, Mom." I rake my hand through my hair. "The exact opposite, actually. Sloane and I broke up."

"Noooo!" Ansley cries. "I love her. She's so cute. You're cute together."

"Thanks, Ans. But things didn't work out." A sharp pang stabs me in the chest and I fight against despair.

"Why not?" Ansley asks, pushing.

"It's complicated." That's a true statement.

"You seem sad about it. I take it the breakup wasn't your idea."

"No, it wasn't."

"You should journal about getting back together. Hang on, let me check my calendar—" There's a pause while my sister consults the astrological signs or the lunar eclipse or some other new-age bullshit. "Yes, it's a triple seven coming up."

"I take it that's good?"

"Very. Here's what you do. Sit down and envision your future, then journal about it. Be very specific. Light a candle and be intentional about the process. Fold the sheet of paper and place it under a crystal and then manifest."

"Should I spin in a circle three times too?" I grumble. Ansley can be a bit much.

"If you want to. But it's not strictly necessary."

Oh geez.

"I have to get going, long list of to-dos before the move. Sorry I didn't call earlier, Mom."

"It's okay, honey. But I better not hear about an engagement through the grapevine," she chirps.

"You don't need to worry about that, Mom."

Because Sloane's not speaking to me. I seriously doubt we're getting engaged.

"Don't be so negative, Cam. Remember, it's a triple seven day! Go manifest right now!" Ansley chides.

"Bye, guys."

I disconnect and throw the pillow back over my face, hoping to drift back to sleep and at least dream about Sloane. That's as close to manifesting as I'm getting.

CHAPTER 41
SLOANE

Cam texts me once a day for the next few days, but I don't respond.

I'm too afraid I'll crack under pressure, toppling like a Jenga game after a bad pull.

No, it's safer to avoid.

Soon, he'll move to Fort Lauderdale and that will be that.

Everything will go back to the way it was before he showed up on my doorstep, asking for my dad.

I suck in a deep breath, an empty hollowness yawning wide in my chest.

A few more days, and I'll be Cam-free. Marked safe from gorgeous pro football players with outstanding internet dick notoriety.

With shaky hands, I stamp the due date on the index card in the back of a Princess Diaries book and hand it to Abigail, the shoo-in for Summer Reading Champ.

"Thanks, Ms. Sloane. Is your boyfriend coming to the

End of Summer Book Bash?" She gazes up at me with bright blue eyes, clearly hopeful.

"No. He's moving to Florida."

"Oh. So you're not getting married."

I half-laugh, half-sob. "No."

"Bummer. He's really cute."

"I know. But he has a job in Florida and I'm working here. So that's tough."

"No biggie. My dad drives trucks all over the southeast and my mom stays home. It's fine. If you love each other, you can make it work."

Her words saw at the open wound, ripping at the jagged edges. The spot may never heal.

"Thanks, Abigail. But I don't think we're meant to be."

She stares up at me, confused. "Because he's moving?"

"No. Because it's complicated."

"More complicated than geometry?"

I have to laugh at this. "Probably about that level of complicated, yeah."

"Wow. That is hard. But my mom always tells me I can do hard things."

This kid isn't letting up.

"You sure can, Abigail. She's absolutely right."

"I'm nine. If I can do hard things, you definitely can. You're way older than me."

Well, shoot. She's got me there.

"Sometimes you have to let people go."

Her small, pink lips downturn. "That's sad."

"It is. But eventually things get better and you move on."

"That's not how all my books end."

Good gravy. Where's this kid's chaperone?

"The books you read are fiction. You learned about the difference between fiction and non-fiction in school, right?"

"Yes. Fiction is make-believe."

"Exactly."

"So happy endings are make-believe?" She squishes her brows together, trying to figure this out.

Same, girl, same.

I bite at my lip, wondering if I should deliver the brutal truth to Abigail right now or let her learn for herself the hard way.

"Not always," I hedge. "Sometimes love works out."

"And you get married?"

Probably not the time to quote current divorce statistics.

"Yeah. And you get married and live happily ever after."

"That's what I want."

"Me too, Abigail. Me too." Well, at least I used to want that. Before I realized every man is a freaking cheater. Or, at least, every man that dates me.

"You still could, Ms. Sloane. Look." Abigail points to the arch of the Children's Department. Cam's leaning against the wall, all broad shoulders, tapered waist, and muscles for days. He waves at Abigail and she waves back, smiling shyly over at him.

"Abby—we have to get going. I need to stop by the grocery and pick up dinner." A blonde woman swings over, taking Abigail by the hand.

"Okay, Mom. See you next week, Ms. Sloane. Good luck!" She waves and wanders off with her mother, leaving me alone in the Children's Department. Well, alone with Cam.

Shit.

There's only two minutes to close and no one left to rescue me.

Cam wanders over, his marine gaze never leaving mine. Like I may scurry off and he'd have to chase me through the stacks or something.

"Hey. Can we talk? Please?" He clasps his hands, his voice tipping up.

I break eye contact, heat unfurling low in my belly even as hot anger bubbles inside me. The man still has an effect on me and it's low-key annoying.

"No. Go away."

"Please, Sloane."

I war with myself for a few seconds, but figure he'll stalk me in the parking lot anyway.

"Fine. As soon as I'm done here. Give me five minutes."

He loiters near the entrance while I shut down the computer and tuck in the chair. The custodian fires up the vacuum cleaner, zooming away without paying us any attention.

We walk in silence out to the parking lot and Cam grabs my elbow, steering me away from the parking lot and behind the building.

"Where are we going, Cam? It's been a long day, I just want to get home."

"Come on. Give me ten minutes."

Because I'm a sucker and a sappy romantic—and Abigail had a few good points, especially for a nine-year-old—I let Cam lead me out to the park in the back of the library. We walk toward the gazebo at the far end of the outdoor space and I suck in a breath.

Twinkly fairy lights drape from the gazebo, a white

tablecloth spread over the old wooden picnic table. There's a fancy charcuterie board, along with a bottle of chilled white wine and two glasses. A huge bouquet of flowers—blue hydrangeas this time—sits in the center of the table and a portable speaker's playing Frank Sinatra's greatest hits.

"Cam—"

"C'mon, Trouble. Can we at least talk?" He cuts his gaze to mine and I feel my resolve crumbling like a sandy shoreline at high tide during a hurricane.

"Fine. But make it quick. Otherwise my dad'll ask questions." A total lie, but what's good for the goose, right?

His hand hovers at my low back, but doesn't dare make contact as he guides me to the picnic bench. I take a seat, perched tentatively on the edge. Ready to bolt at any moment. The sun's setting in the distance and there's a light breeze as Cam folds his tall body down onto the wooden bench.

"May I?" He gestures at the wine, sweating in the heat.

"Fine." May as well enjoy a beverage—it's still sticky and humid out here.

He pours us each a tall glass of wine, screwing the lid back onto the bottle before sliding my glass over.

I take a long slug and he does the same, cicadas humming in the tall grass behind us.

"Sloane, I'm really sorry. I should have told you about the video." He swallows hard, Adam's apple bobbing in his thick neck. "It was one stupid night in Chicago. My buddy's birthday and they invited these women up to the room. We had too much to drink—I should have left. I can sit here and make excuses for my behavior—peer pressure, too much alcohol, blah, blah, blah. All of that is true, but it's also bullshit. I made a big mistake. And it cost me a lot. My spot on the team in Chicago. But if it costs me you—" He gazes out into the field, dark brows knit.

"Hold on. Chicago? Don't sit here and fucking lie straight to my face, Cam. I saw the date on the video. It was a few days ago, when you were in Florida."

"What? No, it wasn't. Swear."

"Bullshit, Cam! It was timestamped!" Fiery anger surges through me. *How stupid and naïve does he think I am?* "Jamie pulled it up on her phone and the date was right fucking there."

"Sloane—I swear to God nothing happened while I was down in Florida. That video was from months ago. That's the main reason I got cut from the team."

"So Jamie found an old sex video on the internet and doctored it? C'mon, Cam. That's ridiculous."

Cam frowns, his lips pressed together. "I guess. I mean, I don't know why she would do that. But I promise you, I haven't been with anyone since we started dating. I'd never hurt you like that, Sloane."

His deep blue eyes slide to mine and a pang radiates through my chest. I want to believe him—so badly—but don't all cheaters say these things? Ratface sure did.

It was only this one time.

I'll never do it again, Sloane.

I never meant to hurt you, baby.

Uh-huh. Right.

"Prove it." I fold my arms over my chest, fortified by anger and chardonnay.

Cam huffs out a shaky breath and slides his cell out of his pocket. Clicking on the search tab, he types in a few keywords and hands me the phone without meeting my gaze.

I hit play and sure as shit, it's the same grainy video. The hotel room, the skyline, the beautiful women. All the same. This time with no time and date stamp in the corner.

Pausing the video, I hand the cell back to Cam, emotions swirling through me.

Cool relief, but also anger. At Jamie, for being a conniving bitch.

But also at Cam.

"Maybe this didn't happen in Fort Lauderdale—"

"It didn't, Sloane. I'd never do that to you."

"But you still lied to me, Cam. You told me you got cut for your attitude, for not making plays. You failed to mention a sex video."

His face crumples, shoulders slumping, and I feel terrible. But not terrible enough to stop going.

"I thought you trusted me, Cam. I thought we were a team. Why didn't you tell me?" My voice breaks and I kick at the gravel on the ground, my throat thick.

"I was ashamed." His voice is a whisper, so quiet I barely catch it over the breeze. "I fucked up."

"Cam—" I fumble for the right words, unsure what to say. "I love you. But you betrayed me. I gave you my whole heart, my body. My trust and my confidence. And now I'm not sure I even know you. Was everything between us a lie?"

Cam grabs for my hands and I let him take them, enfolding my fingers in his large, calloused palms.

"No. Of course not. Everything I said—everything between us—was real. Is real."

The correction gives me pause and I pull away, scrunching my eyes shut tight. After a long minute, I finally face him.

"I'm sorry, I really am. I still love you, but I can't do this. I can't take the risk."

I shove away from the picnic table and dash to my car before I give into the sadness wrapping around and engulfing me.

The last thing I want is Cam to see me cry.

CHAPTER 42
CAM

The wine picnic was a fail.

Telling Sloane the truth was a fail.

You failed.

And now I have to live with the consequences of my actions. Take the knocks and start getting comfortable with the fact that I'm going down to Florida alone.

Back at the house, I lurch up the stairs, my legs heavier than two lead posts and about as useful. The sun's sinking down into the lake, but the bright streaks of orange and pink do nothing to boost my mood.

Walking into the closet, I open the top dresser drawer and pull out the black velvet box I squirreled away underneath the neat stack of boxers and T-shirts. I cradle the square box in my palm, sink down onto the edge of the bed and pop the lid.

All four carats of the princess-cut diamond twinkle up at me and my chest squeezes. So hard and tight I can't breathe.

My sister's intel was right.

I was going to ask Sloane to marry me, to be my wife.

She's my everything and I wanted to be with her forever.

And now I've lost her.

For good this time.

I let her go once back in high school, and I swore I wouldn't make that mistake again.

But now I have no choice.

She doesn't want you.

She'll never trust you again.

I don't deserve her, someone that beautiful and sweet. I held her heart in my hand and fumbled it. I may not have cheated on her like she thought, but she's right.

I wasn't honest with her, wasn't man enough to own up to my mistakes. I kept part of myself from her, hoping she'd never find out the truth.

And now we're done.

Ding-dong.

The doorbell chimes, echoing through the quiet house, and startles me out of my pity party. It's probably a delivery from Troy, some celebratory bottle of bourbon or something. Maybe a packet of papers from HR I need to sign for. I don't dare hope it's Sloane, coming to tell me she forgives me and will take me back.

Shoving the ring into my pocket, I lumber downstairs, the chime dinging again. The delivery must be important.

I freeze at the bottom of the stairs and clutch the railing. I'd love to dash back upstairs, but it's too late now.

Coach already spotted me through the frosted glass.

Shit.

He's the last person I want to see right now. I promised him I wouldn't hurt Sloane and that's exactly what I did.

After everything he's done for me, I can only imagine what he's about to say.

With a deep breath, I open the door. "Coach."

"Camden. May I?" He tips his head at the house and I nod, holding the door for him. He crosses over the threshold and my gut roils.

There are fewer things I want to do right now than have this conversation. But I owe him that much.

"Can I get you something to drink?" I motion to the fridge, but Coach shakes his head.

"No, thanks. This isn't a social call."

"Oh, right." I lick at the inside of my lip, anxiety churning through me in full-force. "Come on in."

I walk to the kitchen and Coach follows close behind me in silence. I offer him a stool at the island, but he declines.

"I'm okay." He removes his hat, clutching the brim with his thick fingers. "Son, respectfully, what the hell were you thinking cheating on Sloane? After you stood in my house and swore to me you wouldn't hurt my daughter. Then the first chance you get, you sleep around on her? You should be ashamed." A vein pops in his neck, his knuckles white from the tight grip on his hat.

"It's not what you think, sir." I swallow hard, my throat tight and dry. "I didn't cheat on her. I'd never do that to Sloane."

"Don't lie to me, son. She told me all about it." Coach narrows his eyes at me and I resist the urge to squirm beneath his steely gaze.

Hot shame washes over me. I hate that Coach knows about all of this, that I let him down, too. I have to set the record straight—say the words out loud—because he deserves to know the truth as well.

"Have you talked to her today? Because what Sloane saw was fake." I take a deep breath, swallow hard over the rock lodged at the back of my throat. "I'm not downplaying my behavior, sir. There is a video—I'm not proud of it and wish I could take it back—but that happened well before I started dating Sloane. Someone altered the date and timestamp on the video and made it look like it happened down in Florida. It didn't, I promise. I'd never hurt her like that. And I should have told her about the video sooner—I know that now—but I didn't. Truth is, I'm ashamed. At how I acted, the things I did. I had my reasons at the time, but still—" I rake a hand through my hair, try to keep the wobble out of my voice.

"Son, are you telling me this is the same video from the winter, when you were still in Chicago?"

I jerk my head up. "What?"

"You think I don't know how to search things up on the internet? You're a good player, Cam. Teams don't cut good players for dropping a pass or two."

"Oh." My voice drops low and I am humbled.

Coach saw the video.

"Yes, sir. It's the same video. I didn't know we were being filmed and I've never done anything like that before —and I'm not planning on ever doing something like that again. I set the record straight with Sloane an hour ago, but she's still upset. She doesn't trust me."

Coach taps his hat against his upper thigh, shoves a hand in the pocket of his cargo shorts.

"Well, I'm glad to hear you didn't do anything to hurt Sloane purposely."

"I didn't, sir. I love her. I asked her to move to Florida with me, before all this went down. I was planning on proposing." My voice catches, despair ripping through me.

The ring in my pocket's suddenly heavier, weighing me down. A glittering reminder of my failure.

"Well, Cam, here's what I'll say about it. One—in the future, keep your damn pants on. You're a professional athlete. That makes you an automatic target for all types of scammers. What you and your friends did, what you engaged in—that was a rookie move."

I lick my lips and rub my clammy palms on my shorts. "Yes, sir."

"Two—don't keep beating yourself up about the video. You paid your penance with the team and now you're suffering again. You've owned up to your mistakes and now it's time to move on. Everyone makes mistakes."

"I'll bet you never made any mistakes like that."

Coach's serious face cracks and he lets out a belly laugh, throwing his head back so far I catch a glimpse of the tan line on his neck from his polo shirt.

"Son, I've made more than my fair share of mistakes. I do believe you dated my favorite mistake of all."

Sloane.

"Nobody in this life is perfect. And thank God, or I wouldn't have my daughter. Sometimes you have to run through the shit before you find out it was manure all along, meant to help your garden grow.

"Sloane is the greatest blessing in my life. If I hadn't fucked up in high school—excuse my French—she wouldn't be here today. At the time, I thought my world was ending. But it wasn't. Sure, it wasn't my plan. But things rarely go the way we plan. On the field or in life. You have to learn how to read the plays and run with it. One thing I'm always looking for in every player, every single season is adaptability. You have that, Cam. That's what makes you a great asset to any team."

I flex my knuckles, my throat thick.

"Thanks, Coach. I appreciate you saying that."

"I wouldn't say it if I didn't mean it, son. You know another thing you have that a lot of players don't?"

I shake my head. "No."

"Grit. When you got cut in Chicago, you could have plopped down on your sofa eating junk food and watching daytime TV. But you didn't. You came back here and trained. Took your knocks and made yourself faster, stronger, better. That's grit, Cam. You didn't quit, didn't give up. You fought for what you wanted. And what you wanted was football."

Tears sting the backs of my eyes, and I fight the surge of emotion swirling in my chest.

"If you want Sloane—and I believe you do, after watching the two of you not-so-covertly sneak around all summer—you need to fight for her. Don't give up yet. She may take some convincing, but if anyone can make her come around, it's you."

"I wish I knew how to do that, Coach. I've tried quite a few things, but she won't even take my calls."

"Well, I'm not too solid in the love department. But I do know my daughter and I'm sure we can come up with a play or two."

CHAPTER 43
CAM

On Coach's advice, I keep trying with Sloane.

I call. I text. I send more bouquets, so many flowers the florist probably thinks I'm a stalker.

But everything I try fails.

She doesn't want me.

I hurt her too badly and there's no coming back from this.

As a last ditch effort, I even take advice from Ansley and light candles, turn around in circles, then search the night sky for shooting stars to make a damn wish.

Nothing doing.

It's over.

I fumbled hard. Had the ball in the end zone and dropped it.

Now I'm leaving Thunder Creek tomorrow. But I still have a few loose ends to tie up before I go.

The first task on the list is one final practice with Langley. Technically, I can't work out with the team anymore, since I signed on with Fort Lauderdale. But tossing balls on a field with a friend?

There's enough of a loophole there.

"Let's run the routes Coach assigned last week. Remember, you don't have to look at your man. I've got you, and your receiver during the season will too. Count it down and let it fly." I slap his back, tossing him the football.

He nods slowly, digesting what I said before running down the field.

As he jogs away, I take a second to soak everything in. Although the circumstances were shitty, it was kind of amazing coming back to my hometown and playing on my high school field. Comparing times and plays and seeing the sport through young, eager eyes.

Being back on this field with Coach Carter was a gift. Not every high school coach would have welcomed a player back with open arms.

But Coach didn't hesitate, not even for a second.

And neither did his daughter.

I shove that thought away as Langley signals to me and counts.

One, two, three…the ball flies through the air and I run the route, jumping to grab the ball.

"Yes!" I fist-pump into the sky. "Perfect. Next play…"

We run every play Coach has in the playbook, including Special Teams and trick plays. Langley nails every single one.

Football in hand, I jog down the field to join him. I'm hot, sweaty, and tired, but satisfied. My work here is done.

As long as he executes, Langley should get the starting QB spot on the team.

"Great job." I toss him the ball. "You've got this. Text

me when Coach makes the announcement. But I expect great things from you."

He beams at me, his chest puffed up with newfound confidence. "Thanks, Cam. Even if I get the back-up position, I still grew as a player working with you. I appreciate it."

My heart swells, throat thick with emotion.

This kid. He's gonna go far with a winning attitude like that. Grateful, humble, talented. He can have it all someday.

"You'll get it. Go out there and execute. You had it in you the whole time." I throw my arm around his shoulder and we walk off the field together.

———

My last stop is Coach's house. I purposefully plan around Sloane's schedule, making sure to swing by while she's at work, but before football practice.

Coach answers the door, sandwich in hand. "Cam. Come on in. Want lunch?" He motions for me to shut the door and I follow behind him to the kitchen.

"I'm good, thanks."

"How about some lemonade? They won't have the good stuff down in Florida." He shoots me a sideways grin and I nod.

"Sure."

Coach pours me a glass of lemonade and I sit with him at the kitchen table. I try not to think back on all the meals I had here with Sloane, my hand resting on her thigh, her bare foot rubbing my calf.

That's all history now and there's no going back.

"You're leaving soon, huh?" Coach interrupts my daydreaming.

"Yes, sir. I'm hitting the road at first light tomorrow. I'm due on the field the day after, and I need to get settled before pre-season starts."

"That's too bad. We're gonna miss you around here." A deep V forms between his brows as he stares across the table at me.

I wonder which *we* he's talking about. Surely not Sloane. She'll breathe easier once I'm out of Thunder Creek for good.

"I'll miss you and the guys for sure." I swipe at a drop of condensation on the outside of the glass and try to ignore the strangled feeling in my throat.

"I take it you and Sloane didn't work things out yet?" He arches one brow high, studying me over the last bite of his sandwich.

"No, sir. I tried, but she's still upset."

"I figured that, judging by the way she's been moping around here. Driving me a little nuts, not gonna lie."

I puff out a breath, my chest tight. "I'm sorry about that, Coach. But I'm not sure what more I can do."

He frowns at me, dusting the crumbs from his hands onto the plate. "Seems like now's the time for a Hail Mary."

I squint across the table at him. "Excuse me?"

"Yep. It's time to break out the big guns, son. You have to put yourself out there, lay everything on the line. It's the fourth quarter here and you're down. There's a risk she'll say no, there always is. No way around it. Do you think you can handle that?" He levels his gaze on me, his stare as intense as it is during the last seconds of a game when we're losing by a touchdown.

"Yes, sir. I'd rather take that chance than live with regrets."

"Atta, boy." He smacks his palm down on the table, rattling the wood. "So here's the scenario—"

Leaning back in his chair, he grabs a pen from the junk drawer behind him and the two of us put our heads together. We come up with a big play, Coach scribbling the route down on a paper napkin, a series of X's and O's as intricate as any football offense.

After thirty minutes, he caps the pen and sits back, arms folded across his chest. "You've got this, son. Give it your best shot."

I grab the napkin and stuff it in my pocket, determined to do everything I can to win back Sloane.

CHAPTER 44
SLOANE

Today is Cam's last day in Thunder Creek.

I shouldn't have it marked on my calendar and I definitely shouldn't care.

But I do.

No matter how hard I try to pretend I'm okay and everything's fine, inside I'm dying. If I were Jane Austen, I'd describe my current mood as 'bereft.' I couldn't sleep last night and haven't eaten anything all day, not even able to stomach the donut Ms. Mabel brought in for me this morning from Java Jolt.

Between the dark circles under my eyes from insomnia and the late summer humidity wreaking havoc on my hair, I'm quite the vision.

Less than twenty-four hours and he'll be gone.

Tears prick behind my eyes as I hurry over to the printer to grab the handouts for romance book club. Tonight's the last meeting of the summer and there's nothing I'd rather do less right now than sit around and chitchat about love.

"Psst—Sloane!"

I swivel so fast my ponytail swats my cheek. "Gracelyn! What are you doing here? I thought you had a client tonight."

"I did, but my mom took her for me. She wanted a single-color process and a tight curl—not really my cup of tea. And I wanted to come to your book club. You know, for moral support."

"Aww, babe. Thanks." I smash her in a quick hug. "But did you read the book?"

"What? Y'all actually read the book? I thought most book clubs sit around and talk and drink wine?"

I chuckle. "Not this one. For starters, no beverages allowed in the library. And these ladies always read the book. But it's okay. Tonight we're talking about *Pride & Prejudice*. We read that back in high school. I'm sure it'll come back to you."

"Girl. You're cute. You think I actually read that book, ever? Um, no. I read someone's notes and copied an essay some upperclassman gave me. But it's cool. I'm great at winging it."

Holding my eye roll in check—because she is here to support me—I link arms with her and together we head to the conference room. Ms. Mabel and Meg Langley are already here, and a few more people stroll in as the clock ticks closer to five p.m.

"Okay, I think we can get started. We have a good crowd tonight." I glance around the circle, noting a new face or two. Word must be spreading about this fun group of readers. Tonight we have eight people, not counting me or Gracelyn.

"First of all, thanks for coming. I picked this month's

book because I love Jane Austen. Any other Jane Austen fans here?"

Several hands shoot up and my lit-loving little heart is full.

"Super. Let's go around the circle and everyone can share their favorite part."

Gracelyn shoots me an SOS stare, and I add, "If you want."

Her shoulders sag with relief as Ms. Mabel takes the floor, launching into a long response about the first ball scene. A few others chime in and the conversation gets going. Gracelyn toys with her stack of silver bangles, but everyone else participates enthusiastically.

After a while, the conversation dies down, so I ask another question. "Why do you think Mr. Darcy and Elizabeth Bennett had such a hard time resolving their issues? Do you think one of them was more in the wrong than the other?"

Meg answers first. "I think they both had a hand in the problem. Elizabeth was stubborn and prideful and Mr. Darcy couldn't get past his biases."

"Isn't that just like a man—" Ms. Mabel mutters and Gracelyn giggles.

"Right?" Grace gives Ms. Mabel an approving look.

"I don't know. I feel like Elizabeth wasn't as much in the wrong as Mr. Darcy," I point out. "He had more power than her and was in a better position. He kept secrets from her as well."

Gracelyn kicks my foot, but I keep talking, ignoring her. "I understand why she was upset with him for most of the novel."

She kicks my foot again, this time so hard I almost fall out of the plastic chair.

"What Grace?" I whisper, spinning to face her.

And there's Cam, standing in the door of the conference room, one hand shoved in his pocket. Face burning, my eyes slide up and meet his marine gaze. He has matching rings circling his eyes and hasn't shaved in a few days, dark stubble peppering his jaw.

Everyone stops talking as they all stare at Cam, then at me, then back at Cam. Gracelyn clears her throat and the sound bounces off the light green walls.

"Quick bathroom break?" she suggests, but I shake my head.

"No. I'm good. Anyone else?" I glance around the circle, but no one moves to stand. "Okay, then." I clear my throat, shifting in my chair. "Let's continue."

Sitting up tall, I try my hardest to ignore Cam. Maybe he'll take the hint and go away.

"Like I was saying—Mr. Darcy kept secrets," I emphasize this last part, to hammer home the point, "and that's not a good foundation for a relationship. So I get why Elizabeth was upset."

"Maybe Darcy had good reasons for keeping secrets." Cam's deep voice carries from across the room.

"Perhaps. But Darcy should have let Elizabeth make that choice." I stare directly at Cam, chin lifted and jaw tense.

"I'm sure he feels badly about it. In the end."

An ache spreads through my chest, radiating out into my arms, my skin prickling.

"You're right, Cam. He does," Meg chimes in, bobbing her head. "That's when the book really gets good. When all the secrets come out and he professes his love for her. Oh —that's the best part." Meg clutches her necklace, swooning over Mr. Darcy.

Cam straightens his shoulders and strides over to me, right through the center of the book club circle. Heat shoots all the way from my chest to my face and my heart's racing.

He sinks down until we're face-to-face and grabs my hands.

"Cam—don't," I whisper, my throat so tight I barely manage to squeeze out the words.

"Sloane Carter, I love you. And I screwed up, big time. Just like Darcy. I should have told you the truth from the beginning and I'm so, so sorry. But I can't take it back."

The entire book club circle shifts in their seats, leaning in closer so they can hear every word of Cam's confession. Blood whooshes loud in my ears and my stomach twists into a knot so tight a sailor in the Coast Guard would be proud.

"What I can do is admit that I was wrong. Wrong to take advantage of your trust, your goodness."

"Ohhh—" Ms. Mabel murmurs, glancing from me to Cam. "A man admitting he was wrong. That's a good one there, Sloane. He's a keeper."

A tingle runs down my spine as Cam grips my hands tighter, moving in close, so close his familiar woodsy scent winds around me.

"What I can do is fight for you. I don't want to quit on us, Sloane. We're a good team—a great team—and that's tough to find and even tougher to keep. Please don't quit on us."

Tears well in my eyes as I take a shuddery breath. "I don't know, Cam. You hurt me, broke my trust. How do I know you won't do it again?"

"You don't," Ms. Mabel says. "It's called faith, child.

Elizabeth didn't know if Darcy would keep more secrets. But she bet on him and took the risk."

Took the risk.

Some people stay.

Cam wants to stay. He could have left. Left Thunder Creek for good without ever looking back.

But he didn't.

Instead, he took a risk and busted into book club to profess his love for me.

I inch to the edge of my seat, so close to Cam I feel his breath on my skin, our noses almost touching.

"Yes. I'll take the risk, Cam."

His tense face breaks into a smile and he presses his mouth to mine, seizing my lips in a passionate kiss. Applause breaks out around us, but all I care about in this moment is Cam.

Eventually, he breaks away. "I love you, Sloane Carter."

"I love you, too. Have you ever read *Pride & Prejudice,* by the way?"

Cam grins, his teeth gleaming in the bright library lights. "No. Me and Coach watched the movie this afternoon. You know, to get ready for book club."

I smack him lightly in the chest. "You talked to my *dad* about this?"

He nods. "Yeah. Who do you think told me to throw a Hail Mary?"

CHAPTER 45
SLOANE

Cam moves down to Fort Lauderdale as planned for pre-season, but I still have some things to take care of in Thunder Creek.

The End-of-Summer Reading Bash goes off without a hitch, with tons of kids and their parents all showing up for the party. We have cookies and lemonade and Abigail wins the award for the most number of books read over the summer.

"Thanks, Ms. Sloane." She smiles sweetly at me, clutching her gold medal and the gift certificate to Swirly-Q, a Thunder Creek tradition.

"You're welcome—you earned it! Thirty-three books is a reading record for the library!"

She flashes a gappy smile up at me and my chest cracks open a little. I'm going to miss working at the library when I move to Florida. Maybe I can find a job at a library or bookstore down there.

"Thanks—it was hard, but we can do hard things!" she chirps and I nod, hugging her small shoulders.

"That we can. Have a great school year, okay?"

"I will."

Abigail and her mom wander out of the library and I squash down my sadness, my eyelids gummy.

"We sure are gonna miss you 'round here, Sloane. Especially since Meg took the job in the front office at the high school. I'm down two helpers." Ms. Mabel shakes her gray head, the chain on her readers tinkling.

"Don't worry, Ms. Mabel. I'm sure you'll find people to take our places."

"I will. But they won't be as lovely as you. You're my girl." Ms. Mabel encircles me in a hug, squeezing. "But I don't blame you one little bit. A man like Cam Crawford swoops in after me, I'm saying yes. Go live your life, Sloane. Be happy." Tears sparkle behind the lenses of Ms. Mabel's glasses and I nod, too choked up to speak.

After a minute, I take a shaky breath. "Thank you. Say bye to Meg for me. I'm sorry she couldn't be here today."

"She had Orientation at the school. But I'll tell her you said bye."

With one last hug, I tuck in my chair for the final time and head out of the library.

Gracelyn comes over to help me pack up my stuff for the move.

"Gah, I hate this!" She throws herself on my bed and stares up at the ceiling. "We were gonna move in together and have a perpetual sleepover!"

That was never going to happen, but I don't tell Gracelyn that.

"Look at it this way—you'll always have a place to stay on the beach in Florida!"

"True, good point. I do love the beach."

"Exactly." I shove the last of my clothing into my suitcase and together Grace and I manage to zip the bag closed.

"I can't believe you're leaving." Grace glances around my room, the closet and dresser empty. "I'm going to miss you, bestie."

She grips me in a tight hug and tears fill my eyes. "Me too, Gracelyn. Thanks for being here for me this summer. And come see me all the time, okay?"

Gracelyn nods, her chin pressing into my shoulder. "Okay."

"We ready? I don't want to be late to the game."

Tonight's the exhibition game at the high school, a pre-season game between Thunder Creek High and our biggest rival, Lighting Ridge.

"Sure, let's go."

By the time we arrive at the high school, the parking lot's packed. We find one of the few remaining spots and hustle into the stadium.

"Is your dad nervous?" Gracelyn asks as we move through the crowd.

"Coach Carter? Nervous? Never." I spot my dad pacing on the sidelines, wearing his coaching uniform: dark blue Thunder Creek polo, khaki shorts, baseball cap, and his bright orange whistle. He's staring at his clipboard, frowning, and tears prick behind my eyes.

I'm going to miss my dad.

He's gruff and quiet, keeping to himself most of the time, and watches a shit-ton of ESPN. But still—he's the best guy I know (Cam's tied, but don't tell either of them).

After Cam showed up at the library, I cornered my dad about the whole thing. He muttered something about second chances and taking risks, then patted Cam on the shoulder and went to Mack's house.

That was it.

The man's a real mystery, but I love him with my whole heart.

He glances up from his clipboard and waves at me and Gracelyn. I shoot him a smile and a thumbs-up and then Grace and I climb into the bleachers, snagging the seats next to Meg.

"Is Langley excited about his first game? I heard my dad tapped him to be QB One." I squeeze her knee and the corners of her lips tip up in a smile.

"He is. A little nervous, but not half as nervous as me."

Good thing, too, because Meg's toe is tapping a mile a minute, shaking the entire metal bleacher. I hope Langley has a lot more composure than his mom.

A cool breeze kicks up, a nice change from the brutal August heat, and the band marches onto the field. The Thunder Creek theme song rolls through the stadium and all the students and alum sing along. The drumline raps on their drums and the cheerleaders line up in two parallel lines, shaking their blue and white pom-poms.

"Thunder Creek, stand up and cheer for your starting line-up!" The announcer's voice booms through the speakers and everyone jumps up from the stands, cheering and screaming.

"Playing Quarterback this season is Beau Langley!"

Meg whistles and claps as Langley jogs through the pom-pom line, waving at the crowd. The rest of the team is announced one by one and then the Lightning Ridge cheerleaders cartwheel onto the field to cheer on the opposing team.

Finally, both teams take the field and the game begins. The first play is an easy pass down the center and we gain a solid thirty yards. Next, we run a slant route for another thirty yards.

"Langley's doing great!" I shout to Meg and she nods, her eyes not leaving the field.

The next play doesn't move the ball forward, so now we're on second down. My dad's pressing his headset and making calls. The team lines up in formation and Langley throws a perfect spiral down the field to his wide receiver. Number 45 leaps into the air, catching the ball and running it into the end zone for a touchdown.

Meg leaps off the bleachers, screaming and cheering for her son. Gracelyn and I jump up and hug each other as the crowd goes wild.

"Thunder Creek's in the lead, 6-0."

My dad consults with Coach Baker and calls the next play. We go for two and convert.

"Yes!" Grace, Meg, and I all high-five and the excitement in the stadium's palpable.

Lightning Ridge's offense lines up and they march down the field, making good plays and gaining yardage. Coach Mack's red-faced, fists balled at his side. Meg's fiddling with her necklace and Grace is so close to the edge of the bleacher she may fall off.

The quarterback lifts his arm, reading the field, and fires off the ball. The defensive back to the right sees the play and jumps into the air.

"Yes!" I scream as the player surges forward, picking the ball and scoring another touchdown.

"Thunder Creek 14, Lightning Ridge 0," the announcer booms and the crowd cheers so loud the entire stadium rumbles.

Lightning Ridge holds us off on the next set of plays, managing to finally score. Then it's halftime and the band

and cheerleaders rush onto the field, music playing and legs kicking high in the air. The team retreats to the locker room for one of my dad's signature pep talks and Gracelyn and I take the opportunity to head down to the concession stand and grab snacks.

And run straight into Jamie.

"Oh hey, girls. Fancy meeting you two here—Mommy give you a night off, Gracelyn?" Jamie arches her brow, smirking. "And Sloane. Here all alone. What a shocker."

I bristle and Grace straightens her shoulders, fists clenched as she steps toward Jamie. Luckily, I'm close enough to grab one of Grace's belt loops, holding her back.

"Shut up, Jamie," Grace hisses and Jamie laughs, flipping her scarlet hair over her shoulder.

"Oh, must have a struck a nerve." She fixes her gaze on Grace and I wonder if I should call security or something before the two of them launch into a catfight.

"Why don't you scurry along, like the dirty rat you are?" Gracelyn waves a hand in Jamie's direction, shooing her away. But Jamie just bats her lashes and acts all innocent.

"So harsh, Gracelyn. It's like you don't remember anything at all you learned in cotillion."

"Like you'd know anything about that, Jamie. You were too busy going down on the entire basketball team to make it to cotillion class." Gracelyn folds her arms over her chest, her skin flushing pink.

"At least they were interested—" Jamie juts out her chest, then turns her eyes on me. "Heard you were following Cam down to Florida. Still the same lovesick school girl you've always been—guess things never change."

"They sure don't, Jamie. Because here you are, still

bullying people." Gracelyn inches closer to Jamie and I tighten my grip on the belt loop.

I want to confront Jamie myself.

"Not that you deserve to know anything about me or my love life after the nasty stunt you pulled at Mustang's with the fake timestamped video. But just to set the record straight—I'm hardly 'following Cam down to Florida like a lovesick school girl.'" I air quote her words, my voice rising, and a group of teenage girls stops to eavesdrop. "I know you don't know anything about real love, but Cam and I are in a very serious, happy, loving relationship—"

"Emphasis on *loving*—" Gracelyn chimes in and Jamie frowns, a tiny furrow marring her brow.

"Despite your attempt to break us up. I should really thank you for showing me that video because it's only made us stronger."

Jamie presses her matte red lips together, holding her chin high.

"Whatever. The two of you have always been boring anyway." Jamie tosses her hair again, faking a yawn. "Have a nice life down in Fort Snoozeville."

"Thanks, we will." I shoot her my sweetest smile, wiggling my fingers at her. She glares at me one last time, then pivots on her stiletto heel and sashays away without another word.

A long exhale seeps from my lungs as I watch her denim-clad rear retreat down the sidewalk, heading toward the sideline. A minute later, she's leaning against the fence, tossing her hair over her shoulder and calling attention to herself as the team and coaches file back onto the field.

"What a bitch. Bye-bye and good riddance," Gracelyn mutters, glowering at Jamie. "Hopefully she picks up a modeling job on the other side of the planet and decides to stay."

I laugh, relief rolling through me. "That would be nice. We can all hope."

Gracelyn and I grab snacks and start heading back to our seats when there's a tap on my shoulder.

I whirl around and there's Cam, wearing his Thunder Creek High T-shirt, matching me and Gracelyn.

"Cam!" I leap into his arms and his deep chuckle reverberates on my chest, sparks of happiness shooting through me. I smash my lips to his, kissing him long and hard. "I didn't know you were coming."

"I wanted to surprise you, Trouble." He grins at me as I slide down his sculpted body, my feet hitting the asphalt.

"Does my dad know you're here?"

"Yeah, I visited the team in the locker room, wished them good luck."

"Of course you did. They only let the real ones into the locker room, you know." I smile, linking my fingers with his.

"The perks of being an alum." He winks at me as we work our way through the maze of people scrambling up the bleachers.

The three of us squeeze next to Meg, who hasn't moved a muscle since we left. She's clutching her hands so tight her knuckles are chalky white.

"Hey, Meg. Langley's doing great out there. He's a natural," Cam says.

She smiles up at Cam, her cheeks turning rosy. "Thanks. He's going to be so glad you made it. Did you see him yet?"

Cam flashes his white teeth at Meg and nods. "Sure

did. Gave him a pep talk, told him to relax and enjoy it. Four years flies by."

The game resumes and Cam gives us all a play-by-play, explaining every single route, every pass in great detail. I know nothing about football compared to him, even after living with the coach. It's fun watching him light up with excitement, talking about his passion.

Finally, we're in the last minute of the game and it's all tied up. Langley has one last shot to win the game outright or we're going into overtime and our team needs a lot of yardage to make that happen. My dad's pacing the sideline, his brow furrowed, one hand shoved deep in his pocket. He makes the call over his headset and Langley backs up, reading the field.

I hold my breath and squeeze Cam's hand tight. His lips move silently—he's reading the field right alongside Langley, willing him to make the right call. Langley releases the football and it sails through the air. Ten, twenty, thirty, forty, fifty yards, landing in the wide receiver's open palms. He tears through the defense and hoists the ball up high in the sky.

"And Thunder Creek wins!" the announcer screams and the marching band breaks into the school fight song, all the students and alums jumping to their feet and belting out the words.

"Fight, Mustangs, Fight!" Applause rattles the bleachers and Gracelyn and Meg jump up and down hugging. Cam grabs me, kissing me right there in the stadium beneath the stars.

"I'm so glad you're here," I murmur against his lips, smiling. "I always wanted to do this back in high school, you know."

He brushes a strand of hair from my eyes and gazes down at me, his marine eyes shining.

"Me too, Trouble. Me too."

All these years later, and Cam still has the same effect on me.

Breathless.

Want to see what Cam does with that ring? Subscribe to my mailing list and you'll get instant access to an exclusive bonus scene!

Want more in the Thunder Creek series? Keep reading for a sneak peek at Gracelyn and Coach Mack's book, CALLING THE SHOTS!

CALLING THE SHOTS
SNEAK PEEK
GRACELYN

should have stuck to my guns.

Stayed off *Blaze* and *Buzz* and *Soulmate.com* forever.

I managed just fine all summer long, while Sloane was here in Thunder Creek.

I lived vicariously through her love life and everything was good.

Great, even.

But as soon as she left for Florida with Cam, I logged back in and started swiping right again. Like a freaking addict, ready for my next hit of oxytocin.

Flush.

The toilet whooshing in the next stall jolts me back to my miserable reality. I have to sashay back out there and bid the fondest adieu to Pixel Pete, the world's most boring IT guy. Why'd I even swipe right on that guy? We have zip in common—I'm pretty sure his idea of a good time is writing code. The man has zero game and may still be a virgin. Not that there's anything wrong with that, I just don't particularly want to have to walk him through the female anatomy.

Hard freaking pass.

With a heavy sigh, I wipe my sweaty palms down the thighs of my jeans and stand tall on my very-much-wasted-on-this-date stilettos. I slide the lock back on the stall and shove out into the dim restroom. Only to make eye contact with Jamie Ware, the biggest bitch in town and my archnemesis.

Fuck my life.

Now I have two choices. I can: A) dip back into the stall and fake a violent retching episode. Or B) waltz over to the sink and wash my hands like a normal person.

Much as I'd love to go with option A, I saunter over to the sink, head held high.

"Hey, Gracie. How are you?" Jamie trills, flipping her long scarlet hair over her shoulder.

I *really* hate when people call me Gracie.

"All alone now that your little friend's shacking up in Florida?"

My gut clenches, bringing option A back into play.

"Great to see you too, Jamie. And not that it's any of your damn business, but I'm not alone. I'm on a date." I wrench at the faucet handle and water sprays out full-force, splattering from the sink and turning bits of my gauzy white blouse sheer.

Shit.

I ratchet the pressure down, meeting her gaze in the dingy mirror. She arches a penciled brow and acts shocked.

"How nice for you. Another one-night stand in the books, then?"

My jaw clenches, hot anger bubbling in my veins. This

bitch has been tormenting me since high school and I am *over* it.

"You'd know a lot about those, I'm sure."

She unsnaps her clutch, pulling out a golden tube of lipstick. Popping the lid, she swipes the deep red color across her bottom lip.

"No, that's not really my style. I'm more of a long-term gal myself. And I'm not into the local dating scene, either. That's so, I don't know, passé, don't you think?"

Considering I told her five seconds ago I was on a date with someone who's most likely a local, no, I clearly do not think. But whatevs…

My cell vibrates in my pocket. Saved by the bell.

Quickly drying my hands, I tap the screen to life and read the text.

> Pete: It was nice to meet you. I had to jet.
> Take care

Well, this is a first. Pixel Pete couldn't even wait for me to get out of the bathroom before he bolted. At least we can avoid the awkward end-of-date pleasantries and the "I'll call you later" lies.

"Lover boy texting you already?" Jamie angles her head, trying to read the message. I shove the cell deep into my pocket. No need for her to know Pete has left the building.

"No. Just Sloane, checking in with me. We always text each other when we go out, to be on the safe side. The old buddy system, ya know? Oh—you probably don't know because you don't have any close girlfriends."

Jamie purses her lips, but doesn't take the bait.

"I'd love to meet your date, Gracie. Care to introduce me?" She smooths an imaginary wrinkle from her satin top, thrusting out her perfect breasts.

Under normal circumstances, I'd say no to this request. Now that Pixel Pete is M.I.A., it's a hard fucking no.

"It's early days, Jamie. Maybe another time."

"Oh, right. I'm threatening, I get it. Happens to me a lot." She fans her delicate fingers over her chest.

Oh, brother.

"No, not that at all."

We lock eyes in the mirror, neither of us breaking. A long second passes and I silently will her to walk out first. I have no plan, other than ducking out the emergency exit and calling an Uber.

The door to the restroom crashes open, banging against the wall, and two women stumble in. Still, Jamie doesn't budge as the ladies crowd us at the sink, giggling and talking loudly about how cute the bartender is. One of them turns on the faucet and water sprays me again, this time thoroughly dousing the lower half of my shirt.

"Ohmygosh, I'm so sorry." She grabs at a stack of paper towels and starts awkwardly blotting my midsection.

"It's fine, don't worry about it." I ease away from her and the geyser of a faucet, Jamie hot on my heels. She's so freaking close to me, the heavy scent of her perfume stings my eyes.

Pushing out into the dim hallway, I frantically try to figure a way out of this jam. There's no way in hell I want to admit to Jamie my date bailed on me. I can't very well walk back to our empty table. That will be a dead giveaway.

Slowing my steps, I cast a quick glance over the crowd in the bar. Sure as shit, Pixel Pete is gone, our table sitting vacant in the corner. A large group of college-aged kids dance in the center of the room, high tops shoved to the side of the makeshift dance floor. The bar's packed, but I don't see anyone I know.

Except Mack.

Sloane's dad's best friend and my mom's next-door neighbor. He's sitting alone near the end of the bar, drinking a beer and watching football on the television.

With a deep breath, I straighten my shoulders and strut confidently in his direction, Jamie right behind me like a fricking drug dog. Hopefully she can't smell bullshit.

"Hey, babe." I sidle up close to Mack, resting my hand on his forearm as if we've known each other for years.

Which technically we kind-of-sort-of have, but not in a touchy-feely dating type of way.

He stares down at my hand for a second, and I silently will him to play along.

"Hey, Gracelyn. Everything okay?" He cocks an eyebrow, a smirk dancing on his full lips.

"Yeah, bathroom was fine. Clean. All good. The bartender didn't come back with my drink yet?" I wave at the server, leaning over the wooden bar in Mack's direction.

"Just go with it, okay? I'll pay you back," I whisper in his ear, the clean scent of his aftershave tickling my nose. I've never been this close to Mack before, never noticed how broad and strong he is, how he fills out his T-shirt in all the right ways.

"Ahem." Jamie clears her throat and I glance over my shoulder.

"Oh, you're still here?" I wrinkle my nose and she stiffens, tipping her chin up.

"Hey. I'm Jamie." She purrs her name, popping her

mouth out in a sultry pout, and thrusts her hand in Mack's direction.

"Uh—hey." He shakes her hand, more out of politeness than true interest. "Mack. I coach over at the high school."

"Oh, I know. I see you at practice every day."

Really? This is news to me.

"You do?" I narrow my eyes at her. "You're stalking the high school football team now?"

Jamie lets out a high-pitched giggle, as if that's the funniest joke she's heard all year.

"No, silly. I took over as assistant coach for the dance team. We've been out on the field once or twice since school started. Most of the time the boys have it all to themselves, though, and we're in the stinky old gym. But I'm so happy to officially meet you, Mack." She flutters her fake lashes at him and I swallow down the vomit, signaling to the bartender for another drink.

Luckily, he's a regular—and took my drink order with Pixel Pete—so he knows I need another tequila on the rocks, stat.

"How long have y'all been dating?" Jamie asks and the corners of Mack's lips tip up the teeniest bit as he takes a long slug from his beer bottle.

"Oh, a while." I stroke Mack's arm, trying to sell the story. His skin's warm and smooth, veins popping over his muscles.

"Like a month or two? Funny you never mentioned such a handsome boyfriend all summer long."

My cheeks heat under Jamie's stare, heart pounding hard in my chest.

"We were keeping things kind of chill this summer," Mack says, snaking his arm around my hips and pulling me closer to him. I try not to panic as my rear brushes against his thick thigh and his fingers palm the round globe of my ass.

"Wow."

For once, I may have actually left Jamie Ware speechless.

Halle-freaking-lujah.

"Well, Mack—I hope to see you again real soon." Jamie flips her hair over her shoulder, locking her gaze on Mack.

"Yeah. See you around." Mack nods at her, then turns his attention back to me, a sexy smile playing on his lips. A fluttery sensation rolls through my tummy and fingers of heat lick at my skin.

I keep my eyes trained on Mack for a full minute, not daring to turn around and risk blowing my cover. He doesn't drop his hand from my ass, either, holding me in place against his hard body.

Now that I'm staring deep into his jade-green irises, I notice the laugh lines crinkling his tanned skin, the light stubble peppering his jaw, the line of perfectly straight white teeth, sandy curls peeking from beneath his ball cap.

The man is low-key hot.

Even if he is at least a decade older than me.

"Is she gone?" I mouth the words, trying to keep my voice low and barely audible.

"Not yet." He leans in closer, his breath warm on my face. "She's over in the corner, chatting with some people."

"Shit," I mutter. "Sorry, but could you just keep this going for like, a few more minutes, until she leaves? It's a long story."

Mack doesn't answer and panic flashes through me. If he bails now, Jamie will know I was lying and that will be a million times worse than Pixel Pete walking out on me. Because how pathetic am I, that I had to lie about having a boyfriend?

Without taking his eyes off mine, Mack sets his beer down on the bar with a clink. He grips my hips and pulls me into him, settling me right between his spread thighs. Then he leans in and presses his mouth to mine in a soft, slow kiss.

He tastes like beer and masculinity, his lips rolling over mine, teasing me. My heart hammers, blood whooshing in my ears as my mind races over nothing and everything all at once.

I'm kissing Sloane's dad's best friend in the middle of Mustang's on a Saturday night.

And damn, it's good.

Very, very good.

This man knows how to kiss, a shiver of pleasure rippling through me as he squeezes my ass. He slides a hand in the back pocket of my jeans and wetness floods my panties.

"How was that?" he murmurs against my lips and I smile, trying to catch my breath.

"Good. It was…good."

"Okay, then." He inches away slightly, cutting his eyes toward the corner. "She's still looking over here, but she definitely bought it. Act natural."

He kisses me again, lighter this time, then the bartender slides a drink in my direction. Mack takes that as his cue to scoot back and I reach for the drink, knowing my entire body's flushed. The curse of fair skin, there's absolutely no way to hide my feelings. I'm a freaking walking mood ring.

"Cheers." Mack picks up his beer, clinking the bottle with my glass and I smile, happy I bested Jamie. At least for for the time being.

"Care to tell me what that was all about?"

Pre-order CALLING THE SHOTS here!

ALSO BY KARA KENDRICK

SEAGLASS BEACH SERIES

Unmistakable

Unstoppable

Unrivaled

Undone

PEACHTREE GROVE SERIES

Rushing Into Love

Turning Up the Heat

Chasing After Forever

THUNDER CREEK SERIES

Out of Bounds

Calling the Shots

MAN OF THE MONTH CLUB: STARLIGHT BAY

New Year's Renovations

Love in Bloom

Stars & Sparks Forever

MAN OF THE MONTH CLUB: SYCAMORE MT.

Snowbody But You

MAN OF THE MONTH CLUB: CANDY CANE KEY

Reeling Him In

Lights, Camera, Christmas

MAN OF THE MONTH CLUB: MAGNOLIA POINT

Brides & Birdies

HOLIDAY NOVELLAS

Christmas in Cayman

Mr. Right Under the Mistletoe

My Charming Holidate

Snowed In With the Scrooge

BILLIONAIRE SERIES

Charming the CEO

Flirt Like a (Fake) Groom

HEART OF A WOUNDED HERO SERIES

Soldier On: Heart of a Wounded Hero

WILD BROTHERS SERIES

Forever Wild

Find them all at www.karakendrick.com

Kara Kendrick writes fun and flirty small-town romance destined to give you all the feels. A reformed English major, she also has a master's in counseling and was an elementary school counselor in her pre-mom life.

She loves the beach, wine, and rock-hard abs, not necessarily in that order. When she's not dreaming up Happily Ever After's, you can find her chasing after her boy-girl twins, working out semi-hardish, or walking her adorable Shiba pups with her husband, who's not too bad himself.

Let's be friends! Sign up for the VIP newsletter and be the first to hear about upcoming releases, promos, and giveaways.

If you enjoyed reading this book, please help spread the word by leaving a review on Amazon, Goodreads, Bookbub, Facebook Reader Groups, Booktok, Bookstagram, or wherever you talk spicy romance books!

To stay in touch, visit www.karakendrick.com

ACKNOWLEDGMENTS

Deepest gratitude to all the people involved in helping me put this book out into the world:

My alpha readers, my sisters and mom; Valentine Grinstead and the entire Valentine PR team; Nicole McCurdy at Emerald Edits; Virginia Carey, line editor; Chelsea Kemp, cover designer; and my ARC team and all the bookstagrammers and bloggers who took a chance on me.

Last, but never least, thank you to my home team—Lance, Luke, and Kinsey. I love you all and am so grateful for the opportunity to pursue my passion. Xoxo.

www.ingramcontent.com/pod-product-compliance
Lightning Source LLC
Chambersburg PA
CBHW070559300726

48975CB00006B/1649